We asked readers what they love about

Danielle Steel

'Danielle's books always make me feel **strong, inspired and happy** – truly a page-turning experience' *Liz*

'She has a remarkable ability to write different stories at an **amazing pace**. Every time I pick up a book I know that I'm going to be taken through **highs and lows**' *Gillian*

'I feel like I've **travelled the world** through her descriptions of the places in her books' *Ann*

'Every book **gets you hooked** from page one' *Julie*

'Danielle Steel takes me to another place with her masterful story-telling . . . **Absolute reading pleasure** from the first page to the very last' *Holly*

'I have **drawn immense strength** from the characters in many of her books' *Sarika*

'I love how she puts **her whole heart** into her writing' *Corina*

'I just love getting lost in her books. I can **stay up all night reading one**, just to know how it ends' *Kimmy*

'Danielle is such **an inspirational writer**, whose experiences are carried into the books. When I read each book, I feel as though **I am there with the characters** . . . They have gotten me through some very tough times and I would be lost if I didn't have one of her books in my hand' *Katie*

'Danielle Steel's books are **the perfect escape** from reality. Every time I read her books I'm transported to another place, ready for a new adventure' *Kelly Ann*

'I have been reading Danielle Steel books for fifty years or more and have kept every one – she is **my favourite author**' *Christine*

'**Gripping** reads that you **can't put down**' *Joanne*

'Her stories are **beautiful** and **gut-wrenching** and **totally unforgettable**. She has to be one of the best in the world' *Linda*

Fall from Grace

Danielle Steel has been hailed as one of the world's most popular authors, with nearly a billion copies of her novels sold. Her recent international bestsellers include *The Cast*, *The Good Fight* and *In His Father's Footsteps*. She is also the author of *His Bright Light*, the story of her son Nick Traina's life and death; *A Gift of Hope*, a memoir of her work with the homeless; and the children's books *Pretty Minnie in Paris* and *Pretty Minnie in Hollywood*. Danielle divides her time between Paris and her home in northern California.

BY DANIELLE STEEL

In His Father's Footsteps • The Good Fight • The Cast • Accidental Heroes
Fall From Grace • Past Perfect • Fairytale • The Right Time • The Duchess
Against All Odds • Dangerous Games • The Mistress • The Award
Rushing Waters • Magic • The Apartment • Property Of A Noblewoman
Blue • Precious Gifts • Undercover • Country • Prodigal Son • Pegasus
A Perfect Life • Power Play • Winners • First Sight • Until The End Of Time
The Sins Of The Mother • Friends Forever • Betrayal • Hotel Vendôme
Happy Birthday • 44 Charles Street • Legacy • Family Ties • Big Girl
Southern Lights • Matters Of The Heart • One Day At A Time
A Good Woman • Rogue • Honor Thyself • Amazing Grace • Bungalow 2
Sisters • H.R.H. • Coming Out • The House • Toxic Bachelors • Miracle
Impossible • Echoes • Second Chance • Ransom • Safe Harbour
Johnny Angel • Dating Game • Answered Prayers • Sunset In St. Tropez
The Cottage • The Kiss • Leap Of Faith • Lone Eagle • Journey
The House On Hope Street • The Wedding • Irresistible Forces
Granny Dan • Bittersweet • Mirror Image • The Klone And I
The Long Road Home • The Ghost • Special Delivery • The Ranch
Silent Honor • Malice • Five Days In Paris • Lightning • Wings • The Gift
Accident • Vanished • Mixed Blessings • Jewels • No Greater Love
Heartbeat • Message From Nam • Daddy • Star • Zoya • Kaleidoscope
Fine Things • Wanderlust • Secrets • Family Album • Full Circle
Changes • Thurston House • Crossings • Once In A Lifetime
A Perfect Stranger • Remembrance • Palomino • Love: *Poems*
The Ring • Loving • To Love Again • Summer's End • Season Of Passion
The Promise • Now And Forever • Passion's Promise • Going Home

NON-FICTION

Pure Joy: *The Dogs We Love*
A Gift Of Hope: *Helping The Homeless*
His Bright Light: *The Story Of Nick Traina*

CHILDREN'S BOOKS

Pretty Minnie In Hollywood • Pretty Minnie In Paris

Danielle Steel

FALL FROM GRACE

PAN BOOKS

First published 2018 by Delacorte Press, New York

First published in the UK 2018 by Macmillan

This paperback edition published 2018 by Pan Books
an imprint of Pan Macmillan
20 New Wharf Road, London N1 9RR
Associated companies throughout the world
www.panmacmillan.com

ISBN 978-1-5098-0043-8

1 3 5 7 9 8 6 4 2

A CIP catalogue record for this book is available from the British Library.

Typeset by Palimpsest Book Production Ltd, Falkirk, Stirlingshire
Printed and bound by CPI Group (UK) Ltd, Croydon, CR0 4YY

Visit **www.panmacmillan.com** to read more about all our books
and to buy them. You will also find features, author interviews and
news of any author events, and you can sign up for e-newsletters
so that you're always first to hear about our new releases.

To my wonderful children,
Beatie, Trevor, Todd, Nick,
Samantha, Victoria, Vanessa,
Maxx, and Zara,

May your falls be as gentle as possible,
and may you rise quickly,
having learned precious lessons.
It is *never* finished, no matter
how things appear.
And may you be blessed always
with wondrous new beginnings.
I love you with all my heart,

Always,
Mom/DS

Foreword

Dear Reader,

This was a very interesting book to write, and touched on some subjects that happen in life. "Evil stepmothers" have gotten a bad rap all the way back to "Snow White," and before. But what about evil stepchildren? Several times recently, I've heard horror stories of kind stepmothers who've been good wives and good to their husband's children, only to have the adult stepchildren turn on them and strip their stepmothers of everything when their father dies. Suddenly a woman who may have lived protected and well can find herself with nothing, not having worked in many years, with no income of her own, barely able to survive. It is truly a fall from grace and a rude awakening, and requires enormous courage, strength, energy, and resourcefulness to rebuild a life and reinvent yourself. To lose your role and status as wife, and all your security, when you lose a beloved spouse is an unimaginable blow.

Another theme that has intrigued me is how, innocently, sometimes people can find themselves on the wrong side of the law by the actions of a business partner, a boss, or their own misguided actions, unaware of the risks at hand. What happens when you are stripped of everything—and suddenly your flawless reputation vanishes too? What happens to an innocent or naive person who is charged with a crime, or goes to prison? It can happen.

In circumstances like these, the rebuilding of a life is no small challenge when everything you counted on is gone, when the person you loved and trusted is no longer there, when evil people use you, circumstances go against you, when life closes in on you and you find yourself in an unfamiliar world with no protection. Step by step, day by day, you have to start from scratch, create a new life and a new world, and go on, with courage and integrity. When everything goes wrong, when you *Fall from Grace* after a golden life and years of safety, which vanish in the blink of an eye . . . then what? That's when you discover who you are, and what matters most, and a strength you never knew you had. I hope you enjoy the story as much as I did writing it!

Love, Danielle

There will come a time when you
believe everything is finished.
That will be the beginning.
—Louis L'Amour

FALL FROM GRACE

Chapter 1

Staring out at the summer rain, Sydney Wells felt as though she were swimming underwater. For the past eight days she had been in shock. Her husband of sixteen years, Andrew, had gone off to do an errand on his favorite motorcycle, on a back road with little traffic near their Connecticut home. He had a passion for fast cars and vintage motorcycles, and had been riding one of his best ones, a Ducati. He had promised to be back in minutes, but four hours later, he still wasn't home. She imagined he had met up with a friend, or thought of other errands once he was out and enjoying the ride on the warm summer day. He hadn't answered his cellphone when she called him. The highway patrol said later that he'd hit a wet spot on the road, and some gravel. He'd been wearing his helmet but the strap wasn't fastened. He was going such a short distance. The bike had slid, his helmet had flown off. They told her he had been dead on impact. At fifty-six. And Sydney was a widow at forty-nine. Everything had an unreal quality to it. Nothing looked familiar, none of it seemed possible, and it seemed even less so once his lawyer came to see her. Andrew had been the head of the investment firm he'd inherited from his father and had been a responsible husband, the father of thirty-three-year-old twin daughters by his first marriage, and stepfather to Sydney's two daughters, Sabrina and Sophie. They'd had what she considered the perfect marriage, and had expected to grow old together. Sixteen years seemed like but an instant now.

She had made it through the funeral with her daughters on either side of her. Her stepdaughters, Kyra and Kellie, were in a pew across the aisle with their mother, Marjorie, who had flown in from L.A., and Kellie's husband, Geoff, shepherding them along. They lived nearby and had left their three- and five-year-old sons at home. Kyra lived in New York with her current boyfriend in the West Village brownstone her father had bought her at twenty-five. To keep things fair to both his daughters, he had purchased Kellie the house she wanted in Connecticut, near his own, at the same time. She'd been recently married, wanted babies, and preferred a country life, but with the birth of their second child, the house was too small for them now, and they'd been talking about upgrading for a while, with her father's help of course.

Their mother, Marjorie, Andrew's first wife, had moved to L.A. after the divorce eighteen years before, a year before Andrew met Sydney. So Sydney had played no part in their separation, nor the dissolution of their marriage, nor the enormous settlement Andrew had given Marjorie. He was a generous man, even to the woman who remained bitter and angry for two decades after he left her. The marriage had simply died. She was an unhappy woman, eternally discontent, and took it out on everyone. Andrew had finally had enough.

Marjorie's rage and jealousy had found an easy focus on Sydney, once she met Andrew, and she had successfully poisoned the twins against her. With no valid reason, except their mother's venom, they had hated Sydney from the first. There had been no turning the tides. They'd been seventeen when their father married Sydney, a pretty blond divorced woman with two little girls, nine and eleven. She had done everything to win over Andrew's daughters, but their viciousness to her and cruelty to her children finally discouraged her. With Marjorie's fury to fuel their hatred of her, there was nothing Sydney could do, and she had finally given up. They had hardly spoken to her in the last week and acted as though she had killed their father, when she was grief-stricken, and so were Sophie and Sabrina.

Jesse Barclay, Andrew's lawyer, had come to the house the day after the funeral. She had to know. Sixteen years had sped past them, and Andrew had never changed his will from the one he'd written before they met. Jesse had looked embarrassed when he told Sydney that he had re-minded Andrew to update his will when they got married.

He'd always intended to but somehow had neglected to do it, and he'd thought he had the luxury of time. He hadn't expected to die in an accident, nor to get sick at his age. They had both signed a prenuptial agreement when they married, which kept whatever they had separate, and he intended to amend that too after they'd been married for a while. He was only forty when they married and Sydney had been the same age his daughters were now.

When he died, Andrew was vital and alive, at the top of his game, and a loving husband. He had never meant to leave Sydney in the situation she was in now and simply hadn't gotten around to changing his will or their prenup. He was engaged in living, not dying. He would have been heartbroken if he'd known what she was facing. The last will and testament still in force when he died left everything to his two daughters. Since he'd written it before he knew her, there was no provision for his second wife.

The house they lived in belonged to his daughters upon his death, and as soon as they were apprised of the situation, on the same day Sydney was, their lawyer advised Jesse that they wanted her out of the house thirty days after their father died. She had twenty-two days left in their home. And in the same spirit, not having met Sydney or remarried when he wrote the will, Andrew had left all of his art, possessions, investments, the contents of the house, and his entire fortune to his two girls. And since the prenup precluded community property, whatever Andrew had bought or owned during their marriage remained his, and now belonged to his daughters. The only exception were gifts he had specifically made to Sydney, with confirmation in writing.

The twins had looked victorious when they showed up at the house together the day they learned of the will and began inventorying the silver, art, antiques, and valuables. Kellie had already taken two expensive paintings and a sculpture to her own home, with her twin's permission, of course. They said nothing to Sydney about it, and she found the empty spaces they had left when she got home from running an errand. She had sat down on the couch and gasped, realizing what would come next, and how they intended to handle it. Kellie and Kyra had already agreed that Kellie would move into the house since she was married and had children, and Kyra wanted to continue living in New York in the house she owned.

The four days since Sydney had discovered her legal situation as Andrew's widow had left her dazed and in a state of panic, which she hadn't shared yet with her girls. She didn't want to worry them, and needed to figure out what she was going to do before she told them. Essentially, according to his will and reinforced by their prenuptial agreement, she now owned nothing that she and Andrew had shared for sixteen years. He had given her some jewelry, which she had a right to keep, along with a small painting of little value that he had bought her in Paris on their honeymoon. And on their tenth anniversary, he had given her a cozy apartment in Paris on the Left Bank and put it in her name. It was a one-bedroom walk-up, in a charming old building in the city they loved. But it had none of the pretensions of opulence that would have attracted the kind of buyers willing to pay a high price, if she needed to sell it now.

She had given up her career as a respected dress designer for a well-known firm when they married. It had been a hard decision for her, but Andrew had wanted her free to spend more time with him, and pressed her to give up the high-pressure job that had supported her and her daughters since her own divorce seven years before they met. The idea of no longer working was daunting but appealing, since she would not only be able to be with him, but with her daughters as well. She had finally succumbed to his entreaties and quit her job a month before they married. She hadn't worked since, and stopped missing it after a while. Their life was full. They traveled and were together and with their respective children, and they went to their favorite city, Paris, for romantic trysts once or twice a year. They loved knowing they had the apartment there and could go anytime.

Other than that, Andrew had handled the disparity in their finances discreetly, with kindness and grace. He kept a joint checking account sufficiently funded so that she could pay the monthly household bills and buy whatever she wanted without asking him or feeling like a charity case. He never questioned what she bought, and she wasn't an extravagant woman. She had worked hard for what she earned before they were married, and was grateful for the life of ease he gave her, and everything he did for her and her two girls. And although she had no income of her own once she stopped working, they had lived well on his generosity for sixteen years. And suddenly, overnight, her situation was dire. The only money she had was what was in their joint checking account, and after she paid their outstanding bills with it at the end of the month, there would be little left. He usually funded the account once a month, so there was almost no surplus in it at the moment, enough to live on for a short time if she was careful, but not for long, and not forever. Had he left her even a small portion of his fortune, she would have been set for life, although she never thought of it.

For four days she had lain awake all night, thinking about her situation and trying to figure out what to do next. She cried for him and the shocking loss she would have to learn to live with, of a husband she had loved profoundly. And in addition she had to find a way to support herself, and quickly. She needed a place to live and a way to pay the rent and eat after the money in their checking account ran out. Everything else belonged to Kellie and Kyra now. They had said she could keep her car and her clothes, and little else. They had finally won the war they had waged on her for so many years. The victory was theirs, and Andrew had played into their hands without meaning to, by never redoing his will once he remarried. If he'd had any inkling something like this could happen, he would never have left her at their mercy. He was well aware of how vicious they were to Sydney, and had complained about it to his daughters many times.

Both her daughters had good jobs and supported themselves, and enjoyed the occasional helping hand from their stepfather. But Sydney was entirely financially dependent on him, and had been ever since she gave up her job when they married. Her first husband had left her with nothing except her salary, and paid a pittance as support for the girls. He had met a wealthy woman and moved to her home in Dallas shortly after the divorce, rarely seeing his daughters. Two years later, he and his new wife were killed when their small private plane crashed while they were on safari in Zimbabwe. Andrew had acted as father to her girls ever since they'd been together, and had supported them too, once Sydney gave up her job, until the girls were employed and could live on what they made. He had put both her girls through college since she couldn't. And he had always been wonderful to them and interested in everything they did. And now they had lost him too.

Sydney's genuine grief over losing Andrew was compounded by her terror over what was going to happen to her, and what she would do when her checking account was empty, which would be very soon. From a life of stability, security, and luxury, she had been cast into uncertainty. And she had been out of the job market and the design world for too many years to find employment easily, especially in her old field. She wasn't even up on the computer techniques designers used to draw today. She still sketched the traditional, old-fashioned way. She was behind the times and virtually unemployable after sixteen years out of the business. It was her worst nightmare come true. She had lost Andrew, and after years of depending on him, she could no longer support herself, except by waiting on tables or selling shoes. There was nothing else she could do. She couldn't even get a job as an assistant or secretary without knowledge of current computer programs. Her only talent was design, but her skills and contacts were obsolete.

Night after night after the funeral, she sat awake in her bedroom with the lights on and a legal pad in hand, listing what she could sell and trying to guess what it might bring her. The jewelry Andrew had given her was handsome and she loved it, but he had never bought her important jewelry, and she hadn't wanted him to. He had spent far more on his art collection, which was of greater value and which they had selected carefully together, and now every piece belonged to his girls, since he had paid for it and had never designated it specifically to her. She owned the apartment in Paris, and she wanted to sell it quickly. She would need the money to live on. No matter how much she loved it, she had to put it on the market now. Her clothes had no major value if she sold them. And she couldn't think of anything else. Everything that she thought of came under the heading of "contents of the house" and was part of his estate and belonged to Kellie and Kyra, according to his will.

Only Andrew's attorney knew how drastic her situation was, and she had sworn him to secrecy. She didn't want to frighten Sophie and Sabrina, who were coping with their own sadness over losing Andrew. Expressing her rising sense of panic to them wouldn't change anything or help her.

A little over a week after the accident, she went into the city without telling anyone. She met with a realtor she had found online who advertised short-term temporary furnished apartments. She had to be out of her home in Connecticut in three weeks. She was trying to think clearly and make a plan, because she knew the twins wouldn't let her stay even an extra day. After seeing five truly grim apartments on the far Upper East Side in depressing, poorly maintained buildings, she found a small one-bedroom apartment, with a tiny second room they said could be used as a closet, an office, or a nursery.

She could put whatever boxes she had in there. The price was reasonable, the building ugly, there was no air-conditioning, and the small kitchen was part of the living room. The furniture was from IKEA and most of it was new, with a few items from thrift shops. The realtor said the owner was studying abroad for a year and was willing to rent it month to month. Sydney knew that her daughters would be shocked when they saw it, and she didn't intend to tell them about it immediately. They didn't need to know about her circumstances yet. Hopefully once the apartment in Paris sold, the money would sustain her until she could find a job. She kept reminding herself that at forty-nine, she was still young enough to start a new life, but her heart felt like a rock in her chest when she signed the papers for the furnished apartment. They had to check her credit references, but the realtor assured her that everything would be in order by the time she needed the apartment. Hearing that made Sydney's heart race. She felt dizzy at the thought of giving up the home where she'd lived for all these years.

She started packing for Paris that night when she got back to Connecticut. Sydney had sent an email to a Paris realtor that afternoon, and they were meeting at the apartment in two days. She hadn't been encouraging about putting it up for sale. Sydney was still deciding what clothes to take and was distracted when the doorbell rang. She was startled to see a woman there whom she had known for years but never been close to. She had noticed her at the funeral and was surprised to see her there too. They had met when their children went to school together, and ran into each other occasionally now at the grocery store, and she was standing at the door with a cake box in her hands, which she held out to Sydney.

"I was on my way home, and thought I'd see how you're doing. Did you eat today?" Veronica asked with genuine concern, as though they were close friends. She was a few years older than Sydney and had been divorced for several years. She was a good-looking woman, played tennis a lot, and stayed in shape, but she talked too much, and Sydney didn't have the energy or desire to deal with her after looking at apartments in New York all day. Selecting her new home that was the size of a closet had been depressing to contemplate, compared to where she lived. And she couldn't even imagine what the girls would say when they saw it.

"I'm okay," Sydney said, looking tired and standing in the doorway. She didn't want to seem ungrateful but didn't want to invite her in. "I was in the city all day. I had some things to do there. And I was just packing. I got home a little while ago." The house looked dark behind her, but Veronica wouldn't take the hint. She seemed determined to reach out to Sydney, who had no desire to see anyone, let alone a woman she hadn't spent time with in years, and had never been close to.

"Are you going somewhere? Are you going to stay with the girls in the city? I can spend the night anytime you want, if you don't want to be alone." It was the last thing Sydney wanted. Although she was sure the offer was well intentioned, it felt intrusive.

"No, I'm fine. I'm going to Paris, to deal with our apartment there."

"Are you moving there?" Veronica looked curious as they continued to stand in the doorway. Veronica wondered suddenly if Sydney was going to sell the house she and Andrew had lived in. It was a spectacular home with extensive grounds and beautiful gardens, although it took a lot of time, people, and money to maintain, but it would be harder for her without Andrew to run things, since she was alone.

"No, I'm not moving to Paris," Sydney said with a sigh, her defenses down, and stepped back so Veronica could come in, which she did immediately and followed her to the kitchen. Sydney offered her iced tea and they sat at the black granite counter for a few minutes. Veronica questioned her about the apartment in Paris, while Sydney put the quiche she'd brought into the fridge. "I can't imagine using the apartment again without Andrew. It was our special place." She looked devastated as she said it. "I'm going to sell it."

"You need to slow down," Veronica said seriously. "You know what they say, don't make big decisions like that for a year after you lose someone. You'll regret it later. You might want to start spending time there, or in New York with Sophie and Sabrina. I wouldn't make any fast moves if I were you." Sydney hesitated for a long moment before she answered. She didn't want to give her all the gory details and confide in her, but she'd find out some of it anyway.

"It's more complicated than that. The twins have inherited this house. I'm moving out at the end of the month. Kellie and her family are moving in. I'm trying to figure out the rest." Veronica looked stunned, as Sydney tried to make it sound commonplace and not like the blow it had been. But Veronica pounced on the news like a cat on a mouse.

"You're *moving out*? In three weeks? Can't you stay here for six months or a year?" She was shocked to hear that Andrew's daughters, and not his wife, had inherited the house. But no more so than Sydney was. She tried to sound calm and at ease with it when she answered, as though she'd expected it. It was too embarrassing to do otherwise, and expose how upset she was. Out of respect for Andrew, she tried to put a good face on it to Veronica, who seemed hungry for information Sydney didn't want to give. But she was in Sydney's kitchen and clearly didn't want to leave. She had traded a quiche for inside information. And Sydney remembered what a gossip she was.

"If I'm going to move, I might as well do it now," she

said bravely. "And I need to get things squared away in Paris."

"Did they inherit that too?" Veronica looked horrified, wanting every detail.

"No, he gave me Paris as a gift. But this house is theirs, and everything in it." Veronica was quiet for a long time as they looked at each other, and Sydney wished she'd leave.

"At least you'll have fun buying a new house or apartment and shopping for it." She tried to sound positive. Sydney didn't comment on what she said, but she wasn't going to be doing any shopping of any kind, if she intended to eat as well. "When are you going to Paris?"

"I'm taking the red-eye tomorrow night. I'll be back in a few days." She stood up then, hoping to encourage Veronica to go. The conversation had depressed her even more, and Veronica finally took the hint as they walked toward the front door.

"Call me. We can have lunch, or I can help you pack up the house or something." Sydney had no desire for an audience while she tore her life apart in honor of the twins. Dealing with them in and out of the house to check the silver, crystal, and art was bad enough. She wanted to spend her last days in her home alone, mourning her lost life in peace. She had not only lost the man she loved unexpectedly, but her lifestyle, her home, her status as a married woman, and even her sense of herself. Who was she now without Andrew? She had suddenly become a pauper, previously married to a very wealthy man. She felt as though she'd fallen off a cliff into an abyss.

Veronica hugged her and then left, and Sydney went back upstairs to finish packing, feeling worse than before her visit. She emailed her daughters and told them that she was going to Paris for a few days, and then lay awake in the clutches of anxiety all night.

Veronica called her in the morning and told her again how sorry she was about the house. "I didn't sleep a wink all night, worrying about you," she said, and Sydney didn't add that she hadn't either. There was no point. And she didn't want Veronica to know how upset she was about the house and why. It was none of her business.

After that, her younger daughter, Sophie, called, concerned about her. "Why are you going to Paris now, Mom? What's the rush?"

"I just want to get everything organized, and it's too sad being here alone. A couple of days in Paris might be good for me." She tried to sound cheerful about it, and she promised to call her as soon as she got back.

Her older daughter, Sabrina, texted her between meetings, and told her to take care and be careful traveling alone. Both her daughters were worried about her, which was new for all of them. They'd never had to be concerned about her before, and she didn't like being the object of their pity. They didn't even know about the house yet.

They knew that Andrew hadn't left them anything, but they would be horrified when they learned that he had left his wife nothing either. It all went to the twins, whether they deserved it or not. And Sydney and her daughters knew they didn't, not by any means.

She took a shuttle to the airport in time to make the ten P.M. flight on Air France. She was traveling business class, although Andrew had preferred flying first, but those days were over for her now. She had used air miles to pay for the business class ticket, as a last moment of luxury and comfort. And she wanted to sleep on the plane.

They offered a full meal on the flight, which she declined. She hadn't eaten but wasn't hungry, and didn't want a five-course meal at that hour. She reclined her seat and closed her eyes, remembering the last time she and Andrew had gone to Paris six months before, for New Year's Eve. It brought tears to her eyes as she thought about it, and the tears squeezed through her lashes and down her cheeks as she tried to sleep. Finally the soothing noise of the airplane lulled her to sleep, and she woke up as they were preparing to land at Charles de Gaulle and a flight attendant asked her to raise her seat. The sun was shining over Paris, the landing was smooth, and moments later, she was standing at baggage claim waiting for her bag. She wasn't traveling as a VIP, as she had done with Andrew. She was just a woman alone, going to Paris to sell the apartment she loved.

She tried not to think about it or how much fun their last trip there had been as she got into the cab and gave the driver the address, possibly for the last time.

Chapter 2

Sydney concluded her business in Paris in a single day. She met with the realtor, who was candid with her. She explained that in the current political climate in France, with high taxes including an aggressive wealth tax, French residents had been fleeing the country for several years, to Belgium and Switzerland. And high-end real estate buyers from Russia, China, and the Arab states wanted showy apartments of great luxury on the Avenue Montaigne, or in the sixteenth arrondissement, and lately they had been going to London more than Paris, out of fear of being taxed by the French, even as foreigners. The government was anxious to bring in revenues from anyone they could. But those buyers were not looking for quaint little apartments like the one she had and loved. The realtor suggested that she might do better renting it at a reasonable price, and waiting until the market improved. After listening to her, Sydney agreed. A modest rental would not solve her financial problems, but it would provide a small, steady income every month, which would help. She told the realtor not to rent it for longer than a year, and to keep it on the market for sale.

She spent that night and the next day walking around Paris, trying to avoid her favorite haunts with Andrew, which was nearly impossible, since they'd loved to walk everywhere. They went to museums, gardens, galleries, famous bars like the Hemingway at the Ritz, and the Café Flore and Ladurée for tea. She stayed away from the shops on the Faubourg Saint-Honoré and the Avenue Montaigne since she could no longer afford them anyway. And when she left the apartment, she took all her small, favorite sentimental objects with her: things Andrew had given her as gifts, things they had bought together, photographs of them all over Paris. She bought another suitcase and took her small paintings with her as well, packing them carefully. She wasn't sure when she'd be back, or even if, and didn't know who the tenant would be.

It had been a whirlwind trip, but she had accomplished what she came to do, and had reassured her daughters by text that she was fine. She looked around the apartment for a last time with tears streaming down her face. It already looked less personal without the familiar things she was taking with her. She took a cab to the airport and watched silently as the city slipped away. She sat in the terminal after she checked in, feeling bruised by the brief trip.

Her long, straight blond hair was pulled into a sleek

ponytail when she boarded the plane. She was wearing a crisp white shirt and black jeans, with flats and a black leather Hermès Kelly bag Andrew had given her several years before. It occurred to her that if she had to, she could sell that too, at a high-end resale shop, if things got desperate enough. She was cash poor now and had to get used to the idea.

She was taking the last flight out of Paris so she could sleep, and planned to skip the meal again. She took her window seat on the plane next to a man wearing a tie and a gray business suit. He loosened his tie before they took off, put it in the pocket of his jacket, which the flight attendant took to hang up, and rolled up his shirt-sleeves. She guessed him to be about her age, with thick well-groomed salt-and-pepper hair. He looked prosperous and was wearing a gold Rolex watch and a wedding band, so she knew he was married. They nodded to each other, but neither of them was inclined to speak, which was a relief to Sydney. She wasn't in the mood. He got busy on his computer as soon as they took off. She closed her eyes and reclined her seat. She had already told the steward she wouldn't have the meal. She'd had a sandwich at a bistro she and Andrew loved near the apartment, and the waiters there had been sad to hear her news about Andrew and offered their condolences.

She was tired from the emotions of being in Paris without him and seeing the apartment, knowing she was going to rent or sell it. She fell into a deep, exhausted sleep, and awoke when the pilot made an announcement, first in French, and then in English, several hours into the flight. His voice was calm as he spoke over the PA system, and told them that they were having a mechanical problem, and were going to make an unscheduled landing within the hour. And in the meantime, they were dumping fuel into the Atlantic. He warned the passengers in case they saw it from the windows. He said they were an hour away from Nova Scotia, and would be landing there. She glanced at the man sitting next to her and he raised an eyebrow at her, not sure if she was American or French or if she spoke English. Her heart was pounding after what the pilot had said. An "unscheduled landing" did not sound good.

"Ever been to Nova Scotia?" the man next to her asked with a rueful grin, and she shook her head.

"No, and I don't want to. What do you think is wrong with the plane?"

"They probably ran out of foie gras in first class, and are stopping to pick some up." He saw how frightened she was and tried to keep the mood light. "I was in a crash-landing situation in China last year, with a motor on fire, and we made it in fine. They're pretty good at bringing these big birds down, even in emergencies. I think it will be okay." He tried to reassure her and saw that her hands were shaking as she took a tissue out of her bag and blew her nose.

"I just lost my husband," she said in a soft voice. "I wasn't planning to join him quite so soon, and I have two daughters in New York." It was more than she would normally have told him, but she was scared and unnerved by the announcement.

"I'm sorry about your husband," he said respectfully. "I have two ex-wives, and a wife I'm married to now, who are all going to be seriously pissed if I go down on this plane, and a son in St. Louis who might be upset about it too." She smiled at what he said. "Was it cancer?" he asked her gently, to take her mind off the plane, and she shook her head.

"A motorcycle accident," she said. "He was only fifty-six." He looked sympathetic. He wondered what she'd been doing in Paris, but didn't want to ask.

"I'm sure we're going to be all right," he said again.

A few minutes later, they were told to put their life vests on, and the plane began to pitch and roll, and instinctively he reached out and took her hand and held it fast in his. He had big, smooth hands that were comforting, and even though he was a stranger, she was glad to be sitting with him and not alone. "I'm not getting fresh," he informed her once he was holding her hand. "I just figure we're in this together. We can discuss the implications of it later. Just don't tell my wife." She laughed in spite of herself at what he said, as land came into view and the pitching and rolling continued and increased. They began losing altitude rapidly and looked as though they were about to crash into the water. Sydney gave a gasp and he tightened his grip on her hand, and they leveled out just above the water and headed steadily toward an air strip. The plane was making a terrifying growling sound, and Sydney thought she could hear a small explosion at the rear, like a truck backfiring, and they seemed to be picking up speed as they proceeded toward what they could see now was an airport, with a fleet of emergency vehicles with flashing lights waiting for them.

"We're almost there," he said in a soothing tone. "And they're all waiting for us. They'll get us out," he said in a strong voice, as she nodded and kept her eyes riveted to the fire trucks and ambulances on the ground, praying he was right. She had nothing to look forward to now, she knew, but she couldn't abandon her kids and die too.

They landed with a hard thump and bounced off the ground several times. The plane was listing severely, and they realized that part of the landing gear on one side had not come down. But other than the angle at which they were leaning, nothing worse happened, and they came to a full stop. She could hear sirens screaming as the flight crew opened the doors rapidly and activated the slides. They were told to leave their shoes and hand luggage on the plane, and head for the exit nearest them, as members of the crew with red insignia on their lapels directed them toward the inflatable slides. One by one they left the plane, and rescue crews on the ground herded them into buses. The evacuation of the plane was conducted in an orderly fashion. A few women were crying, mostly with relief, but no one panicked, and everyone looked shocked but infinitely less distressed as the buses drove them to a small terminal, and from there to a school with a large enough auditorium to house them all. Food service and an infirmary had been set up, but no one was hurt. Paramedics walked through the crowd asking if anyone needed help. The hubbub of conversation was loud as people talked about what had happened, and passengers turned their cellphones on and called loved ones at home to reassure them.

Her seatmate called his wife, and Sydney called both her girls. Neither picked up, they never did, but she left them messages that they had made an emergency landing in Nova Scotia but she was safe and would be home soon.

Her companion looked relaxed after they both finished their calls. "I'm Paul Zeller, by the way," he introduced himself.

"Thank you for holding my hand. I was scared to death," she admitted, but didn't have to, he could see it. "I'm Sydney Wells."

"My wife won't even fly unless she absolutely has to, and then she needs three Xanax, a bottle of champagne, and a psychiatric nurse." Sydney laughed as volunteers set up cots in the gym where they'd been assigned. And paper slippers were handed out to all the passengers. They'd been told that a plane would come for them the next day. So they had a long night ahead of them, and maybe even a long day after that. "What took you to Paris?" He was curious, especially so soon after her husband's death.

"I have an apartment there. I was going to sell it, but I decided to rent it instead. I don't think I'll use it again. I couldn't." He nodded.

"I was there on business. I'm in fashion," he volunteered, and said it with pride.

"I used to be in fashion too. I was a designer before I got married. It was a long time ago."

"Who did you work for?" She told him the name of the firm, and he was impressed. "They were a great house. It's a shame they closed. The owner died, and there was no one to keep it going."

"I missed it terribly at first, and then I got used to not working. I stayed home with my daughters and my husband."

"Do you ever think about going back into the business?" he asked with interest.

"I haven't until now. But I don't see how I could. It's been a long time, and I'm not current with all the new high-tech digital design techniques."

"They're no substitute for real talent and experience. You probably know a lot more than you think. You can learn digital techniques. You can't learn talent and design sense," he said confidently. She didn't want to pry and ask him the name of his firm, and he hadn't volunteered it. "Things have changed a lot since you were in the business. People want accessible price points, and high style at lower prices. Women who don't have a lot to spend still want to be in fashion. We try to deliver it. And everyone has factories in China now, even the high-priced brands. You can't make a profit unless you do, or sub work out to manufacturers in China. We all do."

"We bought our fabrics in France, and used factories in Italy," she said wistfully. "They did some beautiful work."

"And you charged about a hundred or two hundred times what I do." He smiled at her. "You were in a different market, catering to a different customer. That still exists, but the profit margins are better at my end of the scale," he said practically. She could gather from what he said that he sold moderately priced goods, or even lower, which had merit too. And that was big business if they dealt in volume.

"It's a different world out there now," she agreed. "Twenty years ago you couldn't buy fashionable clothes at reasonable prices, now you can. I think that's important. I think fashion should be accessible to everyone, not just women who have ten thousand dollars to spend on an evening gown."

"That's music to my ears." He looked pleased. "You ought to think about designing again," he encouraged her, but she wasn't convinced. She felt too rusty and over the hill to go back into the business, although she had loved it for the ten years she had worked as a designer after graduating from Parsons School of Design in New York. "It sounds like you've still got it in your blood." He had noticed that everything she wore or had with her was of the finest quality, and he could see that she had style, even in jeans and a white shirt, with little gold hoop earrings in her ears.

"I'm just a consumer now," she said modestly. "But it's genetic. Both of my daughters are designers," she said proudly.

"For whom?" It was funny that they had found each other, on a plane full of people, and they were both interested in the clothing business. She told him who Sabrina worked for and his eyebrows shot up. "Now, that is impressive. She must be good."

"Very. And a purist. She thinks fashion exists only in the rarified atmosphere she works in. My other daughter does moderately priced clothes for teens," she told him and he nodded. But both firms she mentioned were out of his league, with a more affluent target customer, particularly in Sabrina's case. All three of them were high-end designers compared to what he did, which Sydney had guessed and respected too. She bought the low-priced goods of lesser companies from time to time, and liked them. She respected good design. The low-priced brands had a refreshing honesty to them, and didn't pretend to be something they weren't. And often she found that what Sabrina did took itself too seriously. It was fun getting a bargain, and she said as much to Paul Zeller, and he agreed.

They talked about it for a while and then decided to head for the cafeteria. They were surprised to find they were hungry after their harrowing experience. Somehow life seemed sweeter suddenly, as though they had been given a second chance at living because the plane didn't crash and they didn't die. Everyone around them was chatting animatedly and seemed to have the same feeling. Wine was being poured liberally for all those who wanted it. There was a spirit of camaraderie and communal survival, which created a party mood.

They lay down on cots set up next to each other, and continued their conversation after dinner. He told her about his son in St. Louis, who was a pediatrician, and he was obviously proud of him, as much as Sydney was of her girls. An announcement was made that a plane was coming to pick them up at noon the next day, and while Paul was telling her about his adventures in China, Sydney fell asleep. And for the first time since Andrew's death, she wasn't afraid of anything and had a peaceful night's rest.

The sun was streaming into the gym the next morning when they woke up. They both agreed that they'd slept well, and went to get coffee together. A local bakery had brought truckloads of pastries for all of them. Afterward, they were allowed to claim their luggage, and waited on line for an hour to take showers. Paul and Sydney met outside when they'd changed and walked around, grateful to be wearing proper shoes again. They'd been able to retrieve their shoes from the plane as well, and their hand luggage. The surrounding area was pretty, and the world had never looked as bright and cheery as it did after their near-death experience the night before.

They chatted easily about what they liked to do in their spare time. Paul said he had been a hiker and serious athlete in his youth, and Sydney told him about a trip to Wyoming with Andrew and the children when they were younger and how beautiful the Grand Tetons had been. He admitted to being a workaholic and loving what he did, and she confessed that she was terrified of having to find a job now and didn't know where to start. He looked surprised. She didn't seem like someone who had to work. He noticed her Kelly bag again. He didn't want to pry into her financial situation and be rude, but she saw the question in his eyes.

"It's complicated," she said simply and he nodded.

"It usually is when someone dies. It's bad enough when you get divorced, and a whole lot worse when there's an estate involved. Did your husband have children too?"

"Yes, he did," she said quietly, and Paul understood.

"It'll all get sorted out in the end. It always does. It just takes a while." She nodded, and sat soaking up the sunshine after that with her eyes closed. He was an easy person to be with, and she could tell he was a nice man. She had been fortunate to sit beside him on the plane. It would have been a lot worse for her if she hadn't, and she was grateful to him.

The replacement plane finally came for them at two in the afternoon, and brought a crew to work on the damaged plane. They took the same seats they'd had originally, and flew to New York chatting occasionally and passing time in companionable silence. They felt like old friends by the time they landed at JFK, and like they'd been through the wars together.

"Can I give you a lift into the city?" he offered as they headed toward baggage claim. They were cleared through customs and immigration rapidly after all they'd been through, and representatives from the airline were standing by to greet them, apologize, and offer any assistance. The emergency had been efficiently handled, and all the passengers cheered the captain and applauded when he left the area with the original crew. He had handled it masterfully, as had the crew.

"I'm actually going to Connecticut," Sydney said once they had their bags and were standing on the sidewalk. "I'll take a shuttle. I live there." At least for the next few weeks, she thought to herself. "I just took an apartment in

New York. I'll be moving here soon." He took his wallet out of his pocket then and handed her his business card.

"If I can ever do anything for you, or you want to come back to work as a designer again, give me a call. If not, let me know when you're in the city, and I'd love to take you to lunch anyway."

"Thank you," she said warmly, as she dropped his card into her bag. "I don't know how to thank you. You made a terrifying experience a lot less so for me." He walked her to the shuttle, and she gave him a hug as he smiled down at her.

"Just take it easy. Everything's going to be okay. Give it a little time," he said, in the same reassuring tone he had used when they were about to crash. "Take care of yourself, Sydney," he said warmly.

"You too," she said, and waved once she was on the shuttle, and then got progressively sadder as they approached Connecticut. She hated going back to the dark, empty house. And that night when she pulled her lists out again, trying to figure out how much money she had left and how long it would last her, she thought of Paul and smiled, and hoped he was right. Maybe everything would be okay in the end. But she had a lot of decisions to make until then.

Sydney had texted both girls that she was home, and they called her early the next morning. Sabrina was calmer, as usual, and Sophie was panicked. Their mother had to describe the whole experience to each of them, and told them about Paul Zeller. Sabrina asked the name of his company, and Sydney said he'd never told her. It was on his card, but she couldn't find it in her bag when she looked for it. She knew it was in there somewhere, but her bag looked like a garbage can by then. It always did when she traveled. She told her she'd find it later.

They promised to come out and spend the weekend with her. She was going to tell them then that she had to leave the house. She knew it would be shocking news, but she couldn't delay it any longer. They had to know what was going on, and that she was moving to a furnished apartment in New York in two weeks. At least she'd be closer to them. And she was planning to start looking for a job as soon as possible, which would startle them too. They could hardly remember when she worked, since they had been nine and eleven when she stopped. It seemed like centuries ago.

When the girls came out on Saturday, she broke the news to them at lunch about Andrew not having a recent will in force, and everything he owned belonging to Kellie and Kyra now. The girls stared at her open-mouthed at first, and Sabrina was the first to speak.

"That's not possible, Mom," she said in a firm voice. "He wouldn't do that to you. He wasn't irresponsible, and he loved you."

"He loved all three of us, and if he'd made a new will, I'm sure he would have left you something too. But he never did. He talked about doing a new will when we did our prenup before we got married, but wills are more complicated, and he either forgot or never got around to it. And we never bothered to alter our prenup, which he wanted to do too. He was too young to worry about dying." He'd been in perfect health. "At fifty-six, you don't expect to die."

"So those bitches inherit everything?" Sabrina said, furious at what it meant for her mother, particularly knowing how vicious her stepsisters had always been to her.

"Pretty much," Sydney said quietly, "except the apartment in Paris, which he gave me as a gift."

"What about this house?" Sabrina asked her, looking worried for her. They had been heartbroken over Andrew's death and heartsick for their mother, but now a new element had been added, which put financial panic into the mix for her. That much was easy to figure out, unless he had provided for her in some other way.

"It belongs to them now, and everything in it," Sydney said softly, hating to say the words. "I have to move out in two weeks, or actually a little less. I got a temporary apartment in New York. It's not pretty, but it's furnished and it's a place to sleep." The thought of their mother virtually homeless brought tears to Sophie's eyes. Sabrina was too angry to cry. She wanted to kill someone, preferably her two evil stepsisters, who would be enjoying a windfall due to their father's carelessness. Sophie hadn't gotten that far yet. And Sydney refused to go there. She had loved him deeply in life, and intended to continue doing so in death. Sabrina wasn't as loyal or as noble as she. She had always had a fiery personality, detested injustice of any kind, and was willing to fight for what she believed.

"You have to *move out*?" Sabrina stared at her in shock and dismay.

"The girls gave me thirty days," Sydney almost whispered.

"And what about everything that's here? The furniture, the art, everything you bought together? He can't have wanted them to have that too."

"Their father paid for it. It's theirs. He didn't know me when he wrote his will." Sydney could almost see steam coming from her daughter's ears, and a look of rage in her eyes.

"And they didn't agree to give you some kind of grace period? Until you can get organized and find a decent place to live?" Sabrina asked, and Sydney shook her head. She didn't want to tell them that she could no longer afford a decent place, and even the tiny furnished apartment in the shabby building would be a stretch. "Have you talked to an attorney?"

"Obviously. There's nothing I can do. The will is what it

is. And our prenup makes it worse, because we waived any right to community property. And since he paid for everything, it was all his, and now it's theirs, except for any gifts he made me and put in writing, like my jewelry and the Paris apartment. All I brought to the marriage was what I had saved while I was working, and I spent that a long time ago." It was hard to admit it to them, but she wanted to be honest with her daughters.

"Did he make any kind of financial provision for you, Mom?" Sabrina asked practically. "Did he put money aside for you? I'm sorry to be nosy about it, but I assumed you'd be okay if anything ever happened to him. I never expected you to lose the house, or have to leave." Both girls looked shaken to the core. What their mother had told them was hard to believe. The estate where she and Andrew had lived was one of the largest and most beautiful on the East Coast.

"We had a joint checking account I ran the house with, and that he let me spend for anything I wanted for myself. I have the apartment in Paris, which I'm going to sell eventually. I'm waiting for the market there to improve, and I'm going to rent it in the meantime, which will give me a small income. I have some jewelry, which I can sell too. And I'll need to work."

"Oh my God, Mom." Sabrina sat back in her chair at the kitchen table and stared at her. They were like two versions of the same face, light and dark. The yin and yang.

Sabrina had her mother's delicate features, but where Sydney's hair was blond, Sabrina's was shining ebony. Sophie's looks were softer, rounder, she wasn't as tall as her mother or sister, and for genetic reasons no one could explain, her hair was red. "When did you find out?" her older daughter asked her.

"The day after the funeral. Jesse came to see me."

"Why didn't you tell us?" Sophie asked gently, her heart aching for her mother.

"It's only been a little over two weeks, and I needed time to absorb it myself. That's why I went to Paris, to put the apartment on the market. I'm going to start calling employment agencies this week. I don't know what they're going to say, though. I haven't had a job in sixteen years. I'm hoping to find some kind of work involving fashion or design, but I might have to do something else." She looked worried as she said it, and Sophie leaned over and took her mother's hand in her own.

"You don't forget how to design clothes," she said gently.

"My skills are totally archaic in today's world. People don't even wear what I used to design anymore. I'm thinking that I may be obsolete." She was frightened and hated to seem so vulnerable to her daughters, but there was no hiding from the truth.

"Will you be okay in the meantime, until you find a job?" Sabrina asked her seriously.

"I will when I sell the apartment in Paris, and am employed. Until then I can manage for a while, but it's going to be pretty tight. There's still enough in the checking account to pay for some essentials, for a short time, but not forever." It was humbling to have to admit to her daughters that she was nearly flat broke. And there was no way she was going to be a burden on either of them or borrow money from them. Sabrina made an enormous salary, deservedly so for the work she did, designing four collections a year, and Sophie did reasonably well, although she made less than her sister, designing clothes for teens, and Andrew and her mother had helped her fill in the gaps occasionally when she needed it. Sydney couldn't do that anymore either, and glanced at her apologetically. This was the ultimate reversal of fortune. One minute she had been living a luxurious and secure life, and the next she would be living in a tiny apartment, desperate to find a job, if she even could. "If nothing else, I can sell clothes in a boutique," she said humbly, willing to do whatever she had to.

"That's ridiculous," Sabrina said through clenched teeth. "Look at this house and everything in it, for God's sake, and now you're going to be a salesgirl somewhere? Come on, Mom. The girls can't do that to you. They don't need the money. Andrew must have left them a huge fortune, if they got everything he had. And he's been giving them money for years. His father left them a trust fund, and their mother has a ton of money." Marjorie was one of the most successful interior designers in L.A., and a favorite among the Bel Air set, and had done homes for some of the big stars, not to mention the settlement she'd gotten from Andrew years before.

"That's all true, but we're stuck with the will. He never changed it. Sometimes life works out that way. I'm not happy about it either, but I have to make the best of it. What other choice do I have?"

Sabrina felt tears of anger sting her eyes as her mother thought of something, left the table, and came back a minute later with Paul Zeller's card. She had found it in her bag the night before and wanted to show it to them. "I told you about the man I sat next to on the plane. He's a really nice person, and he seems to have some huge clothing company. I got the impression that he sells low-priced goods. He said to give him a call if I ever want to get back into design. He has factories in China, and he was terrific to me when I was terrified. I was thinking this morning that maybe I should call him. I couldn't remember the name of his company when you asked the other day." She handed the business card to Sabrina. "It's called Lady Louise." Sabrina closed her eyes when she heard the words, and let out a groan.

"Oh, please, don't tell me that's who you met on your flight. He's the scourge of the industry. You should have pushed him into the Atlantic while you had the chance. Do you know who he is?"

Sydney shook her head. Sophie looked disappointed too. She recognized the name of the firm as well. Everyone in the fashion industry knew it.

"He's the biggest knockoff mogul in the clothing business," Sabrina said. "He copies every decent designer there is. He doesn't even try to disguise it. He hires young designers fresh out of school who don't know better, pays them ten times what they're worth, and has a fleet of people running around to photograph every good-looking piece of clothing that's made. He's shameless. He changes just enough so he gets away with it, and you can't copyright most clothing designs anyway. He produces it all in China for pennies with crap fabrics, and gets it into the stores before any of us can get our products shipped. You can buy his copies before you can buy my designs that he knocks off. There's nothing respectable about him. He's never sold an original garment. He makes schlock of the worst kind."

"He says there's a market for what he sells, and he's bringing real fashion to people who could never afford it before," Sydney said. "The concept is a good one, if that's true. Not everyone can afford the clothes you produce, Sabrina. In fact, damn few people can. What's wrong with bringing real fashion to the masses? Don't be such a purist."

Sabrina looked outraged by what her mother said. "Nothing's wrong with it if his design staff came up with their own creations occasionally, or did 'inspirations.' All they do is copy the rest of us as cheaply as they can, and let us do all the work figuring out which way the winds are blowing every season. He's just a giant copy machine, Mom. I've never seen a single thing they produced that was original. He even copies what Sophie makes for teens. You can't work for an outfit like that. You have a name. People still remember what you did. I find your dresses sometimes in vintage shops when I'm doing research. You made beautiful clothes. You didn't copy anyone. You had your own style. People still respect the name of Sydney Smith twenty years later. You'll be a laughingstock, and so will we, if you go to work for him."

"You can't be such a snob, Sabrina. And sooner or later, I'll need a job to pay my bills. I can't pick and choose."

"Do anything, whatever you want, but don't go to work for someone like him. He's the bottom of the barrel." Sabrina was begging her, and Sophie echoed her sister, although more gently, as usual.

"Mom, no one respects what they do in the industry. Sabrina's right. They even knock us off, and our line is young and inexpensive, not up in the stratosphere like Sabrina's. He copies everyone and everything, without shame. Trust us, he's a bottom-feeder. It's all cheesy knockoffs, they don't respect anyone, and not a single thing they sell is their own design. It's all someone else's, but cheaper and worse."

Sydney was silently wondering if she should look for herself. The concept of Lady Louise was good. The products they manufactured couldn't be all bad. She knew how rabid Sabrina was about her designs. But Sabrina worked for a firm that could afford to charge whatever they wanted, based on the name, and the quality of their clothes was top-of-the-line. Sophie was less of an elitist, and even she disapproved of him. But there was room in the market for low-priced products. It had made sense to Sydney when she was talking to Paul Zeller in Nova Scotia. But she decided not to press the point with them. They both looked seriously upset that she would even consider asking him for a job.

"Anyway, he was incredibly kind when the plane nearly crashed. I was scared to death, and for a while it looked like we were going down in the water. I would have panicked without him."

"Thank God you didn't crash," Sophie said with fervor. "We'd be lost without you, Mom. Brina and I will help you find a job, won't we?" She glanced pointedly at her older sister, and Sabrina nodded, unnerved by everything she had heard during lunch. Their mother was being forced out of her home by her stepdaughters. Her late husband hadn't provided for her and had left her no money, and she had been thinking about going to work for the worst third-rate knockoff outfit in the business. It was fully clear to them that their mother's situation was critical, even if she appeared to be calm about it. But now they realized that the ravaged look in her eyes was not just grief from losing the husband she loved, but also financial desperation and the shock of losing everything to the twins.

"We'll come and help you move, Mom," Sabrina said quietly. "And tell those two witches to stay out of the house until you do."

"I can't do that," Sydney said realistically. "They own it now. And I gather Kellie is moving in. She wants to make some changes, but they needed a bigger house and now she has one." Sydney didn't sound bitter about it, just matter-of-fact and sad.

"Yeah, and that jerk she's married to would like nothing better than showing off with a house like this," Sabrina said vehemently. They hated Kellie's husband, Geoff, too, and Sydney wasn't fond of him either. He was pretentious and arrogant, based on no accomplishment of his own but only his wife's money, which he flaunted and spent at every opportunity. Andrew hadn't been crazy about him, but Kellie loved him, and now they had two kids. He had been a stock analyst on Wall Street when she met him, but had quit his job the minute he married her and hadn't worked since. They had been married for nine years, and now they had hit the jackpot, and he was going to have a field day strutting around. The thought of it made Sabrina sick, even more so than it did her mother. Sydney was still dazed by the wrecking ball that had hit her, and too terrified and shaken up to be angry at anyone. She was overwhelmed with fear of the future.

All three of them were subdued for the rest of the weekend, and the two girls discussed their mother's situation all the way back to New York on Sunday night. They worried that she'd be unable to get a job and would run out of money.

"She can live with me if she wants to," Sophie said generously, but Sabrina was more sensible.

"Neither of you is going to want that forever. She's too young to just live with you like some old dowager. She needs a life, and a job apparently. This is going to be so hard on her," Sabrina said unhappily. "At least we talked her out of going to work for Paul Zeller. That would have killed me."

Sophie smiled at the thought. The idea of it was ridiculous, even to her. "I'm glad he was nice to her on the plane. He must be semi-human after all," she said, giving him the benefit of the doubt, despite the fact that he was the arch-enemy of all talented, creative designers, and copied every item of clothing they made.

"I can't understand how Andrew did that to her," Sabrina said. "You'd think that sometime during all these years, he'd have written a new will to include her. I can't believe the twins are getting everything and kicking her out of the house. I hate them more than ever." But she was angry at Andrew now too. He had disappointed her, and his failure to do what he should have done had hurt their mother badly.

"He just didn't expect to die at his age," Sophie said, but it didn't seem like an adequate explanation to either of them. It was a failure of gargantuan proportions from a man who knew better, and had loved their mother.

"Neither did our father, when he went down on the plane in Zimbabwe. He didn't have a will either," Sabrina reminded her.

"He didn't need one. He didn't have anything. Andrew did," Sophie said, thinking about it again, and wondering what would happen to their mother. Sophie wanted to comfort and protect her. And Sabrina wanted to ride into battle for her. But there was no one to fight. Andrew was dead and had left nothing to their mother. The twins owned everything.

Sophie and Sabrina knew their mother was going to have to figure out a way to survive somehow. But how? There were no easy answers, and tough times lay ahead.

Chapter 3

For the next ten days, Sydney packed her clothes and personal belongings. She went through Andrew's books and all the little things that she knew had meant a lot to him, sentimental objects and photographs, the albums of the trips they'd taken. She packed the souvenirs of their years together. Not necessarily objects of value, although a few were, but they were things that she treasured. She had stacks of boxes to take to the New York apartment, along with her clothes. She weeded through her closets and took out things to sell that she wouldn't wear anymore, and set up several racks for her daughters to go through for themselves, of beautiful, expensive things she thought they'd like. She took a storage unit to put some special clothes away that she didn't need but wasn't ready to part with. It was a full-time job, and the housekeeper worked every day to help her. They both cried while they did it.

She was rolling a rack of things to sell out of her bedroom into the hall when Veronica showed up again unannounced, and looking mournful. She had brought her a sandwich and a Caesar salad in case she was hungry, but Sydney didn't want to waste time eating. Veronica lingered, trying to chat, and Sydney finally told her she was too busy, so she left. There was something invasive about Veronica's visits, though Sydney felt guilty for thinking that as she went back to work. The twins dropped by every day now to check on her progress and see if anything they considered valuable had disappeared. Kyra complained when she noticed that a small pink enamel Fabergé clock encrusted with pearls and tiny rubies was no longer on Sydney's night table, and she asked her stepmother where it was.

"Your father gave it to me for my birthday when I turned forty," Sydney replied, and Kyra shrugged. She could afford to buy a dozen new ones, but had always liked it.

"Dad said I could have it." Kyra tried but convinced no one, and Sydney didn't bother to respond. She had enough on her mind. She had postponed her job search until she got to New York. She had too much to do getting ready to move. And on her last night in the home she had loved and shared with Andrew, she was grateful to be alone. She just wanted to be there, with her memories. She had packed up his clothes along with her own, and sent them to storage. She wasn't ready to dispose of them yet, and didn't want to leave them for Kyra and Kellie to pick through, sell, or give to Geoff. Putting them in storage made it feel like she was taking Andrew with her, although more and more it was becoming a reality that he was gone. And she admitted it to no one but there were moments now when she was angry at him for what he had allowed to happen to her at his daughters' hands. She was being stripped of everything, not only art and furniture, but the home that had been her refuge, her status as a married woman, her feeling of safety, and all the remnants and familiar landmarks of her life with him. All she had left was his name. The twins were claiming almost everything else.

The moving van came the morning she was supposed to leave the house, thirty days after Andrew's death, to take what she was sending to storage, and the rest to the tiny apartment in New York. She stood in her bedroom for a long moment, and then walked quietly down the stairs with a lump in her throat the size of a fist and kissed the housekeeper goodbye. Sydney could no longer afford her, and Kellie had hired her. She needed the job so she was staying, but she said it broke her heart.

Sydney didn't look back as she drove away in her station wagon. She couldn't. She knew that if she did, she wouldn't have been able to go any farther. She had to go forward. And she saw Kellie drive in through the gates as soon as she drove out to follow the moving truck to the city.

It was a hot day and stifling in the apartment without air-conditioning. The elevator was small and slow, so it took forever to unload the truck. Sabrina and Sophie showed up that afternoon as she was stacking boxes at the back of the second bedroom she was using as a closet, and Sophie helped set up racks for her clothes. She had brought all the things she thought she'd wear most in her new city life, or if she got a job. She had brought a few cocktail dresses and evening gowns in case she had a social life, but she couldn't imagine it now. She'd had notes from friends, promising to call her, but no one had so far. Veronica had warned her that as an attractive single woman, she would be a threat to her married friends, which Sydney hadn't believed at first, but maybe it was true. And rumors had spread quickly that she was moving out of the house. Whatever the reason, embarrassment, discretion, or cowardice, she had heard from no one in the weeks since the funeral. Only Veronica called and showed up, and it seemed she always had some piece of bad news to share. Sydney had started avoiding her calls. She just didn't want to hear it anymore. She'd enough bad news of her own, without Veronica making her feel worse.

Sophie had arrived at the apartment in cutoff white denim shorts and a pink T-shirt from the brand she worked for, with sandals that laced up her slim legs. The clothes she designed were young and fresh. Sophie wore them a lot, they suited her and made her appear even younger than she was, with her mane of curly red hair. She looked like a teenager herself, totally different from her sister. Sabrina was wearing a black cotton dress of her own chic design with high-heeled sandals, and seemed like she was going to a fancy lunch somewhere, with her dark hair pulled severely back. And Sydney was wearing jeans and an old shirt of Andrew's and feeling disoriented. This didn't feel real. The tiny, ugly apartment couldn't be hers. The girls were upset when they saw it, and Sabrina disappeared for a while to buy flowers, while Sophie helped her mother hang her clothes and did all she could to make the agonizing process easier for her. She still wished her mother would move in with her, although Sydney was determined not to impose on either of them.

It took them all day to get the apartment organized in order to fit everything into the limited space. By eight o'clock that night they finished. There was nothing left to do. They had done all they could, and most of what she'd brought had to stay in boxes. There was no place to put it. The flowers Sabrina had bought and arranged in vases made the place look more cheerful, but Sydney had the feeling that she was camping out. All she could think of was Kellie moving into her home. She was exhausted when she finally sat down on the couch and gazed at her daughters. There was nothing any of them could say to make the moment better. It had been a hard day. The harsh reality of her life now was staring them all in the face.

"Why don't we go out to dinner?" Sabrina suggested.

There were several restaurants in the neighborhood, but no one leapt at the idea. They were all feeling worn out and no one was hungry, but both girls wanted to bolster their mother's spirits.

"I don't think you can get me off this couch with a crowbar," Sydney said, drained. "I'm so tired I don't think I can walk or eat," she said honestly. It had been a rugged day, leaving one home and trying to turn this place the size of a closet into another. She realized now that there were no window shades and she'd have to buy them, and the towels looked like they'd been stolen from a cheap motel. They were rough and small, gray from too many washings, and she wanted to buy new ones. Kellie had made a point of telling her to leave the linens at the house, and she had. She wasn't going to fight over hand towels and washcloths, although she had brought three sets of her favorite sheets. They had so many, Kellie would never miss them. "I think I forgot to bring soap," she said vaguely in a wan voice, and Sophie volunteered that she had brought toilet paper with her that morning.

The two girls left together, with Sydney still sitting on the couch, and they promised to come back the next day and take their mother out somewhere. The two young women agreed as they shared a cab downtown that their mother seemed battered, but it had been grueling for them too. What Sydney had brought with her had seemed like so little on the truck in Connecticut, but once it got to the apartment, everything seemed to have grown in the shrunken surroundings. It made them realize again how hard this was going to be on her and what a huge change.

She called them both the next day and told them she was too tired to get out of bed. It was raining and she wanted to stay home. They tried to talk her out of it but couldn't, and finally agreed to leave her on her own. She insisted she'd be fine. She set out her photographs of Andrew and the girls on every surface where she could fit them, and she spent the rest of the day in bed, watching movies on the tiny ancient TV in her bedroom.

And on Monday, forcing herself, Sydney went down her list of employment agencies and called them all. She had four appointments for that week, and was determined not to lose momentum. She couldn't look back now, or down, as though she were climbing a cliff and hanging on by her fingernails. She just had to keep going until she reached a place that felt safe to stop, and she hadn't reached it yet. The abyss was still yawning below her, and she was afraid to fall.

All of her meetings at the agencies were discouraging, and by Friday she had heard the same thing over and over again. She had been out of the job market for too long, her experience was no longer relevant, she was too old and competing with people half her age for jobs. They suggested that she consider some other line of work in fashion, instead of design. Editorial assistant at a magazine perhaps, or working in a designer boutique or on the designer floor at a department store. No one took her seriously as a designer, and at four o'clock on Friday, she took Paul's card out of her bag again, where she had left it after showing it to the girls, and called him. She wasn't going to beg for a job she realized she was no longer suited to, but she was going to ask him if he had any suggestions for her. She had no idea where to turn next. The people she had worked with many years before all seemed to have disappeared. She couldn't find any of them listed in information or on the Internet. She was touched when Paul took her call and came on the line immediately. His voice sounded pleasant and upbeat, and was a relief to hear.

"Hi, Sydney, what have you been up to?" He seemed like he really wanted to know, and she wasn't sure if she should tell him the truth or lie. She was running out of steam. It had been a brutal week.

"Well, let's see, since the plane crash I moved out of my house in Connecticut into an apartment the size of a phone booth," she said. "I saw four employment agencies this week, and before I take a job as a waitress, I thought I'd give you a call and pick your brain to see if you have any bright ideas. It's either that or work at Starbucks." He could hear from the timbre of her voice that things were not going well despite her attempt to make a joke of it.

"Have you ever been a waitress before?" he asked, sounding startled.

"Actually, no."

"Then why not stick with what you know? Let's have lunch on Monday, and we'll talk. Don't sign up at Starbucks just yet."

"I'll try to resist the temptation," she said and laughed, feeling better just talking to him. He'd had the same effect on her when their plane nearly crashed and he told her they'd be fine. She believed him.

"What else have you been up to? How are your daughters?"

"They've been terrific. They helped me move over the weekend." He could only imagine how traumatic it must have been for her to leave her house, only weeks after losing her husband. He stayed off painful subjects while they chatted for a few minutes. He told her to meet him at his office, which was in an old warehouse they'd transformed in Hell's Kitchen. They had facilities in New Jersey as well. He told her to come at noon and he'd show her around. There were several good restaurants in the neighborhood, and he'd take her to lunch after the tour. "See you then," she said. "And, Paul, thank you for seeing me. I need some fresh ideas."

"I'll see what I can come up with this weekend," he promised, and her spirits had improved slightly when she hung up. She had something to look forward to, and she was not going to tell her girls she'd called him. They had a visceral prejudice against the kind of clothes he made, and she wasn't going to try and convince them otherwise. They were cheap copies of expensive clothes, but there was obviously a market for them. If nothing else, after their experience in Nova Scotia, she and Paul had become friends. And she needed some of those right now. Her old friends from Connecticut seemed to have disappeared the minute Andrew died. Veronica's theory about married women not wanting divorced or widowed female friends around was proving to be accurate. She had disagreed with Veronica when she said it, but maybe she knew what she was talking about. There wasn't a single part of Sydney's life that hadn't changed.

She spent a quiet weekend since both her daughters were in the Hamptons, and she took a long walk in Central Park and watched couples strolling and families picnicking together. She listened to a reggae band for a few minutes, and sat on a bench and observed the world drifting by, and then she went back to her apartment and tried to read a book, but her mind had been blank since Andrew died and she couldn't concentrate, so she lay on her bed, which filled her entire bedroom, and fell asleep.

And on Monday morning, she headed for Hell's Kitchen on the subway. She was wearing a white linen dress with big turquoise beads, flat sandals, and a chic straw bag, and her hair was pulled neatly back. She looked fresh and summery when she gave her name to a pretty young girl at the reception desk. Suddenly the whole world seemed half her age, and the people she saw coming and going around her all looked like kids. It was a relief to see Paul walking toward her a few minutes later with a smile on his face. He was delighted to see her. He gave her a hug in greeting and told her she looked terrific, and they went back to his office to talk before he showed her around.

"You know, I thought about you all weekend," he said seriously, "trying to come up with some bright ideas for you to reinvent yourself, but I kept coming to the same conclusion. That's crazy. You were a terrific designer when you retired. That doesn't go away. You can't throw away a talent like that, nor should you. It's like teaching Picasso to be a busboy or an engineer. Why would you want to do that? You're an artist, Sydney, a talented designer. You've been out of the business for a while, and you may not have the computer skills that kids do these days. But it wouldn't take you long to get up to speed, and as long as you have a piece of paper and a pencil, who cares how you come up with designs, or what you draw them on? Look at you, you're fabulous. You know just how to put it together. Why would you want to give that up? You took a break. Now you want to come back. Why not give it a shot?"

"Because no one will hire me," she said honestly. "At least that's what the employment agencies told me last week. I've been away from it for too long. My point of view has changed, the world has changed, I don't have a commercial touch anymore, and everyone in the business is half my age. Look at my kids, they're twenty-five and twenty-seven, and they're at the top of their game. I'm over the hill," she said, trying not to sound as discouraged as she felt.

"That's bullshit. You have experience they don't have, and perspective. You have an overview of fashion, which adds dimension. You know what's already been done, what worked and what didn't. A lot of these kids are still very one-dimensional. They haven't seen enough yet. And too many of them rely on their computers and don't really have talent. How many really do? You know it as well as I do. They can draw, but they can't design. They don't have enough to bring to it yet. They've seen last year, and two years ago. You've seen a hell of a lot more than that. It matters. And you have your own style, most of these kids don't. They all look like bums sleeping under a bridge." And she knew he wasn't wrong about that. It was the current style.

"So what are you telling me? I did give it a shot, going to see the agencies." Listening to him, she almost believed him, but it wasn't happening. In fashion now, youth was king. And the one thing she couldn't do was erase her age.

"I'm telling you, give *me* a shot. Give *us* a chance. Come to work for me. If you talked to your daughters about me, I'm sure they tried to scare you off. They're at the top of their field. They work in an elitist world, even the line for teenagers your younger daughter works for. Their prices are still above ours. But the truth is that isn't always what sells. Designers like your kids hate people like me, because we borrow, heavily, I admit it, but we bring fashion to everyone. We make looking great accessible to the masses, at prices they can afford. And if you want to try it, you can work in some original designs and do some signature pieces for us. I'd really like to give it a try, and if it doesn't work, then we'll have learned something from it. I think we need each other, and if you want to use your name here, you can. I have no objection to it. I'd love it. We can give you your own label for what you design. Sydney Smith for Lady Louise. That was my grandmother's name, by the way. She was a seamstress and a cool old dame. I named the company after her. She came here from Poland and taught me everything I know about life and clothes. What do you think?"

Sydney could just hear Sabrina shrieking in horror if she heard their conversation, but so much of what he said made sense, and he was right. Designers like Sabrina were enormous snobs about fashion, and created for an elite few. There was plenty of room in the market for a different kind of customer. It sounded challenging to Sydney, and like fun.

"I'll give you a tour," Paul said. "I want to show you our design studio." She followed him out of his office and up a flight of stairs. The building had an industrial look to it, which appealed to her. It was all very different from the lofty atmosphere she'd worked in before. This was fresh and young.

He led her into an enormous room where twenty designers were working at tables, sketching, working on computers, and correcting designs, with color swatches and bits of fabric hanging over their desks. Some of them had photographs on their screens of clothes she recognized, and she knew what that meant. They were copying more expensive designs, but Paul didn't deny it, and he assured her that they modified them enough to keep them from being exact copies. Most clothing designs couldn't be protected or copyrighted, but he still had his designers change a pocket or a sleeve length or a skirt to keep them from being identical to the designs that "inspired" them. They gave them a new twist the original designer may not have thought of, dared, or been allowed to do.

She walked from table to table quietly, and was shocked at the youthful age of the designers. They were dressed like orphans and street people, there were as many girls as boys, and they all looked intent on their work. It was an impressive operation, and on the floor above them were the patternmakers, working diligently, adjusting the designs to make sure they worked. It was exciting being back in the familiar milieu, on a much larger scale. Paul had more of everything. There were so many of them it looked like a school, and in a way it was. They were all learning something new, and she had new techniques to learn too. She toured the building with him, and they wound up back in the lobby, and then he walked her down the street to an Italian restaurant with a garden for lunch. The day was just cool enough to sit outside. He ordered a Bloody Mary, and they ordered lunch, and she talked about what they'd seen. She asked him a lot of questions, and his answers seemed straightforward and sounded right to her. She was touched that he was willing to give her a chance. She had a feeling that no one else would, and certainly not a firm like the one Sabrina worked for, or others like it. She'd been gone for too long. But not for Paul.

"I'll do it," she said, halfway through lunch, and he glanced at her in surprise.

"Do you mean what I think you mean . . . what I hope you mean?" he asked, and she nodded and broke into a smile.

"If you want me, yes, I do," she confirmed.

"I can't pay you what you made before, when you stopped working. But in the long run, you'll make more here. A lot more if you take the kind of strong role I hope you will. Sydney, we have a home for you for the long haul, if you want it. You could have a major impact here." He made her feel competent, relevant, and important, and not like a has-been. He gave her hope that she could work her way out of the financial mess she was in.

"I do want it," she said seriously, and suddenly nearly dying in a plane crash with him had become the best thing that had happened to her in a long time, and recently for sure.

"When can you start?" he asked, beaming at her, and she laughed.

"Tomorrow?"

"Sydney, you're on!" He got up and walked around the table to hug her, and it reminded her of Nova Scotia again, when he had told her that everything would be okay, and she believed him. And now he was making that promise come true. She clung to him for a moment and thanked him, and he ordered champagne when he sat down again. "My grandmother would approve," he said, smiling at her, and she laughed. Things were starting to look up. She had a job. The only thing she couldn't do was tell her girls where she was working. In the five weeks since Andrew's death, she had nearly drowned, and now, thanks to Paul, she was swimming to the surface again, and she knew she would survive.

Chapter 4

The morning after her lunch with Paul, Sydney woke up feeling anxious and excited. It seemed like a hundred years since she had last gone to work, and now she had a job at a successful company again, no matter how different it was from where she designed before. Her heart pounded when she thought of it, but she could hardly wait to get to the office. She had no idea what assignment she would get at first. She had a lot to get familiar with.

She took the subway downtown and walked into the Lady Louise building in Hell's Kitchen at five to nine. Paul had told her to report to HR to fill out paperwork when she arrived. She took the elevator to the top floor of the remodeled warehouse complex, found the human resources office, and introduced herself. A girl who looked about Sabrina's age smiled at her, handed her the employee handbook, and put the papers to sign in front of her. She noticed that she would be getting health insurance, which was important to her, since hers got canceled when Andrew died, and she couldn't afford to get sick now. The entire process took half an hour. The girl was brisk and efficient, and asked if Sydney had any questions. She had one last paper to sign, which was her work contract. She and Paul hadn't discussed salary, and Sydney stared when she saw the amount listed on it. It wasn't even close to what she used to make when she was the head designer of a high-end fashion line, but it was far more than she had hoped to make now, or thought she deserved after a long hiatus. It showed Paul Zeller's respect for her and her talent, and what he thought she could do for his firm. Five minutes after she signed the contract, she walked into his office and thanked him profusely.

"You're paying me too much," she said, looking embarrassed, and he laughed and invited her to sit down.

"You're the first employee who's ever said that to me. I think you're worth it, Sydney. I want you to give Lady Louise a touch of class we don't have now, just a little edgier and upmarket from what we've been doing. I think some of our clients are ready for it. We want to attract that client, and for those who aren't, they'll still have our lower-end lines." He looked at her thoughtfully, admiring what she'd worn that day. She had picked a short black linen skirt, a simple white silk T-shirt, and high-heeled black linen pumps for her first day at work. She looked elegant and youthful, and everything she had on was chic and expensive. Sabrina would have approved of her outfit, but not the job she had just taken.

Sydney knew she was damn lucky to have it. She just hoped she could justify his faith in her. "I'm going to put you in the hands of our head of creative and design today. I want you to be his shadow for the next several months. He can teach you everything about our business. I had a meeting with him yesterday after our lunch. He's going to give you some projects so you can get your feet wet. He's a great guy, and is responsible for some of our biggest successes. He has an unfailing eye," he said, smiling at her. "A lot like you. He'll be here in a few minutes," and as he said it, a tall, thin, young Chinese man walked into his office in a black T-shirt and black jeans, wearing high-topped black Converse. His hair was jet black and as long as Sydney's, and hung straight down his back, nearly to his waist, and the look suited him. He had a beautiful, delicately carved face, like an ivory statue, yet his whole style was modern, simple, and sleek. He greeted Paul in a businesslike way, and looked Sydney over appraisingly. She couldn't tell if he liked what she was wearing or not, or if he approved of her getting the job. She wondered if people would be jealous of the fact that she'd been hired, or bothered by her age. She hadn't seen anyone even close to her age, except Paul, since she walked in. And so many of the design staff she'd glimpsed the day before looked like kids fresh out of school to her.

Paul introduced them. The young Asian man's name was Edward Chin. He was twenty-nine years old, and he had a British accent. Paul said he came from Hong Kong, had worked at Dior for two years, and been employed by Lady Louise for three, and he had risen to stardom in the company quickly. She thought it an interesting contrast that he had gone from high-end, high-priced fashion to the low-priced lines Lady Louise produced. They spent a few minutes chatting in Paul's office, and then Edward said he had work to do and invited Sydney to come with him. She felt suddenly overdressed compared to her new boss, but she had thought it best to dress well for her first day at work. She could see now that she'd be fine at work in future in jeans and even T-shirts, as long as she looked neat and presentable. Edward's outfit almost disappeared, and all that she noticed and was riveted by was his finely chiseled face, and his intelligent dark eyes.

She followed him to the design floor she had seen the day before, with the twenty young designers frantically at work. None of them had private offices. They all worked in the big open space that looked like a loft, with brick walls, long, tall windows, and high ceilings. He walked her over to the table he had assigned her close to his own. Hers had an enormous desktop computer on it. There were several sketch pads, a box of pencils, erasers, sharpeners, and everything she needed. She felt like a kid on the first day of school.

"Paul said you don't design on a computer. You'll learn," Edward Chin assured her. "We're working on next spring right now. Half the group is working on tops and blouses, the more senior designers are working on jackets."

"What would you like me to do?" she asked, feeling slightly overwhelmed.

"I'll show you what we've got so far, and what's been approved," he said seriously, and she followed him to the large computer on his own desk, where he brought up a slew of designs. She was impressed by how clean and straightforward they were, could see easily that many of them were variations of the same pattern, which was economical for them, and admittedly some of the designs and styles looked familiar to her. She concentrated on what he was showing her. "Why don't you work off some of these today, and see what you come up with? Try and stay within the parameters of what you're seeing, using the same bodies, and adding something new with collar, sleeve, detail, and stitching. Our size runs are pretty broad, so it's got to look good on a size twelve too, and no tricky hidden closures, which are too costly to produce. This isn't what you're used to."

She nodded, not sure if he was being critical. So far, he had been direct and matter-of-fact. He was intent, and hadn't smiled at her yet. His clipped British way of speaking to her sounded educated. She noticed that he had long, graceful hands as he pointed to the designs on the screen. And then, while he was showing her a sketch on the computer, he picked up something that looked like a pencil, and added some corrections to one of the designs on his computer screen. It was a special program, and he was literally drawing on the computer. It looked like magic to her, and she smiled as she watched him.

"I feel like I'm coming out of the dark ages," she admitted to him. "Twenty years ago what you just did was science fiction." He smiled at what she said.

"I had to learn it too. I attended the Royal College of Art in London. They didn't believe in things like this ten years ago. I did an internship with Stella McCartney, then worked for Alexander McQueen before I went to Dior. It's a big transition coming to work here, and Paul likes to keep everything digital, but a lot of the old principles apply. We just simplify and digitize them." Sydney knew they also copied other people's designs a lot, and only modified them slightly, so they didn't have to start every design from scratch, the way famous designers did. "I've seen a lot of your work," he said in a soft voice. "I'm a big fan. I did a project on just your coats once when I was in school. Your structure was fantastic. You taught me everything I know about working with stiff fabrics, which I prefer to softer ones, like Nina Ricci or Chanel's evening gowns. We don't do a lot of evening wear here, at least not yet. We're stronger in day wear and we have a bigger market for it. Evening wear is a much smaller market, and it's harder to produce. You can waste a lot of fabric if something goes wrong." All of which she knew from experience. She was impressed by his history, and whom he'd worked for before Lady Louise. It spoke well for the brand that he had chosen to work there.

He printed out some of the designs on his screen, of blouses and jackets for her to work on and modify if she chose to, and handed the sheets to her. "You're going to do just fine. I know Paul has some big plans for you, if things work out. But first you need to learn the basics, and how we do things. And I'm taking you to China with me, when I go to see our factories in three weeks. That's not a problem for you, is it?" He looked at her questioningly. "We'll be gone for about three weeks. It'll be miserably hot there, but I'm overdue for a visit, and Paul wanted you to see it. Coordinating with our factories and keeping them on track is a big part of what I do," he explained to her, and just talking to him, she could tell that Paul's faith in him was well placed. He was brilliant and made everything simple and clear for her.

She took the pages he gave her to her desk then, and tried to focus on what she was doing, adding to basic designs to make them slightly more interesting without making them more expensive to produce. Two or three of the young female designers wandered by and shyly said hello to her, as she sketched all morning. By lunchtime she had only one design that she liked. The others still didn't seem right to her. She felt both rusty and green at the same time. When Ed Chin came by at twelve-thirty to see what she was doing, she wasn't satisfied with her work yet, but he was pleased.

"I like that one," he said, pointing to one she had discarded and glancing at the others. "Those pockets would cost us a fortune," he said, indicating the one she liked, "and the double stitching. It's a great look, but we can't afford those touches here. We need to create that illusion, but find a cheaper way to do it. You have to keep your eye on cost at all times. It's all about the look, without the high-end touches to back it up. You have to give something up in every design," he said, and smiled at her. "It's a whole new ball game, and a challenge to let go of what we love most. You have to remember who our customer is, and what they want to pay. We have a standard to uphold on pricing. That's our strength in the marketplace."

He hadn't mentioned copying other people's designs, and seemed more interested in what she could come up with on her own, to get a feeling for the flavor she could add to their line. And his pointers were helpful to her. She saw that he was eating a salad at his desk a little while later, and didn't go to the cafeteria in the basement with the others. A lot of people went out for lunch, although one of the other designers told her that the food downstairs was good. But she decided to stay at her desk and work through lunch.

She worked on the blouses and jackets all afternoon,

and stayed till six o'clock. Ed was still at his desk when she left and said good night to him.

"How did the first day feel?" he asked her with interest. He didn't let on to her, but it impressed him that she was working there.

"Thrilling, scary, new, and familiar in some ways. I'm excited about the trip to China you mentioned. I've never been to Asia before."

He smiled when she said it. "It's an education, especially in this business. Everyone produces there now, even the big-ticket name brands. It just doesn't make sense to produce mass market goods anywhere else anymore. The factory towns in China are miserable, the pollution is awful, and working in Beijing can be rough. It's a lot less sophisticated than here, but the work ethic is tremendous, and the sheer number of workers at their disposal. I'm planning to visit my family in Hong Kong on the way back, and you're welcome to join me. I think you'll love it. It's a fantastic city." He looked at her warmly when he said it.

"Thank you." She was touched by his invitation, and couldn't wait for the trip. "Does your family mind your being here?" Paul had hinted that he was from an important Hong Kong family.

"They expected it. They want me to get experience in the States. My family is in manufacturing for all the high-end European and American brands, so they encouraged me to see and experience how it all works here. Lady

Louise is a little bit of a detour for me, but it's an important market too. Our factories produce all the goods for Chanel that are made in Asia, Prada, Gucci, and the big-name American brands. China is where it's all happening now. I'll go back eventually, but I'm not ready to yet. I still have a lot to discover here." He seemed to be learning his lessons well, since he had such an important job with Paul. She knew from Paul that they relied on him heavily for the look of their brand. And he wouldn't be designing if he went home and got involved in the family's manufacturing business, so he was savoring it for now, even at Lady Louise. He seemed to think of it as a challenge, not a step down.

She said good night to him then, and thought about him on the subway ride home. He was a very intelligent man, and clearly had an enormous talent. She would have liked to introduce him to her girls, although they would have been critical of where he worked, but he had a lot in common with them, and a pure eye for fashion. He had kept one of Sydney's designs that afternoon, and wanted to do a little work on it himself with his magic computer pencil, but he had praised her and said she was on the right track. She was a fast learner now that she had a better understanding of what he expected of her. She was trying to keep things simple, cheap, and clean.

As she ate a salad for dinner in her small, airless living room, she wondered how she would explain a three-week absence when she went to China with him. It might prove to be a turning point for her, when she'd have to tell the girls about her job. She couldn't just disappear.

Sophie called her and asked what she'd been doing that day. She had tried to reach her mother's cellphone and was surprised to find it turned off. Sydney knew that Sabrina was already working hard on her collection for Fashion Week in September. Sophie's firm did presentations for buyers, but she didn't have the pressure of elaborate fashion shows the way Sabrina did. She didn't get the glory her older sister did, but she preferred her less stressful world and the whimsy of designing for teenagers, which suited her. It was a niche she really enjoyed.

"I was at a lecture at the Metropolitan all day," Sydney lied, referring to the museum, and hoped that would satisfy her. "It was fascinating, on Etruscan art."

"I wondered where you were," Sophie said, sounding surprised. She told her mother that she and her boyfriend, Grayson, were going to Maine for the weekend, to sail with friends if he felt like it, and she wanted to let her mother know. Sydney knew Grayson had severe social anxiety, which made him unpredictable. But Sophie seemed to accept his eccentric personality without complaint. "Maybe you should go away for a weekend sometime too, Mom. You can't just sit in that apartment and boil."

"I'm fine." She couldn't tell her that she'd been in the

air-conditioned studio at Lady Louise all day, and it had been nice to get out of the heat. Her apartment was stifling at night.

They chatted for a little while, and Sydney went to bed early, surprised by how tired she was. She wasn't used to working anymore, and she had been tense wanting to do everything right on the first day.

The weeks after that flew by, and her fellow designers often stopped to talk to her when they walked past her desk. They'd been impressed by her drawings and the old-fashioned way she achieved them, which was far more challenging and less forgiving than designing digitally, with programs that corrected everything. And she had glanced at their work too, and saw the meat and potatoes of Paul Zeller's line. They were, in fact, copying many big designers, making small adjustments and minor changes so they couldn't be accused of copying them identically, but the similarities to the originals were strong. There was no denying it, but what they did no longer seemed so wrong to her. They were making high-priced fashion available to women who couldn't have afforded it otherwise, and wanted to be well-dressed and look great for play and work. She talked to Ed about it one night over a drink after work. He had invited her for a glass of wine at a small neighborhood bar they all went to down the street.

"My daughters are outraged by what happens at Lady Louise. They think it's a copy mill, but I don't see it that way. I think we provide a valuable service. Not just women with six-figure incomes should be able to buy chic clothes," she said, justifying it. She had seen a lot of the copying on the computers around her desk but Ed hadn't asked her to do any of it herself.

He laughed at what she said. He was easy to be with, hardworking, talented, and conscientious, and she liked him more and more as she got to know him. And little by little he was showing her the ropes of her new job. "Be careful you don't drink the Kool-Aid, Sydney," he warned her. "Let's face it, we are a copy mill. We just do it better than anyone else. We know what to keep and what to change, so we don't get totally vilified, but we deserve a lot of the criticism people aim at us. And yes, it does seem right to bring fashion to women with smaller incomes, at prices they can afford. But we knock off a lot of great designers, and people in the industry like your daughters have no respect for us. It's inevitable. But Paul is a smart guy. He knows what he's doing and his market. He fills a need, and our prices are better than our competitors'." Lady Louise's knockoffs were cheaper and better made than anyone else's.

"Has he ever gotten in trouble for copying other designers too closely?" Sydney asked, curious about Paul. She had hardly seen him in the weeks since she'd started working for him, although she was forever grateful for the job he'd given her and the salary he paid her, which had saved her in her hour of need. But he was occupied running the business and didn't spend time with his employees, and she didn't expect him to now that she was one of them.

"You can't get into trouble just for copying a dress. Only with signature pieces where there are trademarks involved. Paul is a high risk taker in a lot of ways, but he's a businessman above all. He sank a lot of money into the factories in China when he bought them, and they're some of the best I've seen. He's not afraid to spend money to make money, and he always has a plan. He's not going to blow everything he's built by crossing the line and letting us get sued. The fashion press crucify us regularly, but I don't think he would do anything illegal, although he may get pretty close to the line."

She nodded. It sounded about right to her too.

"He's a genius at loss leaders," Ed continued. "He knows just what items to lose money on to make a big splash, like our cashmeres last season. He does it to highlight something else we make twenty or even fifty times our money on." And from all she knew of him, Sydney agreed. "He's counting on you to give us some 'class,' as he puts it. I think it's a good idea. You came through the door at just the right time. He was looking for something new."

"So was I," she said quietly. "It was the right time for me too." Ed had no idea why she was working now. She didn't look as though she needed the money, and all her clothes were expensive. He wondered if maybe she was just bored, and had decided to come back to the fashion industry after so long. She didn't explain it, and he didn't ask. He was polite and discreet about others and himself.

Ed had mentioned to her over a drink that he didn't have a partner, and she could see he worked too hard, just like Sabrina, and even Sophie. Sophie had a boyfriend, but when she was working on a new collection, she spent less time with him, and she wasn't too serious about the relationship. Grayson was a complicated person and liked to be on his own. Sabrina flatly said she had no time to date. And Ed was the same way.

"You all work insanely hard in the business now," Sydney commented. "My oldest daughter has no partner either, and says she never has time to date. She's in the office till midnight most of the time, and I think she sleeps there for a month before and during Fashion Week."

"You probably worked as intensely as we do," Ed reminded her, but she disagreed.

"I don't think the business was as extreme then. It's always been stressful, but now it's increased to an incredible degree."

"There's nothing like it, though," he said passionately. "I wouldn't want to do anything else."

"I wouldn't know how to." Sydney laughed. Although she no longer burned with the fire that Sabrina and Ed did, she knew that there were other things in life, like children, a husband, a family, which none of them seemed to want yet. And no one cared about getting married. She had married and had her kids young, and worked too. This generation was completely focused on their careers, to the exclusion of all else. After she spent two pleasant hours with him, talking about fashion, art, and his earlier life in Hong Kong, she was sorry all over again that she couldn't introduce him to her girls. At least until after she told them about her job at Lady Louise.

The moment of truth came, finally, three days before she and Ed left for Beijing. She had been at Lady Louise for three weeks by then, and was beginning to feel comfortable and loved working for him. And she was excited about the trip. The girls had complained recently that she was much harder to reach. She claimed that she was at museum lectures, the movies, sleeping, or that her phone battery had died, but she was running out of plausible excuses, and there was no way she could explain being out of touch for much of her Asian trip. And she had no idea if her phone or Internet would work in the places where they'd be. Ed had told her that the factory towns were very remote.

She waited till the end of dinner at a sushi restaurant downtown that they liked. She couldn't have them to her apartment, or they'd see the suitcase she had packed. She was only taking one bag, which was rare for her. When she'd traveled with Andrew, she had taken two or three, or even four, depending on the length of the trip. But she didn't need anything fancy on this trip, just clothes to work in that were suitable for the heat, except for Hong Kong, where she wanted to be better dressed when she met Ed's family, shopped, or went to restaurants.

"I have something to tell you," Sydney said seriously, as they both looked at her in surprise.

"The two stepwitches have decided to give you back the money, and let you keep the house?" Sabrina asked in a sarcastic tone.

"Hardly. They sent me a stack of bills last week, for expenses that Andrew and I incurred, like some new carpeting in two of the guest rooms and a new refrigerator. We had the garage painted, and our grocery bill came in late." They had sent them all, which was a crushing load for Sydney now.

"Don't pay for the improvements," Sabrina said harshly. "They've got the house. You didn't take the refrigerator and the carpeting with you. You shouldn't even have to pay for the groceries, screw them. Why should you give them a penny now?" Sydney had been debating about it herself. She wanted to be honorable, but not be a fool or their punching bag. She had already tolerated a lot from them for Andrew's sake, too much. But she thought she might turn the bills over to the lawyer to negotiate for her.

"That wasn't what I wanted to talk to you about," she said quietly. "I need to tell you something." She took a breath as Sophie looked panicked.

"Are you sick, Mom?" she asked immediately.

"No, I'm not. I'm fine. I should have told you weeks ago, but I didn't want to upset you. I took a job."

Sabrina looked instantly suspicious. "What kind of job? Not as a salesgirl in a department store, I hope." Her mother had mentioned it as a possibility at one point, and Sabrina wanted an easier life for her than that, and a better job.

"No, not as a salesgirl. I'm designing. Not at your level, of course. I can't expect that. I've been out of the business for a long time."

"So for whom?" Sabrina tried to get her to the point, but she thought her mother seemed guilty and uncomfortable, and she hadn't looked them in the eye.

"I know you won't approve, either of you. But beggars can't be choosers. And that's what I am now. The employment agencies I went to had nothing for me, and said I've been out of the industry for too long. I took the only offer I got, at a very decent salary. For Paul Zeller. I wouldn't have told you, but I'm leaving for Beijing to see their factories in three days. And I didn't want to just disappear." She felt better having gotten it off her chest, and Sabrina gasped, sat back in her chair, and stared at her with a fierce expression.

"Oh my God, why didn't you talk to us first?"

"I did before I called Paul. And you both jumped down my throat. I need a job, girls. I have to work now. I don't have a choice, and he gave me a good one, and is paying me more than I deserve after being out of it for so long. No one is going to hire me to be a head designer, the number two, or even an assistant at a major house. And I don't care what you say, there's merit to what he does. And his head design consultant is fantastic. I'm going to China with him. His name is Ed Chin and he's from Hong Kong. We're stopping off there on the way back." She had a whole new life now, and hadn't consulted them. It upset them both.

"Do you have any idea how embarrassing this is for us?" Sabrina said in a belligerent tone. "It reflects on us to have you work for a crap house like that." Sophie didn't appear quite as upset, just disappointed. But Sabrina was furious.

"It's *not* a crap house," Sydney insisted, "and he might let me do some signature pieces, using my old name."

"Of course he will. He's exploiting you, and trading on your name and the house you used to work for to lend cachet to the garbage he sells." There was no convincing them, and Sophie looked almost as unhappy as her sister. Sabrina just had a faster, sharper mouth, and had jumped in first, speaking for them both.

"I'm sorry you don't approve," Sydney said simply. "This is what I'm doing and I thought you should know. I'll send you my itinerary before I leave." Her daughters sat at the table in glum silence, although they insisted on paying for dinner. The evening had ended on a very sour note. She kissed the girls when they left one another.

In the cab after dinner, Sabrina was beside herself. "You have to give her credit for finding a job," Sophie said generously.

"Do you realize what it will look like if someone at *Women's Wear Daily* finds out? Her name will be mud and ours by association," Sabrina said, looking desperate.

"Don't be so self-centered," Sophie chided her. "She has to pay her rent somehow, and she's being very brave. She's not sitting home crying. She's out working. You've got to admire her for it."

"I don't admire her judgment," Sabrina said sternly, with a worried expression. "Let's hope no one finds out, or makes the connection to us." She dropped Sophie off first, and then went to her empty apartment, still angry at her mother. She didn't like the idea of her going to China either. It would be dangerous and exhausting for her, and anything could happen.

Sabrina sent Sydney a blistering email telling her what a terrible idea it was for her to work for Lady Louise, and what a fool she had been to fall into Zeller's trap. She said that their mother was disgracing both her daughters, and they would be mortified to tell anyone where she worked. They used to be proud to tell people in the fashion industry that their mother was Sydney Smith, and now she was debasing herself and them. She read the email with tears in her eyes.

When she thought about it, Sydney wasn't just angry at her daughters, she was even angrier at Andrew than she had been until now. No matter how vicious his daughters were and how easy it was to focus her anger on them for throwing her out of her home, it was Andrew who had put her in this position, by not writing a will after he married her. It came back to him. The twins couldn't be her only scapegoat anymore. Andrew had a part in this too. It had started with him and his failure to provide for her. She was furious with him, as she lay awake in bed. It was his fault that her own daughters were angry at her now. She had no allies left, and no friends, no money, and no one to turn to for help. All she had was a job. Her girls hated her for it. But at least she had that, no matter what the girls thought of it.

Sabrina was angry at Andrew too. After doing so much for them, he had behaved irresponsibly and left their mother in a hell of a mess. And now look at what she'd done. All because of him. She was far angrier at Andrew than at her mother, who was being naïve about Paul Zeller, and thought of him as some kind of hero for giving her a job. None of them were heroes in Sabrina's eyes, and Andrew least of all, for leaving her mother unprotected in a world of sharks. And from all she had heard in the industry, Paul Zeller was the king of sharks, and her mother had no idea what she was doing by working for him. And the last thing Sabrina wanted was for her mother to get hurt, even more than she already was.

Chapter 5

The plane took off from Kennedy Airport for Beijing, and Ed and Sydney were in business class together. Paul provided business class to his top executives for long trips, and Ed always upgraded his ticket to first class at his own expense on the New York to Hong Kong leg of the trip. But he had graciously decided to fly business with Sydney, and they chatted for a while as they ate a meal, and then Ed watched a movie and Sydney fell asleep. She woke up after several hours and Ed was working on his computer, getting ready for their meetings. He briefed her on some of the people they would meet. Ed thought about work all the time, and liked to be prepared for every possibility, which was why he was so good at what he did and why Paul trusted him so much.

"Did you tell your daughters about the trip?" he asked her when they were finished, and she nodded. "How did that go?" He knew she had been worried about telling them about her job.

"Not so well," she sighed. Sophie had sent her an email the day after Sabrina's. It was more gently said, but the underlying message was just as harsh. Their conclusion was that by working for Lady Louise, she was an embarrassment to them both. But they weren't paying her bills, and there had been no other options for a job. "They're fashion snobs. They don't approve of what we do." Sydney had had no part in the knockoffs so far, but it was what the house was famous for, and she didn't try to deny it. But she still insisted that there was a valid market for what they did, and women with small budgets had a right to good fashion too.

"Maybe they'll come around," he said kindly. He liked her. She was smart, sensible, easy to work with, and a good designer. And even though she hadn't worked in a long time, she was talented and professional to the core. He could also sense that she was an honorable woman and loved her daughters, and their disapproval was painful for her. She worked hard and had turned out to be even more dedicated than he originally thought she'd be. She was willing to put in endless hours, just as he did, and wanted to learn as much as she could about the business.

"I doubt it," Sydney said, looking sad about her daughters. "They can be very stubborn, and they're backing each other up on this. My older daughter says it could even impact her job if someone finds out I work for Lady Louise. I would hate for that to happen. But I don't want to give up this job just to please them." And she couldn't afford to.

The money in her checking account had almost run out. She needed the job desperately.

"I hope you don't quit," he said fervently and meant it. "They'll calm down. Some people are such purists and elitists about fashion, especially at the high end of the industry. It's ridiculous sometimes. I saw it at the other houses I worked for. And everyone told me I was crazy when I took this job. I was afraid they might be right, but I love it, and it's been a great experience. I learned a lot I wouldn't have otherwise. Paul and I don't always see eye to eye, but he's a good person to work for, as long as you set clear boundaries about what you will and won't do. He respects that. He's a very fair boss. And he listens when I tell him I think we've gone too far copying someone's designs. He always pulls back."

Sydney was relieved to hear it and that Ed thought her daughters were wrong. She had come to respect him in the short time she'd worked for him, and she was convinced her daughters would like him too, if they ever met, which seemed doubtful now. They wanted no part of her job or her new life, or the people in it.

They'd been booked on a flight to Beijing with a three-hour layover in Hong Kong. Sydney was tired after the sixteen-hour flight but had slept for half of it, and did some shopping in the airport before they took off again. They were booked into the Fairmont Hotel in Beijing, where Ed usually stayed, in the Chaoyang District. They spent a night there to recover from the trip, and then flew a half hour to Shijiazhuang the next day, where Lady Louise's factories were. The hotel there was a lot less pleasant and less comfortable, and not a single person spoke English. Sydney was completely dependent on Ed, who spoke fluent Mandarin. But at the factories, which were impeccably run, there were a few people she was able to speak to, and she asked many questions to better understand the volume they dealt with, the problems they faced, and what they needed from the designers. She wanted to learn the business from the ground up, and Ed was impressed. They spent two weeks in Shijiazhuang, going to the factory every day, and then traveled to a different city to look at another factory Paul wanted to buy. Ed wasn't enthusiastic about it, and said it would cost them a fortune to bring it up to their standards. After two and a half weeks in mainland China, they headed for Hong Kong, which was a whole different world.

The moment they stepped off the plane and walked through the airport, Sydney knew she was in a fascinating place that was an intoxicating mix of cultures: British, European, and Chinese, with a million subtle variations. The people were sophisticated, the stores fabulous, it was easy to communicate, and Ed's family had sent their Bentley and driver to pick them up. He had invited her to stay at his parents' house with him, and insisted it would be no trouble and that they were anxious to meet her. Their home was enormous and in the Victoria Peak area of town, with beautiful views of the harbor and the city. There was an army of servants to tend to them, the house was magnificently decorated in a combination of English, French, and Chinese antiques, and the guest suite they put her in had a spectacular view and was the most elegant, comfortable room she'd ever stayed in. Seeing it all, she couldn't understand why Ed wanted to live and work in the States, and she said as much to him. He smiled at her when he answered.

"It's easy to get spoiled here, and my parents still treat me like I'm twelve." He was an only child, and his father and two uncles ran the family empire. His mother was a beautiful, cultured woman who had studied art history in Paris. She was one of the most stunning women Sydney had ever seen, and she had a long rope of imperial jade beads around her neck. Everything about her was exquisite. "I'll come back here to work with my family eventually, but I wanted to see more of the world than just this." But realizing what his family could offer him, and coming to understand the magnitude of their business, she couldn't imagine Ed staying away for many more years. There was too much to draw him home, although he seemed to enjoy his independent life in New York, where he didn't have his family looking over his shoulder all the time, and they were well known in Hong Kong. In

New York, he could be anonymous, and he loved it. He had told her that his family had no problem with his being gay. One of his older cousins was too. He said his mother occasionally regretted not having grandchildren, but he thought he might adopt a child one day, when he came home to Hong Kong. But he wasn't ready for that yet, any more than Sydney's own children were ready to settle down. Marriage and children were the farthest thing from their minds. They were completely focused on their work, and so was he. He had a lot in common with her girls, although he seemed more mature.

They spent two days with Ed's family in Hong Kong, and were treated to sumptuous meals, went to stores she wouldn't have found otherwise, and Ed gave her a tour of the city himself. It was extraordinarily civilized, and exciting at the same time. One of his uncles took them to Macao to gamble late one night, in a private speedboat. It was a life of comfort and luxury that reminded her of everything she had lost, but it was even grander, in the best Chinese style. It was easy to deduce that Ed's family fortune was vast. He had a lot to look forward to in the future, and on the plane on the way back to New York, he told her that sometimes he dreamed of creating his own line, but he wasn't sure about it. It was very tempting, and for a minute, Sydney envied him the ease he had. He could do anything he wanted, and he said his family would back him up. It was a rare position to be in. And yet he was modest and discreet and never showed off or bragged about his family and their circumstances. She admired him even more after their trip, and felt they were becoming friends.

They had been on the plane for an hour, as she thought about the trip and savored the memory of everything they'd seen and the private, harder-to-find places Ed had showed her, when the pilot announced that there was a minor electrical problem on the plane, and they were deciding whether or not to return to Hong Kong. He said the passengers would be advised in a few minutes.

Sydney looked nervous when he said it, and groaned as she glanced at Ed. "Oh, shit. Not again."

"What do you mean 'again'?" He was puzzled by what she said. He wasn't normally a nervous flyer, but he didn't like announcements about mechanical problems while he was on a plane at thirty-five thousand feet.

"That's how I met Paul," she explained. "We almost crashed into the Atlantic, and made an emergency landing in Nova Scotia. He held my hand when we thought we were going down. We were stuck there for fifteen hours. We felt like old friends by the time we landed in New York."

Ed rolled his eyes. "It's your fault, then. You have bad airplane karma. I wouldn't have flown with you if I'd known." He was teasing her, but they were both concerned. The plane circled for half an hour, and then the

pilot came back on and said they were able to fix the problem, and would be continuing to JFK. "I forgive you this
time," Ed told her, and she thanked him again for letting
her stay with his family in Hong Kong. After the arduous
trip to the factory, and two weeks of hard work, it had
been an enormous gift for her.

"We'll be going back again," he told her. "You'll have to
come for Chinese New Year. It's a lot of fun then."

"I still don't know how you can stay in New York when
you have so much waiting for you there."

"It's not going anywhere, and I've had a great time
living in London and New York for the last five years." She
had loved seeing Hong Kong for the first time and sharing
it with him. It had been very special. She and Andrew
had never been to Asia. They usually went to Europe,
and South America a few times. Ed had introduced her to
Hong Kong as only a native could.

When they landed in New York, she thought of her girls
immediately. They had exchanged texts several times
during the trip. Sabrina's were a little chilly, and Sophie's
warmer, but she hadn't spoken to either of them since she
left. The time difference was always wrong at hours that
were convenient for her, and she had the feeling they were
both avoiding her and punishing her for taking the job,
which wasn't fair, but it was how they felt about it. She
wasn't about to give it up for them. She couldn't.

"What are you doing this weekend?" she asked Ed as they shared a cab into the city. It was a far cry from the Bentley his family had sent for them. But nothing about the way he looked, dressed, or behaved suggested that kind of wealth, and she respected him for it.

"I have a date." He smiled at her, looking faintly mysterious. She knew he didn't go out often, and was happy for him. "What about you?"

"I hope I get to see my girls, if they're speaking to me," she said ruefully. She had missed them during the trip.

"They should be over it by now," he said with a disapproving look. She was a wonderful woman, and he had grown fond of her. She didn't deserve her daughters giving her a tough time, after everything she'd been through. He didn't know the whole story, but knew enough to be sympathetic. She had briefly talked about her stepdaughters, who sounded like a nightmare to him. And he didn't know they'd gotten the money too, just the house. She was too proud and too private to tell him the rest.

"We'll see how it goes. They might be busy." She hadn't seen them for three weeks, and hoped they had gotten over their anger at her.

She called them as soon as she got home. Sophie picked up, Sabrina didn't. But Sophie was with her boyfriend and said they had plans the next day. She promised to see her mother for dinner in the coming week. And

Sabrina called her back later and seemed to have calmed down, but she had things to do too. She said she was up to her ears in fittings for their show during Fashion Week. These were always frantic days for her, and she promised to see her mother as soon as she got a break, which her mother knew wouldn't be till after her show and after they'd shot the photos for the lookbooks buyers used to place orders.

"How was the trip?" Sabrina asked her mother politely.

"Fascinating. We stayed with my boss's family in Hong Kong. It was amazing, and the time at the factory was interesting too." She knew that Sabrina had put on a fashion show in Beijing two years before and had hated it. Everything possible had gone wrong. The air-conditioning had died in the hall they rented, three of the models had fainted on the runway from the heat, and she'd gotten bronchitis from the pollution. Sydney's trip had been a lot smoother, mostly thanks to Ed, and it made everything easier because the language wasn't a problem for him.

She said as much to Paul Zeller when he took her to lunch the next day to debrief her. She reported on everything they'd done, gave him her impressions, and raved about Ed, about how competent he was, how efficient, how well he handled everything, and how smooth he had made the trip for her.

"I know," Paul said with a sigh. "I've made a couple of factory tours with him. He's a gem. Unfortunately, I always know the clock is ticking. No matter what I offer him, sooner or later he'll go back to his family in Hong Kong. It's inevitable. I can't compete with them. They're among the most powerful people in manufacturing in China. He'll be running that for them one day, if he wants to. I'm just happy to hang on to him as long as I can. Speaking of which . . ." He turned to a subject he'd mentioned to her before, but now wanted to get started on. "I think it's time you start putting some thought into your Sydney Smith signature pieces for us. It's an experiment, but if it works well, it could evolve into your own line one day, down the road." It was a huge plum to entice her with.

"What kind of clothes do you have in mind?" she asked him, flattered that he wanted to pursue it with her. "Dressier? Casual? Just a little step up from what we do now?"

"Yes, a step up. See what inspires you. I'm giving you carte blanche." She was thrilled and couldn't wait to tell Ed. Sydney mentioned it to him that afternoon, and she was surprised to see him frown at the mention of her eventual signature line. She wondered if he was jealous, but she'd seen no evidence of it and he had no reason to be. He was the creative director of Lady Louise, a far more important job than hers.

"I may be crazy or paranoid," he said cautiously, "but after three years, I know Paul. Sometimes he has a hidden agenda, and he'll dangle a big carrot because he has another idea behind it. I got that feeling from him this morning, and I can't tell you why. It's early for him to be talking to you about your own line with your name on it. You haven't been here for that long, and he hasn't tested the market with individual signature pieces yet. I have a strange feeling that he has something up his sleeve." Ed looked troubled and Sydney didn't know what to make of it.

"Like what?" She was puzzled by what he'd said. He had said before that Paul was a good guy and a fair boss. Why was he thinking differently now?

"I have absolutely no idea," Ed admitted, "and I'm probably wrong. I just know that sometimes when he offers a big reward, he has something simmering on the back burner. And I'm pretty sure he was going to wait awhile to give you your own line. I'm not sure why he stepped that up. He didn't tell me. Sometimes he gets a little too ambitious. Just keep your eyes and ears open and see what happens. He'll tip his hand sooner or later. He's not as subtle as he thinks." She thought it was a somewhat alarming warning, and made a conscious decision to be alert. But she was almost certain that Ed's odd feelings were unfounded, and she was excited about the prospect of an eventual signature line, and wanted to put some real thought into it for the future. Paul was talking about introducing a few special pieces of hers in the spring, as a surprise for their higher-end buyers.

She put Ed's concerns out of her mind after that, and

concentrated on getting ready for their presentation during Fashion Week. Because they were a lower-priced line, they didn't do a full fashion show, but only a presentation at a venue they rented, with models wearing the clothes, somewhat like the shows they did where Sophie worked. It was a lot less stressful than the high-end fashion show Sabrina did with forty top supermodels.

Ed had already told her that he would be taking her to all the big shows with him, along with one of their young designers, as he did every season. He mentioned that they'd be going to Sabrina's show as well. Sydney knew that after the shows, they worked on their knockoffs and developed their next line in record time. The designers at Lady Louise worked under brutal deadlines. It was a given and a reality they had to live with. Sydney wasn't proud of the knockoffs they did, but she understood the reason for them from how Paul had explained it. And she hoped that they'd be able to modify their copies slightly this season so the similarities weren't too glaring. It was one of her longer-term goals. Ed liked keeping an eye on that as well, although Paul never minded copying the originals closely. Mimi, the young designer they were taking, was one of Paul's favorite designers. She was French and she never changed enough elements to satisfy Ed, who frequently argued with Paul about it. He was determined to preserve their integrity, to the degree he could.

Sydney had managed to have dinner with Sophie once

before Fashion Week started and she got too swamped to get together. She had talked to Sabrina on the phone several times, but hadn't been able to see her. The first glimpse she got of her was at her fashion show. Sydney was sitting with Ed, and she was beaming with pride when Sabrina took a bow at the end, after all the models had come out for the last time. It was a spectacular show, one of her best, Sydney thought, and Ed agreed. He had followed her career closely because he admired her work, long before Sydney came to Lady Louise.

As soon as the show ended, Sydney went backstage quickly to give Sabrina a hug, and then they left and saw two more shows that afternoon. Mimi, the designer, didn't sit with them, but went to all the shows. A week later, Sydney saw why Mimi went on her own. She happened to walk past Mimi's desk and could examine her drawings closely. She thought the copies were almost identical, and said as much to Ed.

"They're just too close. They look almost the same as the originals," Sydney said. "It's going to make us look bad in the fashion press." He went to check for himself and came back to Sydney's desk and agreed. She knew that legally, in most cases, the original designs weren't protected, but designers who made copies usually tried to change four or five elements. Mimi had only altered one or two, which were barely noticeable because she had modified them so slightly.

"She has a tendency to overdo it," Ed told Sydney. "She can knock off damn near anything. But she has to simplify them, take off some of the details, and give them a little twist. Thanks for mentioning it to me." Sydney realized then that Mimi had been assigned to the shows because she copied the collections so exactly. And whenever possible, she circulated at the ordering venues to get a closer look and examine the details of the big designers' clothes. She was an anonymous face in the crowd, and what she did was exactly what Sabrina objected to about Lady Louise, and why she hated Paul Zeller and her mother's new job. They weren't using other designers' work for "inspiration" as they claimed, they were copying them identically, or more so than they should, and making almost exact copies.

Sydney went back to study Mimi's work again, and the copies she had made from Sabrina's collection. Sydney thought they were the most imitative of all, because Sabrina's work was hot these days.

"I think you need to tone those down a little," Sydney suggested to her.

"But that's what Mr. Zeller wants," the young French designer said firmly.

"Not that close, I'm sure." She complained to Ed again and he promised to have another look.

*

It wasn't until Fashion Week was over that Sydney had dinner with both her daughters. Sabrina looked exhausted, but her show had gone well, and the orders from store buyers afterward had been better than ever before. Sophie's presentation had been a huge success too, with record-breaking orders, and her employers were thrilled.

Sydney got a chance to tell them about her trip to China, and at the end of the meal Sabrina turned to her with an irritated expression.

"So did your slaves knock off everything in my collection?" she asked unhappily, with an accusing look.

"I hope not. I've already made comments to them twice. Paul wants us to do some more innovative things in the future. We don't want to be known just as a knockoff house. The line is actually better than that."

"You're the only one who thinks so," Sabrina said grimly. "I wish you hadn't taken a job with them."

"I didn't have any other choice," Sydney said quietly, and then gave them the only good news she had. "I just got a tenant in the apartment in Paris, so that will help." She'd received another stack of bills from the twins that they wanted her to pay. She had refused, but she didn't mention that to her daughters. But it added to the stress of her current life. They dunned her constantly with bills they should pay themselves and she couldn't afford to.

"One of these days, his knockoff factory is going to

blow up in Zeller's face, and yours, if you're standing too close to him. Be careful, Mom," Sabrina warned her.

"I am, and the head design consultant keeps an eye on all of it. He's an honorable guy."

"If he were, and a serious designer, he wouldn't be working for Paul Zeller," Sabrina said coldly.

"I'm sorry you feel that way, I'd love you to meet him sometime. He's about your age, a little older. And his family was wonderful to me when we went to Hong Kong." Sabrina didn't comment, and it was obvious that neither girl wanted to meet him. This was the second time their dinner together had ended on a tense note because of their criticism of her job. They were intransigent about it. And she was convinced that they were wrong. Although knockoffs weren't admirable, she thought there was merit to bringing great design to people at affordable prices. It was the whole mission of their business, and Paul made it sound like a sacred crusade. But Sabrina and Sophie didn't buy the noble party line.

Two weeks after Fashion Week in New York, Sydney and Ed went to Fashion Week in Paris, to see the collections by French ready-to-wear designers. At Paul's request, they took Mimi with them, and she never sat with them, just as she didn't in New York. She saw every show, as they did, and she had gone to Milan and London Fashion Weeks as well, in the weeks before they arrived. Sydney loved the

French shows, but she thought Sabrina's in New York had been just as good.

When they got back to New York, Sydney started working on the rough drawings for her signature pieces, and was very busy. She had wanted to check Mimi's drawings after Fashion Week in Paris, but she didn't have time and Ed said he would, just to make sure that nothing was too close or an exact copy. But when Sydney saw the first samples from their line in early November, she knew that something had gone wrong. There was a huge problem she'd missed. She could tell she hadn't seen all the designs, they'd withheld some from her. She knew she hadn't seen these. All the major pieces in Sabrina's collection had been reproduced as exact copies, and in some of the photographs, you couldn't tell which was which. There was an enormous article in *Women's Wear Daily* about it, lambasting Lady Louise and their "unethical design staff" and practices, and they called Paul Zeller the chief parasite of the fashion industry. And there was a mention that Sabrina Morgan's mother, the former Sydney Smith of long-ago design fame, now worked for Lady Louise. And the writer suggested obliquely that Sabrina might have leaked her designs to her mother, or even sold them to her for Zeller to reproduce. Sydney felt sick when she read it, and an hour later Sabrina called her. She was in tears, and sobbing when her mother answered the phone.

"I hope you're happy, Mom. I just got fired. They said that what happened is unforgivable and they blamed me for it. They think I sold you my designs for that shit house you work for. I promised them that I didn't, and they said they can't take the chance. I got fired on the spot. They had security escort me out of the building." Sydney's heart turned over when she heard her.

"Oh my God . . . I'm so sorry . . . I warned the designer about it. She's not supposed to copy anything that closely," Sydney said, crying herself by then. They all knew the rules about changing enough elements to make them respectable, but Mimi hadn't followed them, and had done exact copies instead.

"She shouldn't be copying anything at all," Sabrina said, sobbing, but they both knew it was the nature of the business, and Lady Louise wasn't the only house that did it. "My career is over, thanks to you," she accused her mother, and then hung up on her. Sydney was so angry she went to see Ed in a fury. He already knew about the article and the tornado that was happening as a result.

"I'm really sorry, Sydney. I told her they were too close. I think Paul overrode me on this one."

"Sabrina just got fired," Sydney said, looking distraught. "They think she sold us the designs. They had security escort her out of the building. I have to quit." How would she ever make it up to her daughter? She had cost her a wonderful job, and maybe even her career. Sabrina had been right from the beginning. She'd been playing with fire working for Paul Zeller.

"You can't quit. I just talked to Paul, and they're pulling all of Sabrina's designs to make modifications on them. I agree with you, this never should have happened, but we're not the only ones who do it." But it still didn't excuse it, and Sabrina was the one who'd gotten hurt.

"But she's my daughter and she blames me. She expected me to protect her, and I didn't."

"Do you think they'll take her back, if we tell them we're modifying them?" He was desperate to help, but it would be hard to undo the damage, and the shadow it had cast on both Sabrina and her mother. "Tell her to get a tough lawyer and negotiate a deal with her employers. If they fire her, they should give her a great severance package without a noncompete. That's important."

"I'll tell her," Sydney said grimly. "But I can tell you one thing. My relationship with my daughter is a lot more important to me than my job." And she needed the job desperately. She couldn't survive on just the Paris rent from her tenant. And she wasn't likely to get another job, particularly after this. She texted Sabrina what Ed had said immediately. And Ed went to talk to Paul about it.

It was a stressful afternoon, and Paul pointed out to Ed that they were already doing everything they could, by modifying the drawings, and he had even agreed to withdraw one design completely. He admitted to Ed that the copies had been too close, and agreed to promise Sydney it would never happen again. He apologized profusely to Sydney when he called her into his office with Ed. They didn't want her to quit.

"My daughter will never forgive me for this. I just cost her the best job she ever had, because I work for you." Sydney was angry at Paul, and at herself for unwittingly being a part of it.

"You can't quit now," Paul pleaded with her. "I want to give you a full signature line of your own in the coming year, not just a few pieces, and with profit sharing for you on the line." He was using everything he could to tempt her, and she knew she couldn't afford to lose her job. But she felt as though she had sold her soul to the devil. And Sabrina had paid the price. To make it up to Sabrina, she was willing to quit.

Sydney went to see her late that afternoon. Sabrina was sitting in the living room of her Tribeca apartment, crying, and shouted at her mother as soon as she walked in. Sophie had left work and was there to console her too. She had her arms around her sister when Sydney walked in. Sophie was always the peacemaker in their midst.

"I told you to stay away from him, Mom. He's a lowlife in every sense of the word," Sabrina said immediately. Her mother tried to hug her, but she wouldn't let her, understandably. The loss of the job she loved was her mother's fault, indirectly, because of the shoddy practices where she worked.

"I feel terrible about it, worse than terrible. He pulled all of your designs and is modifying them. And he canceled one of them completely. If we tell your employers that, do you think they'll give you back your job?" Sydney looked as heartbroken as her daughter. "Did you call a lawyer?" Sabrina nodded that she had.

"He's working on it. They have no evidence that I showed you my designs or sold them to Zeller, but my boss is a dick. You're not the only firm that ever copied us. Others do too, but these were exact copies, not just 'inspirations,' and the writer of the article jumped on the link with you. It's all over the Internet. I think my boss just wanted to blame me," she said fairly, "but they have no proof because I didn't do it."

"I told Paul I'd quit over this," Sydney said in a subdued voice, crushed for her daughter.

"Can you afford to do that?" Sophie asked her mother, and Sydney hesitated before she answered. She couldn't, but she was willing to, out of loyalty to her daughter.

"Not really," Sydney answered honestly, "but I'll do it in a minute if it will make you feel any better," she said, and Sabrina smiled and was touched. The fire had gone out of her, but she was deeply upset over losing her job, especially if they blocked her from getting another one, which would be disastrous, and they could.

"I can get another job easier than you can," Sabrina said hopefully, "and both of us being unemployed doesn't make much sense. But for God's sake, Mom, be careful of him. I know you think Paul Zeller walks on water, but he's unethical, and he'll use you if he can."

"I trust Ed Chin, who's my direct boss. He keeps an eye on him."

"Well, he didn't stop him this time."

The three of them sat and talked for several hours, and Sophie stayed to spend the night with her sister, and Sydney went back to her own apartment. It was as cold and drafty in the fall as it was hot in the summer. But she didn't care. She poured herself a glass of wine when she got home to calm down, but took only a sip. She had no idea how she would ever make up to Sabrina what had just happened. And what if her daughter couldn't find another job, if it really did ruin her career? Sydney had lost everything herself, and now she was destroying her children's lives. It was the darkest night she'd had since Andrew died. And then she remembered the sleeping pills her doctor had given her when she had told him she couldn't sleep. She hadn't taken any, and the bottle was still full.

She got the bottle of pills out of her medicine cabinet and sat holding it in her hand. She felt as though she had ruined Sabrina's career, and her own life wasn't worth much to her anymore. She was barely scraping by, and doing no one any good. And now she had caused Sabrina untold grief and harm. She had the apartment in Paris to leave them, which was all she owned, but it was something. She suddenly thought she'd be more useful to them dead than alive. It didn't even occur to her that they would miss her or see it as an abandonment. She thought she'd be doing them a favor if she died, to atone for her mistakes. She had nothing left to live for, and nothing to give them. And her career as a designer for Lady Louise was a joke. They didn't need her. They could copy every major designer in the world. All she wanted now was out. And if Andrew had really loved her, how could he leave her without providing for her? The strain of the last five months had been too much.

Her mind was whirling, as she took another sip of the wine and opened the bottle of pills. The phone rang but she didn't answer it. She had nothing left to say to anyone. She had made up her mind. It stopped ringing, and then rang again. She saw that the call was from Ed Chin and she didn't care. She didn't want to talk to him either. She kept the vial of pills in her hand, put her glass down on the coffee table, and finally picked up her cell when he called again.

"Sydney, are you okay?" He was worried about her. He had seen the look of desperation on her face when she left work.

"Yes, I'm okay," she repeated mechanically in a rough

voice. The wine had had little effect. She wasn't a drinker, and alcohol usually hit her pretty hard.

"How's Sabrina?"

"Terrible. What would you expect?"

"We pulled everything for modification. I confirmed it before I left the office. And Paul wants to make it up to you however he can."

"He can't get her job back," Sydney said in a tone of deep despair. "And I can't afford to quit. Isn't that a joke? I'd be worth more to them now dead than alive. I'm not doing anyone any good." Her thoughts sounded disjointed and very dark.

"Don't talk like that," he said, feeling a wave of panic rush over him. His best friend and first lover had committed suicide when they were in college, and he had gotten her drift. "They need you, you're their mother. They have no one else."

"I just cost my daughter her job. She loved that job. And I can't even help her. I'm dead broke. I'm just a headache for them now."

"Every firm in New York is going to want her as soon as they hear she was fired. She's one of the hottest young designers in the States. What are you doing right now?"

Planning to kill myself, she thought, but didn't tell him. "Nothing, I'm having a glass of wine."

She sounded dangerously bad to him. "I'm coming over."

"Why?" She didn't want him interfering with her plan. "You can't. I'm busy." But Ed wasn't going to let it happen. Not a second time in his life. He had been at the library, studying, when his lover had committed suicide, because he didn't have the courage to tell his parents he was gay. He had preferred to die instead. They were twenty, and it had marked Ed forever. He hadn't been in a committed relationship since. He was too afraid to.

"I'll be there in five minutes," he said, and hung up on her. He was there seven minutes later. He didn't live far away, and he had run as fast as he could to get to her apartment. He could see how devastated she was when he got there. She still had the bottle of pills in her hand, and he took them away and shoved them deep into his pocket. "You can get drunk if you want, but you can't kill yourself. You'll only make it worse for them. You have to stick around and help them. They're not old enough to lose you," he said sensibly, worried about his friend. "This will blow over. She'll get another job. I'm not even sure they can enforce a noncompete, firing her like this, because they can't prove she sold us anything. She didn't. A good lawyer will get a big severance package for her because of this. This wasn't her fault. Why don't you stick around and help her with that?"

Sydney looked at him remorsefully, and he saw sanity begin to return. "I'm sorry I dragged you over here," she said, apologetic.

"You didn't. I came because I wanted to. Why don't you go to bed? I'll sleep on the couch tonight." He went to the bathroom then and flushed the pills so she couldn't take them while he was sleeping. He didn't trust her. She still looked ravaged, although she had calmed down a little. She melted into his arms then and started to cry, and he held her while she sobbed. It was all too much for her, and he was her only friend now. He put her to bed with her clothes on, and lay down next to her. He held her until she fell asleep, and then went and lay on her couch. And when he woke up, she was sitting next to him, looking battered, with dark circles under her eyes.

"I'm sorry. I think I kind of lost it last night. I wasn't even drunk. I just had a few sips."

"I know," he said gently. "Sabrina's going to be okay." He tried to reassure her.

"Do you mind if I take the day off today?" she asked and he shook his head.

"I'm not leaving you alone. I don't trust you. You're coming to work. I need to be there." He was her self-appointed bodyguard now.

"I'm fine. Really."

"I'm not convinced. Tell me that when you're dressed and have makeup on, and you're sitting at your desk." She groaned when she stood up to go and take a shower, and then she turned to look at him gratefully.

"Thank you . . . you saved my life last night. I was going

to do something stupid." He nodded with tears in his eyes, remembering his friend.

"I know you were . . ." He pointed at the bathroom then and she padded off to take a shower.

He handed her a cup of coffee when she came back wearing jeans and a black sweater. She looked better, but still not great. Sabrina called a few minutes later. They had offered her her job back, but she was so upset about their unfair accusations that she had decided to get a hefty severance package with a noncompete, so she could look for a new job.

"Maybe this is for the best in the end," Sabrina said, sounding better than her mother. "I'm going to stick it to them, Mom."

Sydney laughed, relieved to hear her daughter in fighting mode. Sydney looked a lot better when she and Ed left the apartment half an hour later.

"I'll treat you to a cab," he offered generously, and hailed a taxi. As they headed downtown, she didn't say anything, but she reached over and held his hand, and he leaned down and kissed her on the cheek. "You scared the shit out of me last night," he whispered to her and she nodded. She had scared herself too. All she'd wanted was to die, and if he hadn't come over, she probably would have. It was a sobering thought as the cab wove through traffic, and the two of them sat silently in the backseat, holding hands.

Chapter 6

When Sydney got to the office the day after Sabrina had been fired, Paul took her to lunch and laid out his plans for her. He was deeply apologetic over what had happened. He renewed his offer of a line of her own, a full signature line for Sydney with profit sharing. He also had a new project he wanted to discuss with her to convince her to stay. He said it was a line of extremely well-made leather goods, copies of expensive purses at great prices, and he was going to put her name on them too. He said they were the best copies he'd ever seen. They were made in China, and he was offering her a share of the profits on the new line of purses too. He said it was an opportunity for her to make some real money. Lady Louise was well known for their high-quality leather goods at impressively low prices, and they sold out every time. She told Ed about it after her lunch with Paul.

"He wants me to be in charge of the line and put my name on them. I don't know anything about leather goods. I've never dealt with bags before," Sydney said, looking intrigued but nervous. He was luring her into areas she wasn't familiar with that he said were big money makers.

"How do they look?" Ed asked her, curious about the purses. Paul hadn't mentioned the project to him yet, but he knew that the purses they brought in from China always did well and had a high-priced quality look.

"I don't know. He said he'd show me this afternoon. He already has samples at the warehouse. He's having someone drive them in."

Paul called both of them to his office later, and they were startled when they saw the bags laid out on a table. They looked like expensive designer bags, the real deal, and even better than the ones they usually sold.

"Who's been making these?" Ed asked him, checking out the silk linings, and Paul mentioned a firm they'd never used before. Ed examined them closely, and so did Sydney. The workmanship was beautiful. There were four different styles, in shapes they all recognized by a familiar high-end brand. Ed opened them and looked for signs that they were real designer bags and not copies, but there were none. He looked impressed and pleased when he nodded at Paul. "They're great," Ed complimented him. Paul was going to call them the Sydney Smith line for Lady Louise, and he quoted an unbeatable price for the purses that their customers wouldn't be able to resist.

"I need you to go back to China and sign them up for production. We have to get them from the supplier. We don't have the machinery to make leather goods like that in our factories," he explained to Sydney, and Ed confirmed it. The bags were a more sophisticated product than they'd made so far, even though they were cheap.

"When do you want us to go?" Ed was worried. "I've got production meetings here for the next month, lookbooks to oversee, and we're already up to our ears getting ready for the presentation of the fall line." They worked almost a year ahead, like every other major design firm. "I can't go back to China yet." He looked panicked at the thought and overwhelmed by his work.

"I need Sydney to go over in the next two weeks," Paul said practically. "I don't want to wait. The bags are already manufactured, so all we have to do is pick the styles and colors we want and import them. They won't do modifications on these styles, and we don't need them to. The bags are gorgeous. Sydney can handle it. The company that makes them is a couple of hours out of Beijing. We'll get her a translator and a driver. She can manage without you this time," he said confidently, but Sydney wasn't so sure. He was giving her a lot of responsibility, and going to China without Ed was going to be difficult. He knew the customs so much better than she did. But the opportunity Paul was giving her was so enormous that Sydney didn't dare turn him down. It was a challenge she'd have to meet.

She and Ed talked about it on the way back to the design floor, and he looked worried about her.

"Think you can do it? It's a lot of paperwork to export them, and he wants you to make sure that what they're manufacturing is as good as what we've just seen. We don't want a bait and switch, where the product they ship is inferior to the samples we saw. I haven't handled the bags before and I don't know this supplier."

"They do beautiful work," Sydney commented. They looked like some bags she had herself, and had sent to storage. They were almost too good to be true, and Ed said they were the best copies he'd ever seen. Paul swore by them and loved the price, and said he was doing Sydney a favor, giving her the project, and Ed agreed. With profit sharing, the bags could be a windfall for her.

Paul had told her she only needed to stay in Beijing for two days, and they would have it all set up for her. Translator, driver, good hotel. She had an appointment with the manufacturer. All she had to do was inspect the bags, pick the ones they wanted, fill out the customs documents, arrange for shipping to New York, and get back on a plane.

She left a week later, and everything went smoothly on the way to Beijing. There was a car waiting for her at the airport to take her to the hotel, and the translator appeared the next morning to join her at the meeting. The bags they showed her were of the same high quality she'd seen in New York, in the same familiar shapes, with only the shoulder straps slightly different from the ones they'd copied, by a well-known designer. It was going to be a fabulously successful line, and the wholesale price was incredibly low. Lady Louise was going to make a fantastic profit on the new bags, which was what Paul loved about them. And having her name on them was an incredible opportunity for her.

She got back on the flight to New York on schedule. They had promised that the bags would arrive within two weeks. They were shipping them air freight. She reported everything to Ed as soon as she got home. The trip had gone without a hitch. She had bought two hundred of the bags, which was a lot for a new item they hadn't tried out yet, but the price was so low, she could afford it on the budget Paul had given her. And she was sure they would be a huge hit, and they would be buying many more in future.

She had signed all the purchase orders since Ed wasn't with her, and the customs documents. Going to China on her own had given her new self-confidence, and Paul said he was impressed with how efficient she'd been.

She called Sabrina and Sophie the night she got home. Sabrina had just interviewed at a firm where she'd always wanted to work, and had signed an excellent severance package, with her lawyer's help and some heavy negotiation and legal threats against the employer that had fired her. They had accused her prematurely with no proof and damaged her reputation. They had given her two years' salary with no restrictions and no noncompete clause, a vital benefit for her. She was thrilled. And *Women's Wear Daily* had printed an apology to Sabrina, after being threatened by her lawyer.

"I think you did me a favor, Mom," she said on the phone, and Sydney was relieved. They had snatched victory from the jaws of defeat. She shuddered thinking that she had almost killed herself out of remorse and guilt the night that Sabrina had been fired. So much had happened to her in recent months, and suddenly it was all too much. Costing Sabrina her job had been the last straw.

Sophie didn't answer when she called her, and as soon as Sydney hung up, Veronica called her. She had heard from her contractor that Kellie was doing a major remodel on the house before she moved in, and thought Sydney should know.

"It's her house now, she can do whatever she wants," Sydney said. "To tell you the truth, I don't really want to know about it. It just upsets me to think about the changes she's going to make. There's nothing I can do. And I don't want progress reports on it once she gets started," she warned Veronica.

"I thought you'd want to hear about it," Veronica said again, sounding miffed. She was the only person from Sydney's past life who still called her, but she only called when there was something upsetting to relate. She was the constant bearer of bad tidings. And she managed to slip in, with her pseudo sympathetic voice, that everyone was saying Andrew had left her nothing and she was broke, which upset Sydney too. "They probably think that because you went back to work. But what else are you going to do? You might as well keep busy since you have no husband and no house to run anymore." Their conversations always took the same negative turn to unhappy issues for her. And Sydney guessed that if it was true that people were talking, the rumor had probably been started by one of her stepdaughters.

"I like working," Sydney said, which sounded stupid, even to her.

"I read somewhere that Sabrina got fired from her job," Veronica said in a snotty tone, to get even for Sydney not wanting to hear about the remodel of the house.

"Not really. She had a disagreement with them, and they acted hastily. They recanted the next day. In the end, she quit. She's interviewing with other firms now." Sydney wondered why she always felt compelled to justify herself to Veronica. Both of her own daughters were perennially unemployed, and one was getting a divorce. Why wasn't she explaining that? Why was Sydney's misfortune always her focal point of interest?

"And what have you been up to?" Veronica persisted.

"I just got back from China, for the second time," Sydney said, feeling pleased with herself for what she had accomplished.

"I guess you don't have time for your old friends anymore," Veronica said, sounding insulted, as though Sydney had slighted her, when in fact she was working and trying to keep her head above water.

"Not at all. My 'old friends' haven't called me since Andrew died," Sydney tossed back at her. It was true. She'd been very hurt by it at first, but was too busy to think about it now.

"They probably don't want to intrude," Veronica suggested.

"Or you were right the first time, when you said they wouldn't want a single woman around. I haven't heard from a soul." And she no longer cared. She had enough on her mind. But she didn't like the idea that they were saying she was broke. It made her sound like a loser, but if Kyra and Kellie were saying it, there was nothing she could do to stop them, and, in fact, it was true.

Veronica promised to call soon and hung up then. Sydney hoped she wouldn't, but didn't have the guts to say it to her. Somehow whatever mood she was in, it always made Sydney feel worse whenever Veronica called. At least she didn't drop by in New York. She never came to the city.

For the next two weeks, Sydney worked closely with Ed on preparing the presentation of the new clothing line for the fall. And she was working on inspiration sketches for the Sydney Smith line they were developing. They still had a long way to go. Her line of signature purses would be presented first, and would be a good test of how strong her name was.

She had Thanksgiving dinner with Sabrina and Sophie at the restaurant at the Greenwich Hotel, close to where the girls lived. It was their first Thanksgiving without Andrew, and predictably hard. Sydney was happy to get into bed that night after dinner when she got home, and grateful that the day was over. She bounced back and forth between missing him acutely and remembering every happy moment they'd ever shared, and at the opposite extreme, being angry at him for the life of financial insecurity she led now, constantly worried about money and trying to pay her expenses and bills on what she earned because he had left her nothing else. It reminded her of when she was first divorced twenty-two years before, trying to make ends meet, but at least this time she didn't have two little girls to support. She had managed well on her salary then, and Andrew had come along and made everything easy for her when they got married. He had led her into a life of luxury she had never aspired to, but had gotten accustomed to, and then on his death he had tossed her into the deep end of the pool, without a penny. And the only asset she had was an apartment in Paris she couldn't find a buyer for.

She spent a lazy weekend at home, reading, after Thanksgiving. It rained all weekend, and she was happy to be at home in her tiny apartment, which had begun to feel like home, and a cozy cocoon.

On Thursday morning, their customs broker called her. Their bags had arrived from Beijing, all two hundred of them, and since she had signed the customs documents in China, he wanted her to clear them with him. She told Ed where she was going shortly before noon. He had a mountain of things on his desk and half a dozen designs on his computer screen and looked distracted.

"Call me if you have any problems," he said vaguely as she left for U.S. Customs at the airport.

"I won't," she reassured him. "The broker will be with me. Everything was very straightforward at the other end." She sounded confident.

"You never know with customs. They get upset with some minor detail, a zipper or the thread content of the lining. It depends on their mood of the hour and the alignment of the stars that day, and if the customs agent wants to do it by the book."

"I'm sure it will be fine." She had never cleared a shipment on her own, and normally she wouldn't have had to, except that she had filled out all the forms and signed every document herself, as Paul had instructed her to since he had made her responsible for the line, and it was a first for her.

She ran into Paul as she left the building, on his way to

lunch, and he smiled broadly when he saw her. He looked very dapper in a dark gray suit with a white shirt and red tie, a beautifully cut overcoat, and shoes she recognized as John Lobb by Hermès. He never skimped on himself. He sold low-priced goods, but bought the best for his personal use. And his wife had the reputation of costing him a fortune, which he complained about good-naturedly from time to time. But he seemed to accept the high cost of marriage and divorce as a fact of life.

"Where are you off to?" he asked easily as she hurried to the Uber car she had called, waiting at the curb.

"The airport, customs, to clear our bags. They arrived. The broker just called me." She knew that Paul would be pleased. She had bought them in black, brown, a natural color, and a few in red. And she agreed with him that they were going to be their new hot item for Christmas. They were beautifully made. Even the lining was attractive, in matching high-quality silk.

"Let's get them into the stores as soon as we can," he said, and then hurried off with his collar turned up against the cold, as she nodded agreement and got into the car.

She gave the driver the address of the customs office at the airport, and sat back to answer emails on her iPad, since she had the time. There was one from Kellie and Kyra's attorney demanding payment for the carpeting she'd already told them she wouldn't pay for, since they had the house now. He kept saying that her stepdaughters didn't like the color and wanted it replaced. She forwarded it to Jesse Barclay, and asked him to respond again. She was not going to pay them a penny, but they kept trying. And she had to pay Jesse for his time out of her own pocket, since the estate wouldn't pay him. But it was cheaper than giving them money she didn't owe them and didn't have.

It took them forty minutes to get to the airport from Hell's Kitchen, and their customs broker was waiting outside for her when she got there.

"Did they release the goods to you?" she asked him, hopeful that they had, and he shook his head. They were going to the office for commercial shipments.

"They said they have to see you in person. They're being a pain in the ass." She wasn't surprised and strode inside the building, with the broker right behind her. She had never met him before; his name was Dan Parker. There were three customs agents waiting for her when they walked in, and they asked to see her identification. They wanted to know if it was her signature on the documents, and she confirmed it. They could see that it was.

"Did you purchase these purses for commercial use?" one of them asked her and she started to feel annoyed, but was polite.

"Yes, we purchased them wholesale directly from the manufacturer in China. I went over to do the transaction myself and approve the finished product." She didn't want to admit that they were knockoffs, or they might accuse her of bringing in counterfeits, exact copies, but these bags weren't illegal. They complied with all the norms for copied goods, made in cheaper leathers, with different linings from the originals and different shoulder straps. She had inspected them herself according to Ed's specifications and Paul's directions.

The second agent held up one of the bags for her to identify, and she confirmed that it was one of their shipment. It happened to be a brown leather bag with a brown silk lining that differed from the original brand that had been copied. The originals, she knew, were lined in high-grade leather. And as she watched him, the agent sliced open the lining with a knife and removed it, and laid it on the counter, and Sydney didn't look happy about it. She would be even less so if they removed all the linings because they didn't like the fabric content, or charged her higher duty.

"You're not supposed to damage the merchandise," she reminded him.

"Take a look at the inside of that bag," he said, his eyes expressionless as he watched her, and she glanced inside and saw the familiar leather lining she recognized from the similar bag she owned herself, by the original designer. There was a small silver plaque with the name of the expensive brand it had supposedly been copied from, with the clearly marked words "Made in Italy." She looked up at the agent in amazement, not sure what to make of it. The lining had obviously been carefully fitted and sewn in to hide the original interior of the bag with the famous brand name of the maker. And it did not appear to be a counterfeit. It looked like the real deal, the original bag, to Sydney. Clearly someone had altered the handle and masked the lining to disguise it.

"And you're not supposed to be bringing stolen goods into the country," he said coldly in response to her complaint about his removing the lining.

"I didn't see any sign of that when I inspected them in China," she said in a much smaller voice.

"Who added the shoulder straps and lining to disguise them?" he asked her.

"They were sold to us as modifications of the original design when they were copied," she answered, suddenly confused by what was happening. "There was nothing to indicate that they weren't what they claimed they were. Good-looking copies."

"Very good-looking," the first agent commented with a scornful expression. "We've seen products from this outfit before. They're either counterfeit or stolen. These aren't counterfeit, so they're stolen." Once the lining was removed, all the markings were evident. They were expensive bags that were being sold for a fraction of what they were worth and would have been sold for by their rightful maker. They were obviously stolen goods, being sold in large volume to be distributed in the States. An outfit like Lady Louise could sell many more bags than the black market could handle.

"Then clearly we got burned when we bought them." Her voice wavered a little, while Paul's customs broker watched her and didn't say a word. "I'll have to call my employer about this. He won't be happy." In fact, what they had spent on them had gone up in smoke. It was clear to her that the customs officers were going to confiscate them, and prosecute the people who had sold them.

"Your employer's name isn't on these documents," the agent told her. "Yours is." And as he said it, he took a pair of handcuffs off his belt and clipped them on her wrists before she could react or object, as she stared at him in horror. "You're under arrest, Sydney Wells, for trafficking in stolen goods." He read her her rights as her eyes filled with tears and she turned to the broker with a look of desperation.

"Call Mr. Zeller immediately, and tell him what just happened. Do you have his cellphone number?" Her voice was trembling as he shook his head, and she told him the number from memory. "Tell him to get a lawyer and get me out of here ASAP." This wasn't her problem, it was his. She had purchased the bags for him, and they'd been planning to put her name on them, which panicked her even more. Then she turned to the agents again. One of them was calling for a female agent on his walkie-talkie.

"Can I make one phone call?" she asked them, praying that they'd let her.

"To your attorney?" She nodded, lying to them. She was going to let Paul's attorneys handle it. But she wanted to call Ed Chin and tell him she'd been arrested. She knew he'd find Paul and get her out immediately.

"All right, one call," they conceded, and handed her a phone. She called Ed's cellphone and he picked up on the second ring while she prayed it wouldn't go to voicemail. He sounded busy and distracted.

"I just got arrested at the airport," she rushed to tell him. "The bags aren't knockoffs, they're stolen Prada. The manufacturer put in a fake lining to conceal it. If you cut it out, all the markings are clearly there. That explains the high quality. Fuck the bags. Find Paul and get me out of here. They arrested me because I signed all the import documents."

Paul had told her to sign everything and she suddenly wondered if he had known what he was doing when he sent her. She couldn't believe that of him. But he had let her bring them in, on her own, and take the fall when they got caught. Surely he didn't know they had been stolen either. They had been duped by the merchant in China.

"Are you kidding? Where are you now?" Ed asked, incredulous, when she told him what had happened.

"At the commercial customs office at the airport." The female agent had appeared by then. She was a hulking woman who looked extremely unpleasant. And Sydney's expensive shearling coat and Hermès boots didn't impress her.

"Are they taking you to jail?" he asked, and tears filled her eyes as she turned to the agents.

"Are you taking me somewhere?" she asked them, and one of them answered and told her to wind up the call.

"We're taking you to a federal holding facility here at the airport. We'll take you to the federal jail in the city tonight. Your attorney can see you there tomorrow."

"Can he see me here now?" All three of them shook their heads and she told Ed, and where she was going. "You have to find Paul right away. They can't arrest me. I was shipping the bags as an agent for the company. He has to take responsibility for this, I'm not going to. Find him, Ed, *please.*" She was terrified of what would happen to her now.

"I'll take care of it this minute, and Sydney . . . I'm so sorry. I never should have let you go back to Beijing alone. Just sit tight, we'll get you out by morning."

"Oh my God, I have to spend the night in jail?" She was panicked.

"I'll see what I can do tonight." He wanted to kill Paul Zeller for letting Sydney put herself on the line. There was always the risk that goods were counterfeit or stolen when buying cheap copies, especially in Asia. She should never have signed the export documents. The manufacturer should have, but Sydney's name was all over them.

The female agent took the phone away from Sydney, handed it back to her co-workers, confiscated Sydney's handbag, and led her outside to a waiting car to move her to the holding facility. She pushed Sydney roughly into the back of the car, which looked like any ordinary police car except that it was marked "Department of Homeland Security" with a government insignia and an eagle on it, and they drove half a mile away to a building marked "U.S. Customs." Inside, it looked like a jail, with bars everywhere. It was used to hold drug dealers they apprehended and other criminals, and there was a small area for women. There was only one other woman in the cell they put her in. They had found five hundred grams of heroin on her, taped between her legs, and she started screaming at the customs agent as soon as she saw her. She was demanding a lawyer. Sydney felt as though she had been dropped into someone's nightmare, and surely not her own.

Her cellmate in what looked like a cage appeared to be in her twenties, and turned to Sydney to ask her what she was in for.

"There's been some confusion about stolen purses." Sydney felt ridiculous as she said it, and the other woman laughed.

"There's been some confusion about half a kilo of

heroin taped to my crotch," she said, and started shouting again. But no one came to help them. And all Sydney could hope was that Ed and Paul would do something quickly and get her out. This just couldn't be happening, and it wasn't her fault. It never even occurred to her that Paul Zeller might have known that the purses were stolen, and he had knowingly used her, an innocent, to get them into the country.

Chapter 7

As soon as Ed hung up on Sydney's call, he raced downstairs to Paul Zeller's office, and was told by his assistant that he was out to lunch, and probably wouldn't be back for another hour.

"Find him," he said tersely. The idea that Sydney had been arrested and was being taken to a federal jail was unthinkable, and he wanted to get her out immediately, not just as her boss but as her friend.

This was the last thing he wanted to happen to her, and he kept wondering over and over again if Paul had known that the bags were real and probably stolen. The supplier had given him a fantastic deal on them, but Ed couldn't believe Paul would set Sydney up like that and let her take the risk of bringing in stolen goods. He felt guilty for what he was thinking. But whatever he thought, they had to get a lawyer and get her out, and untangle the mess about the allegedly stolen bags. There was a huge market for stolen goods in the fashion industry, particularly leather goods of all kinds. Vuitton, Chanel, Prada, Gucci, it happened to all of them. Thefts were committed, and the bags were trafficked all over the world. And a lot of the stolen articles were shipped from Africa and Asia into Europe and the States.

Ed called Paul on his cellphone and it went to voicemail. He paced up and down outside his office and was waiting for him when he got back from lunch, looking relaxed and pleased, and he seemed startled to see Ed, visibly upset and tense.

"Sydney got arrested in customs. The bags are stolen goods. Her name is all over the documents, so they arrested her. You've got to call a lawyer and get her out. The poor woman doesn't deserve this. She's been there since one o'clock." It was almost four by then. The words came out in a rush. Ed had been going crazy waiting for him. Paul indicated to Ed to follow him into his office, where he took off his coat, dropped it over a chair, sat down at his desk, and stared at Ed.

"First of all, I had no idea the bags were stolen," he said, clearing himself as the first order of business.

"That's beside the point, we can talk about that later. You need to call a lawyer right away. She can't take the blame for a corporate entity. We were duped by the manufacturer, or at least I assume we were. They can't expect her to take responsibility for it. You have to send someone down there to get her out."

"I'm not sure who to call," Paul said slowly. "She needs a federal attorney, and to be honest we don't have one."

And he seemed to be in no hurry to find one, much to Ed's dismay.

"Has anything like this ever happened before?" Ed asked, still looking frantic.

"Once, about five years ago."

"What happened?"

"The employee got five years in prison, and served four. That was different. He had knowledge that the goods were stolen, or he suspected it, and never warned us. He was getting a commission from the vendor who sold them to us."

"Sydney had no idea those goods were stolen," Ed assured him. "She's an innocent and this is all new to her." But Paul was well aware of that himself.

"She probably didn't know," Paul conceded, "but let's be honest here. She's a sophisticated woman. She knows what expensive handbags look like. She may have recognized what these were, even if you and I didn't. And she didn't say a word about it to me. For all we know, she may have been getting a commission from the vendor, to bring them in anyway. You and I weren't in China. We don't know what went on there."

"Are you saying she knew these were stolen goods? Are you kidding? She's a babe in the woods. She's a terrific designer but she's never dealt with purchase and importation. She wouldn't know the difference between a good copy and the real thing. And she trusts us. She had no reason to suspect the merchandise was stolen." He had no qualms about vouching for her, and no doubt in his mind.

"I certainly hope not," Paul said, looking righteous, as Ed began to wonder how much he'd had to drink at lunch. He was moving very slowly, while Sydney was sitting in a federal jail at the airport.

"Why are we sitting here talking about this, wasting time? Why aren't you calling an attorney?" There was a long pause as Paul looked at him.

"Ed, have you ever read our employee handbook? We have a very clear policy about incidents like this. If an employee gets arrested in the course of the work they do for us, in any form, at any time, in any country, we are not responsible for their legal counsel, nor to defend them. It is entirely their own responsibility. We can't be responsible for three hundred employees who can get arrested at any time for any reason. When you sign your work contract with us, you indemnify us from any responsibility to defend you. Sydney will have to find her own attorney to defend her in this matter. I have no way of knowing if she knew if the purses were stolen or not. I can't vouch for her. The manufacturer may have offered her a cut when she was in China. She may look lily pure, but you never know what people are capable of." Ed couldn't believe what he was hearing. His eyes looked like they were going to fall out of his head as he listened to Paul.

"Are you telling me that you're going to step aside and

let her take the fall here? What kind of human being are you? The poor woman was bringing those purses in for you, not to sell on a street corner somewhere. And now she's been arrested for trafficking in stolen goods."

"Maybe the manufacturer or someone else offered her a better commission than I did. But whatever happened, she is responsible for her own defense. We'd go under if I had to provide every employee here legal counsel every time they get in trouble."

"You had her sign all the documents, for chrissake!" Ed was shouting at him, and Paul only nodded. "You could have had anyone sign them, and I heard you tell her to do it all herself. You used her, didn't you, just in case you got caught on this one. How many times have you done this before and never got caught?" Ed was livid. "And now you're not even going to get a lawyer for her?"

"No, I'm not. If she read her employment contract, she would know that."

"What is it, in microscopic print in Chinese somewhere on the flip side of the contract? I read contracts very carefully and I never saw that clause when I signed up."

"Then you should have read it more carefully, and so should she, if she decided to take a better commission behind my back, or took the responsibility for goods she may have known were stolen. You and I will never know the truth," Paul said, and Ed had to force himself to remain calm so he didn't hit him.

"So that's it? You let her take the blame for something *you* did? You cut your losses over two hundred cheap purses that you probably knew were stolen and she didn't?" Ed realized now that Paul had been testing to see how easy it was to get them in, and let Sydney be the one to do it and be responsible if anything happened.

It was obvious now that Paul was going to do nothing to protect her. Ed slammed out of his office and went back to his own desk. He wasn't sure what to do, but first he had to find a lawyer for her. And he did the only thing he could think of. He called his youngest uncle in Hong Kong, who was only ten years older than Ed, waking him up at 6 A.M. Hong Kong time. He explained the situation to him, and said he needed to find a federal lawyer for her in New York, and he had no idea who to ask. His uncle had met Sydney with Ed, and knew immediately who Ed was calling about.

"And you're sure she had no idea they were stolen goods?" Ed's uncle sounded faintly cynical, and knew what a kind heart his nephew had and that at times he could be naïve. Sydney was, after all, a grown woman who had been in the fashion business. He had to take into consideration that she might be guilty.

"I promise you, the woman is innocent about this kind of business. Her husband died six months ago, and I think our shit of an employer set her up and used her as a convenient person to blame if things went wrong."

"That's entirely possible. Is she in need of money?" he asked reasonably. It would explain why Sydney might have taken the risk and made a deal with the manufacturer to bring in stolen goods, and Ed hated to tell him the truth.

"I think she probably is short of money since her husband's death. He died without a recent will, and there were some problems with the estate, but that doesn't mean she'd become a criminal to solve the problem."

"No, but stranger things have happened. And why do you want to find her an attorney?"

"Because our employer isn't going to, I just found out. She has no one else to help her. I'm her boss, and she's my friend."

"I'll see what I can do," he promised. "I'm not sure I can come up with a name immediately. I'll let you know what I can find out. I have a friend I went to school with at Oxford who's a lawyer in New York. He may know someone who can help her. But she needs a federal defense lawyer who specializes in criminal cases. That's not as easy to find as a good tax attorney. I'll see what I can do. And Edward, be careful. You may not know this woman as well as you think." He tried to warn him, and Ed was instantly annoyed.

"Yes, I do." He thanked his uncle for trying to find a lawyer for him, and then walked out of the office at not quite five P.M. He didn't tell anyone that he was leaving, and he didn't care. He took a cab home and called the customs office at the airport from the taxi. But all he got was a recording, telling him their location and no hours. He thought about going to the airport and trying to see her, but she had already told him he wouldn't be able to, so he called the federal jail in the city instead, and was told that no prisoner by that name had been transferred from the airport yet. They refused to tell him when she might come in. They told him to call in the morning. All he could do now was wait to hear from his uncle with the name of a federal criminal attorney, or for Sydney to call him herself. Until then, there was nothing he could do.

By six o'clock, Sydney had been in the cell at the airport federal customs facility for five hours. She had heard from no one, no attorney had shown up, the customs broker had left as soon as they took her away, and she hadn't been able to get calls from Paul Zeller or Ed Chin. She was sure that they were both doing everything they could, and a lawyer would show up any minute and get her released. The federal agents who had locked her up told her nothing either. They acted as though she didn't exist. The only human who would speak to her was the girl who had smuggled the heroin between her legs, and she had lain down on the cot in their cell and gone to sleep. She had flown in from Mexico City, she had told Sydney, and had been awake all night.

At seven o'clock, they brought each of them a sandwich on a tray, and a bowl of instant soup. They had no catering facility there, and had to buy airport food for their prisoners. It was just a holding tank, and they shipped anyone incarcerated there into the city as fast as they could. At nine o'clock that night, two female customs agents walked in, handcuffed her and the sleeping drug smuggler, who woke with a start, and led them outside to a small van. They put them in the back to take them to the federal jail in the city. Their valuables, like Sydney's purse, cellphone, watch, earrings, and wedding ring, were in a plastic bag given to the agents who drove them, to turn over to the jail when they took them in.

The drug smuggler fell asleep again on the short ride to the city, and Sydney watched the familiar route slide by from behind the iron mesh on the windows. She had never in her worst nightmares imagined that she could be in this position. But she was sure that Paul Zeller would straighten it out by the time she got into the city, and she would be released.

Instead, when they arrived at the federal jail facility, the Metropolitan Correctional Center on Park Row across from the courthouse on Pearl Street, she and the smuggler were herded into another holding tank with six other women, and told to strip. They were in the receiving and discharging area, and had each been given a federal register number to identify them. The rules were posted in

English and Spanish. Sydney stared at the federal deputies in disbelief. This wasn't possible. It was like a bad dream. The others took off their clothes rapidly, and seemed used to the routine. They were all in for various forms of drug charges, and crossing state lines with possession with intent to sell hard drugs. One woman was in for trying to smuggle firearms into the airport, and a pale young girl who looked like a teenager was high on crystal meth and had tried to rob a bank with two friends. They were an unsavory-looking group, and all of them stood naked in a matter of minutes in the drafty cell. All the guards were women, and Sydney shivered as she took off her clothes. Within minutes, she was as naked as the others, while a federal officer gathered up their clothes and threw them into plastic bags with their names on them. And then one by one, handcuffed again, they were led into a dismal-looking room, while six tough-looking female guards stood around and watched.

All the guards surrounding them were women, and one of them put on rubber gloves. They were told to bend over and hold their ankles for a cavity search, and for a minute, Sydney thought she was going to faint. She forced herself to think of something else while they searched her, and then pushed her toward a shower, handing her a towel, some rough cotton underwear, a denim jumpsuit, and "bus shoes." There were tears in her eyes when they took her mug shot, and finally led her to a cell where she was alone. It had a cot, a toilet, a tiny sink, and a shelf with nothing on it. They handed her a toothbrush and a bar of soap, and left her there to wonder what was happening in the outside world, and if help would ever come. She couldn't believe that Paul and Ed had abandoned her, nor could she understand the delay in getting her out. They left the lights on in the jail all night, and she lay awake on the narrow cot, listening to the sounds of the jail around her, the catcalls, the screams, the women who sounded insane, and the conversations among the guards as they walked by. She did breathing exercises to try to stay calm. All she wanted was to be released. And she was sure that by morning she would be. The whole thing was a terrible mistake. She thought of Sabrina and Sophie, and was determined not to call them, even if she could. There was no way she was going to call her daughters and tell them she was in jail.

Ed's uncle Phillip called him at ten o'clock that night. It was eleven A.M. in Hong Kong, and he had finally reached his friend in New York, who had given him the name of a federal defense lawyer who he said was expensive, but a good guy. He had gone to Harvard Law School with him.

"Are you paying for this?" Ed's uncle asked him.

"No, I'm sure she'll pay for it herself. Our employer certainly isn't going to. Apparently it's in the small print in our work contracts that if we get in trouble in the line of duty, we're responsible for the legal fees ourselves."

"Nice people you work for," Phillip Chin said in a tone of disapproval. "When are you coming home?"

"One of these days."

And then Phillip asked his nephew a question he'd been curious about for the past five hours. "Are you in love with this woman?"

Ed laughed. "No, I'm not. I'm still gay. But I was her immediate superior. I should have protected her and I didn't, and I feel responsible for her now. We're friends and she doesn't deserve what happened to her. And I'm not convinced of our boss's innocence. This is all I can do to help. At least I can contact an attorney for her."

"And you're planning to continue working for this man?" His uncle sounded shocked.

"No, I'm not." He had made the decision that night, while he thought about the whole sequence of events. He realized now that Paul had used Sydney, dazzled her with a profit participation in the sale of the bags and using her name for a "signature line" to get the goods into the country, and let her take full responsibility in case something went wrong. Sending her to China to sign all the papers and be responsible for the deal had been a way of shifting all the risk onto her. And it had worked. Sydney was in jail now, and Paul was not. And he was even willing to suggest that she might have double-crossed him, to make her look guilty and absolve himself, which was even worse. Paul Zeller was a despicable person, and Sydney had been his unwitting victim. There was no way Ed was going to abandon her now. He had a strong suspicion that Paul knew the bags were stolen. And if so, he had probably done it before. Their leather goods were famous for their high-class look. Maybe this was why. "I just haven't had the chance to tell him yet," Ed said in answer to his uncle's question. "This all happened this afternoon. I haven't even been able to speak to her again since she got arrested."

"If she's innocent," his uncle said cautiously, "this must be a shocking experience for her." He was beginning to feel sorry for her, if everything his nephew said was true. He had found her to be a kind, charming person when they met, with great dignity.

"I'm sure it has been. The first thing I want to do is get her out of jail. And I'll call the name you gave me tomorrow. I'll let you know how it works out."

"Good luck," Phillip Chin said and then hung up, and Ed sat staring at the name he'd written down. Steven Weinstein. He just hoped he could help her and get her off the hook. It was Paul Zeller who deserved to be in jail, not her. Ed sat awake all night worrying about his friend.

Ed called Steve Weinstein on his cellphone at eight A.M. He apologized for calling him so early, and Weinstein said it was fine, he was on his way back from the gym. Ed explained how he had gotten his name, via his uncle in

Hong Kong, and told him what had happened to Sydney at the airport the day before, and that he believed she was being transferred to the federal jail in New York.

"Your employer sounds like a nasty guy," Weinstein said coolly.

"I guess he is, while he pretends to be everyone's best friend. I always thought he had a shady underside, but nothing like this."

"And you don't think it's possible your co-worker had some part in this, or knew what was going on?"

"Absolutely not." Ed vouched for her without hesitating. "She was a very successful designer until sixteen years ago when she remarried."

"Who was she married to? Or is she still married?"

"He died about six months ago. Someone called Andrew Wells."

"Of the investment banking firm?" The attorney sounded momentarily impressed.

"I believe so. She doesn't talk about it a lot. I think there have been problems with the estate and her husband's daughters by his first marriage. They inherited everything, so she went back to work."

Steve Weinstein was thoughtful for a minute. "If she's who I think she is, this is going to get some attention in the press, which will be unpleasant for her until we clean this up. They may use her as an example and prosecute her vigorously to make a point."

"Can you at least get her out of jail immediately? She must be totally freaked out. She sounded hysterical when she called me, and she must be wondering why no one has shown up. I thought Zeller would send his attorneys to her, but apparently it's against company policy, which none of us knew. I'm planning to quit today. The guy is a sonofabitch and I'm convinced now he's a crook," Ed said heatedly.

"Are you romantically involved with her?" Weinstein wanted to know as much as possible before he saw her.

"No, I'm not," Ed said matter-of-factly. "I was her immediate supervisor. She reported to me, and we became friends."

"Does she have kids?"

"Two daughters. They're both designers too."

"In answer to your earlier question, I can get her out of jail, but I'm not sure when. Today is Friday, and she has to be arraigned, and the judge has to set bail, unless we can get him to dismiss the case. If he doesn't dismiss, there will have to be a grand jury hearing, probably after the arraignment. But that will all depend on how bad this looks, especially if her employer is throwing her under the bus, which you seem to indicate."

"It's the impression he gave me yesterday. He's protecting himself. If they go after him, it could be really bad for him. He'd rather sacrifice her. I should have seen it coming, but I didn't," Ed said, feeling guilty again. The idea that they might use her as an example made him even more frightened for her.

"I'll try to get in to see her this morning, and let you know what I find out." Ed liked the sound of him. He seemed young, smart, and down to earth. At least she'd have a lawyer now and be in good hands. And maybe Weinstein could even get the case dismissed. Ed didn't see how they could charge her with the crime. She'd been operating under direct orders from the owner of the company. How could they prosecute her? It didn't make any sense. He hated Zeller for that. He seemed far more Machiavellian now than Ed had ever feared. He had thought him a little sleazy, not an outright crook.

An hour later, Ed walked into Paul Zeller's office. He had already been upstairs and collected his things, and the sketches in his desk. The door to Paul's office was open and he was drinking a cup of coffee his assistant had brought him, and he looked up with a broad smile when he saw Ed.

"I was just going to call you. We have to figure out some special promotion to replace those bags." But he didn't look worried about it as Ed stared at him, and he never mentioned Sydney's name.

"That's it? You're worried about a new promotion, while you let Sydney rot in jail?"

"She's not 'rotting.' She's a well-connected woman. I'm

sure she's called an attorney by now. She made a big mistake."

"No, you did," Ed said bluntly with fury in his eyes. "The only mistake she made was taking a job here. And so did I. I'm here to correct that mistake this morning." Paul looked surprised. "I quit," Ed said, looking at him directly.

"Without notice? You can't just walk out like that. You're our chief design consultant and creative director. You have a responsibility to the company and to your team," Paul said angrily. He hadn't expected to lose Ed in the bargain. Sydney was expendable, which was why he had used her. Ed was not. Not easily in any case.

"And you have a responsibility to your employees, but apparently you don't see it that way."

"I warn you, Ed, if you walk out now, your name will be mud in the industry."

"I doubt that. Your name is already dirt. I've been defending you for three years. That was my big mistake. I'm done," he said, and turned around to walk out as Paul stood up at his desk, with a wicked look in his eye.

"If you walk out now, I can still say that you were in on it with Sydney. You're not clear of this either," he said in a menacing tone. Ed turned to face him again, with an expression that was rock hard.

"If you even think about doing that to me, my family will put you out of business. You'll lose every factory worker you have in China, and your factories. You're a scumbag. Don't *ever* threaten me." And with that, Ed walked out as Paul stared after him, and sat down in his chair without a word.

Sydney was brushing her teeth in her cell when a guard came to tell her that her lawyer was there to see her. She had no comb or brush for her hair, and she tried to smooth it down with her hands. The blue uniform they'd given her was enormous on her, and so were the "bus shoes" she'd been given. They handcuffed her again, let her out of her cell, and walked her through three locked gates and into the attorney conference room where a man in a suit was standing, waiting for her. She assumed that he had been sent by Paul Zeller. It never occurred to her that he had been referred by Ed, or the lengths he'd gone to to find a lawyer for her. She had no idea that Paul would abandon her, since she'd been acting on his behalf, on his orders, as part of her job.

Steve Weinstein introduced himself and said he'd been sent by Ed Chin, and she looked surprised.

"You don't work for Paul Zeller?"

"No, I don't. As I understand it from Ed, your work contract with Zeller states that if something like this happens in the line of duty, you're responsible for yourself. Zeller is not going to help you. He washed his hands of you when you got arrested." She was shocked by what he said. "Why don't you tell me the whole story, starting with the trip to China and what happened there, and what happened in customs yesterday." He took notes while she explained it all to him, and by the end of it, he agreed with Ed. She'd been set up to be the fall guy for Zeller if anything went wrong. And he strongly suspected that Zeller knew he was buying stolen goods, and probably not for the first time.

"Did you ever suspect the bags were real and maybe altered in some way, and not copies?"

"No, I didn't. I thought the quality was unusually good. But they make some remarkable products in China. Everyone in the fashion industry uses their factories now. But I never, ever suspected they were stolen." Everything about her suggested honesty and innocence to him. She looked dazed by what was happening to her.

"Just so you know, Zeller is claiming now that you were in collusion with the manufacturer, and got a commission from them to bring stolen goods into the States."

"Oh my God." She was horrified. "Do you think the judge will believe him?" There were tears in her eyes as she asked. This was the worst thing that had ever happened to her. Much worse than Andrew having left her out of his will, and losing everything.

"Possibly," the lawyer answered her honestly. "It's my job to convince him that you're innocent, which I believe is the truth."

"I am. I swear to you. I never suspected they were

stolen goods. What are we going to do?" She looked bereft as she sat there, staring at him. "Can I leave now?"

"Unfortunately, you can't. The judge isn't sitting today. I checked. Your arraignment is set for Monday, so you're stuck here for the weekend. You can't leave until you've been arraigned. That's where you plead guilty or not guilty, and the judge will set bail. Probably for around fifty thousand dollars. I assume you can post bond," he said, watching her face, and seeing panic in her eyes. She didn't have fifty thousand dollars left, or even close. And she had no collateral to get a loan.

"And if I can't?" she asked in a small voice.

"Then you wait in jail for a grand jury hearing and eventually a trial. Or maybe I can get you released on your own recognizance. You're not a flight risk. It depends what judge we get. We might even be able to get the case dismissed, if they don't have a strong case against you. But I think Zeller would testify against you, to avoid prosecution himself. Everything he did was designed to make you responsible if he got caught. And so far, it worked. My initial fee to represent you is twenty-five thousand dollars. It goes up to fifty if I get the case summarily dismissed. And a hundred thousand if we go to trial. And criminal law fees are payable in advance. But I don't think it will get to trial. At worst, I think they'll make a deal for probation if you plead guilty."

"But I'm not guilty," she said desperately.

"There's always a risk if you go to trial. Things could go wrong. Juries are unpredictable."

"Do you think I'll go to prison?" she asked in a whisper.

"Hopefully not." But he didn't want to promise what he wasn't sure he could deliver. "But it could happen, if everything goes wrong, and if Zeller is out to bury you to save himself. I don't want him on the witness stand against you. According to your friend, Zeller is a liar and a convincing one, and possibly a crook. I'm sure he knew they were stolen goods, but he's not going to admit that to anyone. I'm going to do my very best to keep you out of prison, if you hire me. I'm sorry you have to sit here until Monday. There's nothing I can do about that." He was thorough, honest, and matter-of-fact.

She nodded, unable to speak. She was thinking of what she'd say to her girls. She would have to tell them the truth. She just didn't know when. And if she couldn't make bail on Monday, she'd have to wait for trial in jail. And Steve Weinstein told her it could take up to a year to go to trial. "If you do hire me," he went on, "I'd like to engage some detectives and see if we can find someone who can testify that Zeller knew he was bringing in stolen goods, and maybe even that he's done it before. If we get lucky, someone will talk and you'll be off the hook." She was panicking as she listened to him. If everything went against her, she could wind up in prison. And as far as she was concerned, she might as well be dead. She was beginning to wish she were, not for the first time in recent months.

"I'll see you on Monday, Mrs. Wells," he said as he stood up. "You can hire another lawyer after the arraignment if you prefer. But at least let's get you out of jail." She nodded and didn't dare ask him how much he'd charge for that.

She thanked him for coming to see her, and was taken back to her cell in handcuffs again when he left. She lay on her bed, thinking about everything he'd told her. She felt as though her life was over. She hadn't moved, eaten, or gotten up, when Ed came to see her during visiting hours that afternoon. She had been advised that she had the right to a one-hour social visit per week. The guard told her she had a visitor, and she asked who it was.

"I'm not your social secretary," the officer snapped, put the handcuffs on again, and took her to a room where she was strip-searched before entering the visiting area. She saw Ed waiting for her and began to cry the moment she saw him. It tore his heart out when he looked at her and was allowed to hug her, and then they sat down in a small room full of inmates and their visitors. She was desig-nated as a pretrial inmate. She looked terrible, as though she was in shock. She hadn't felt that bad since Andrew's death that summer.

"Are you okay, Sydney?" he asked her, and she nodded

as they held hands. She could hardly speak she was so upset.

"Sort of. Thank you for finding me a lawyer. I never thought something like this could happen, or that Paul would turn out to be such a shit, and a dishonest person," she whispered to him.

"He's very slick. I never trusted him. I told you that in the beginning, but I never thought he'd go this far. I quit this morning. He's trying to claim you made a deal with the manufacturer to get himself off the hook."

"Steve Weinstein told me. I'm sorry you quit your job over this."

"I'm not." He smiled at her. "It was time. I don't want to work for a bastard like him."

"What am I going to tell my girls? They're going to be mortified. Especially if it hits the papers."

"It could," Ed said honestly, especially if they made an example of her, as Weinstein had suggested to him.

"Imagine if I go to prison," she said, looking terrified. Just the past twenty-four hours had nearly broken her spirit. Time in prison would kill her.

"You won't. You're innocent. Maybe he can get the case dismissed." She nodded but he could tell she didn't believe him. She was humiliated and desperately afraid, and he couldn't even hug her to console her, except at the beginning and end of the visit. But at least they could hold hands. And after an hour, they were notified that their allotted time was over. Ed hugged her again and she thanked him for coming and waved at him miserably as he left, and when he got outside in the cold December air, tears rolled down his cheeks. Sydney was being strip-searched for contraband by then, and was led back to her cell afterward.

She lay on her bed after his visit and didn't get up again. She didn't eat, and on Saturday morning, she called Sabrina. She had to call her collect, and Sabrina took the call sounding puzzled.

"Where are you?" There was an endless pause before she answered, as she choked back a sob. She could barely get the words out.

"I'm in jail," Sydney said miserably. "I didn't want you to worry if you tried to call me." But Sabrina was even more worried knowing where her mother was. Sydney told her the whole story, and Sabrina was almost too stunned to speak.

"I told you that guy was scum," Sabrina said angrily, not sure who she was angrier at, Paul Zeller or her mother for being so foolish and naïve. The story didn't surprise her, but she was horrified for her mother. "He has a terrible reputation. Can I bail you out?"

"Not till Monday. The judge won't set bail till then. And it might be very expensive." She didn't tell her she might not have the money to pay for it. She'd been careful with her salary, but her funds were running low.

Sabrina asked for her lawyer's name, and her mother gave it to her.

"I don't want you to come to court, though. Wait until I get home. And you can't visit me. I only get one visit a week, and Ed Chin came to see me. He found the lawyer for me." They talked for a few more minutes and then hung up. Sabrina called the lawyer immediately and discussed the whole situation with him, and he told her how bail worked and how much it might be. And then she called her sister, and Sophie cried pitifully when Sabrina told her what had happened. They both cried, worried about their mother, and Sophie was distraught that they couldn't visit her. The situation was unbelievable.

The two girls spent Saturday night together, and Sabrina told Sophie everything the lawyer had said. She had already made the decision to pay her mother's bail. Sabrina owned her own apartment and would use it as collateral with the bail bondsman. She wasn't going to leave their mother in jail a second longer than she had to. Steve Weinstein had said he would walk Sabrina through the process on Monday morning before the arraignment.

It was an endless weekend for all of them; Sabrina and Sophie worrying about what would happen to their mother, and Sydney lying silently in her cell, wishing she were dead.

Chapter 8

The arraignment on Monday morning was just as Steve Weinstein had told her it would be. It was uneventful, and there were no surprises. Sydney wore her own clothes to court. She pleaded not guilty to the charges of trafficking in stolen goods and attempting to import them. Steve first tried to get the case dismissed, but with her signature on all the importation documents, the evidence was too strong against her. And when Steve tried to get her released on her own recognizance, the federal prosecutor objected, and the judge refused. He set bail at fifty thousand dollars and moved on to the next case. Steve Weinstein's worst fear was confirmed, that they wanted to make an example of her. The judge could easily have let her out on her own recognizance. She wasn't a flight risk, but instead he had set bail. Sydney stood staring at the judge in despair for a minute, and then spoke to her attorney.

"I'll have to stay in jail," she whispered. "I can't pay the bail."

"It's already been taken care of," he answered quietly.

"Your daughter Sabrina set it all up for you. As soon as I notify the bail bondsman you've been arraigned, and the amount of bail, you'll be free to leave." Tears rushed to Sydney's eyes immediately.

"I can't let her do that. It's not right."

"She also gave me a check for twenty-five thousand dollars for my initial fee, until we know if it's going to trial."

Sydney was horrified by what she was costing her daughter, and she was out of a job too. She didn't want to be a burden to Sabrina. The whole situation was mortifying. Steve tried to reassure her.

"Let's just get you out on bail, and we can worry about the rest later." She looked even worse than when he'd seen her on Friday, and he knew she wouldn't survive it for a year, if she didn't let Sabrina post bail. And Sydney knew that too. Now she really had to sell the Paris apartment. It was all she had to sell to pay Steve's fee for the trial. And she wanted to pay Sabrina back as quickly as possible.

A guard led her away, and Steve went to post bail for her. Sabrina had already taken care of the financial details that morning, and half an hour later, Sydney was on the street with him, in her own clothes, and she let him take her home. She felt shell-shocked from everything that had happened. Glancing around at all the trees and buildings and people walking in the streets, she felt as though she had come back to earth after being terrified she was never going to be free again. They had been the four most frightening days of her life. And the guards and criminals were like actors in a bad movie. Only it was real.

She walked into her apartment, sat down on the couch, and looked around as though seeing it for the first time. She called Sabrina and thanked her for posting bail, and promised to pay her as soon as she could. She was ashamed that her daughter had had to use her apartment as collateral.

"What are you going to do now, Mom?" she asked her quietly.

"I don't know. Look for another job, I guess." And she couldn't even use her one recent job as a reference. "What about you? Have you heard back from any of the places where you interviewed?" She was worried about Sabrina now too. Everything was in a mess again.

"Not yet." They both tried to keep the conversation normal, and not mention the fact that she'd just been in jail. Her life had become a sordid tale of losing her husband, her home, her money, being arrested, and going to jail. And what if she was convicted and went to prison? She couldn't even let herself think about it. She had an appointment at Steve Weinstein's office the next day to discuss the grand jury and what lay ahead. Sabrina promised to bring dinner over that night, and said Sophie was coming too. Sydney said she was too tired to go out. She had hardly slept in four days.

And as though on cue, the phone rang again when they hung up. She hadn't bothered to look at who was calling, and almost groaned when she heard Veronica's voice. It was laughable. She had called to tell her that the twins were selling some of her favorite paintings at Sotheby's. Veronica had seen them in the catalog and recognized them immediately.

"I thought you should know," she said sympathetically, and this time Sydney was in no mood to be polite to her.

"Why? Do you think I'm going to buy them back?"

"Of course not, I just thought . . ."

"That it might upset me more than I already am? As a matter of fact, it does. Why don't you call me with good news sometime? That would be a lot more fun."

"Fine. I'll do that," she said brusquely and hung up a minute later. Sydney was totally fed up with people who wanted to take advantage of her, like Paul, or wanted to make her feel bad, like Veronica. She felt better after she had brushed him off. Ed called her after that. On the spur of the moment, she invited him to join them for dinner that night.

"After all this, I want you to meet my girls." He sounded hesitant, not wanting to intrude, but he agreed to come, and she thanked him again for finding Steve Weinstein for her.

"I'm seeing him tomorrow to discuss the case," she said.

"They should be putting Zeller in jail, not you," Ed said angrily.

"Steve said he wants to hire a detective to see if he can get someone to admit that Paul knew they were stolen goods."

"That sounds like a good idea." She told him to come at seven, and he arrived before the girls. He brought her a bunch of flowers to cheer her up, and a bottle of wine to share with her daughters. And he invited her to lunch the next day.

When they arrived, the girls were startled to see someone in the apartment they didn't know. Sydney introduced them, and they were all shy at first. Ed was nervous that they would hate him because of where he'd worked. And the girls were uncomfortable for the first few minutes. They had brought Thai food and sashimi from downtown, and by the time they set it out on their mother's small dining table, they were talking about fashion with Ed and had found common ground. Sydney smiled as she listened to them, and life began to seem normal again. They didn't bring up the court case until the end of dinner, and by then they were into their second bottle of wine, and everyone had relaxed. Ed liked both of Sydney's daughters, and they all agreed that they hated Paul Zeller and what he had done to her.

It was after midnight when they all left. It had been a nice evening, and Sydney sat in her living room, thinking of where she had been the night before. She still couldn't believe she had been arrested and now she had to go to trial. And she was embarrassed that her daughter had had to post bail for her. But if she hadn't, Sydney would still be in jail. It was the first time she had ever been dependent on her children, and it wasn't a good feeling. She felt like an utter failure, and things had been going so much better for a while.

Sydney was up early the next morning to go to Steve Weinstein's office, downtown near the federal courthouse. They spent two hours going over every detail of the case. She agreed to let him hire a detective to see what they could find out about Paul. She didn't know how she was going to pay for it, but she knew she had no choice. And they discussed the grand jury investigation that would be conducted in secret and would determine if the case went to trial.

Sabrina called her as soon as she left the lawyer's office, with good news for a change. She had gotten the job she wanted, for a higher salary than she'd had before. Sydney hoped it meant that their luck had changed. At least something wonderful had happened to her daughter. It buoyed her spirits as she rode the subway back uptown. Sophie called her as soon as she got home.

"Guess who's on Page Six today," she said, almost chortling as her mother groaned.

"Please don't tell me I am for going to jail."

Sophie read her the piece. It intimated that Kellie's husband was having an affair. The woman he'd been seen with at a hotel recently was a well-known heiress around town, his specialty apparently. And Sydney smiled as she listened.

"It's karma, Mom," Sophie said. "She deserves it." And Sydney hated to admit it, but she agreed with her.

She met Ed for lunch shortly afterward at a restaurant they both liked, and he told her he was going to Hong Kong.

"For good?" She looked devastated. He had become her closest friend, her only friend now. And she had hoped he'd stay around and get another job in New York.

"No, just for a week. I want to talk to my father."

"About going into the family business?" Now that he had quit his job, she realized that he was likely to go back and go to work for them. He had gotten all the experience he needed in Europe and New York. But he surprised her with what he said.

"I want to start my own line. I think I'm ready. I want to know if they'll help me do it here. I want to stay in New York." And then he looked at her seriously. "Would you work on it with me, Sydney? It'll probably take me six months or a year to get it off the ground. But I want to start setting it up right away. I looked at a space in Chelsea this morning. What do you think? Would you do it with me?"

"You know a lot more than I do about running a business. I'm just a designer." But she had learned a lot at Lady Louise too, mostly from him. "And a year from now, I might be in prison," she said, looking grim for a minute.

"Not if Steve Weinstein is worth what you're paying him," he said soberly, and she gave him a small, wintry smile in response.

"I'm not paying him. Sabrina is. I want to pay her back as soon as I can. I can't until I sell the apartment in Paris. And I still have a tenant there for now."

"I could give you stock in the company, so you'd have equity. I want to keep it small at first. I want to start with casual day wear. I don't want to get too grand." She loved the idea, and they took a long walk after lunch to talk about it. He was leaving for Hong Kong the next day. He had already told his mother about the project, but he wanted to discuss it with his father face-to-face. He would be harder to convince. He still wanted his son to come home and join the family business with him and his uncles. But Ed didn't want to live in Hong Kong yet. "I'm happy here," he told her. She was excited about his project, and smiling when she went home. If he convinced his father to help him back it, she would have a job again, doing work she could respect this time, working for an honest man. She was in a good mood all that night, until Sabrina called her the next day.

The story of her arrest was in *Women's Wear Daily*, and they had quoted Paul Zeller talking about how severely disappointed he was that a designer of such great talent would stoop to illegal activities. It made him sound like the injured party, and her like a criminal. It was mortifying, and she was worried about Sabrina immediately.

"Do you think this will impact you in your new job?"

"I don't think so, Mom," she said quietly. "I called them about it this morning, and they were very nice and felt terrible for you. Paul Zeller doesn't have a lot of fans. I think most people will know you didn't do it and took the rap for him. But in any case, they weren't upset with me, and assured me it wouldn't affect my job."

Sydney was relieved to hear it. "When do you start?"

"In a week. It gives me a little time to get organized and catch my breath." Sydney was especially happy that Sabrina would be employed again, since she had spent most of her savings on her mother's bail and legal fees.

Things were slowly turning around for them. Sabrina had a new job she was excited about at an even better firm. Ed wanted Sydney to start a business with him, if his family agreed to help him financially. And hopefully Steve Weinstein would be able to help her with the legal proceedings, and keep her out of prison.

She was still living on a shoestring, and she had criminal charges against her, but at least some good things were happening. She could see daylight slowly streaking across the sky. The dawn hadn't come yet, but Sydney had hope again. It was a start.

Chapter 9

Ed came back from Hong Kong a week before Christmas. And as soon as he landed, he called Sydney with good news. He had met with his father and uncles, and after some debate, they had agreed to finance his clothing business. He had an excellent track record, and had held design jobs with important, responsible firms. He knew the business and was capable of pulling together a talented design team. He had presented Sydney's CV and credentials to them as well. They had given him the green light, and he wanted to get started as soon as possible. His goal was to have his first fashion show on the runway during Fashion Week in September, nine months from now.

"It's a go!" he said when he called Sydney, and then told her all the details. He wanted to look at the Chelsea location with her in the next few days and rent it immediately, if she liked it as much as he did and thought it could work as a home for their fledgling business. It was an exciting time for him. At last he wouldn't be working for someone else, and could do everything the way he wanted. He had no investors to satisfy, only his family. "Do you have time to look at the Chelsea location with me tomorrow?" he asked her, and she said she did.

"This is so wonderful!" She was as thrilled as he was. He sent the realtor an email that night, and they made an appointment for ten o'clock the next morning. When Sydney got there, he was relieved to see that she looked much better and more relaxed than when he'd left. Her four days in jail had been harrowing and taken a toll on her.

They went over every inch of the location, and tried to envision where they would put everyone and how it would work, and by their estimation it was perfect. The realtor promised to have the lease to him by that afternoon.

"Let's go to IKEA tomorrow and buy furniture," Sydney said enthusiastically. The place had been freshly painted, and there was no construction work to do. It was in move-in condition. Ed wanted to start hiring people as soon as possible. He had already made a list of his dream design team, with Sydney and himself as the lead designers. But they needed design assistants too, preferably recently out of school so they wouldn't be too expensive, or too inflexible, and would have fresh, innovative ideas.

They went to buy desks, tables, chairs, file cabinets, and shelving the next day, and outfitted a small kitchen. They bought comfortable desk chairs, and Ed was going to buy the computers. They had rented a truck to bring everything back from IKEA, and unloaded most of it themselves when they got back to Chelsea. They had hired someone to put the furniture together. They sat back and admired the results at the end of the day, and then Sydney got ready to leave to buy a small Christmas tree for her apartment.

"What are you doing on Christmas Eve, by the way?" she asked him before she left.

"Nothing much. I haven't had time to think about it."

"Why don't you come to dinner with me and the girls? Just casual, at my place." Sophie had already said that her boyfriend would probably join them, if he was up to it, and there was room for six people at her table, if they kept their elbows close to their bodies and used her narrow chairs.

"I'd love it," Ed said, smiling broadly. After that, she went to buy her tree, which took up a corner in the living room, but looked festive, and she had bought decorations. She didn't allow herself to think of the fourteen-foot tree they'd had in the living room in Connecticut every Christmas, or the garland of white flowers over the main doorway, or the wreath on the door. She had bought a tiny one with bells and pinecones on it, and attached it to the front door. And even though the tree was small, it smelled like Christmas, and filled the apartment with the scent of pine. The ornaments she'd bought for the tree were all red and gold, with some tiny teddy bears and toy soldiers. It looked cheerful and happy when she was finished.

Steve Weinstein called her after that, to give her the date of her next court hearing in April. It was months away, but would give them time to pursue their investigation of Paul Zeller and what he might have known about the stolen purses. And the grand jury investigation would go on during that time. After Steve had told her about her hearing date, she decided to invite him to dinner on Christmas Eve too.

"I usually go home to Boston for the holidays," he told her, touched to be asked to their family Christmas dinner. "But this year, my brother and sister are with their in-laws, and my parents are in Florida. They might be moving there." The invitation sounded warm and friendly to him, and he liked his new client and the idea of getting to know her better. He had already told her that he had never been married, had no children, and was thirty-eight years old. And she thought her girls would like him. "My family is Jewish," he added, "but we're not religious, and we always celebrate Christmas. We get the best of both worlds that way."

"I love Christmas too." She sighed softly then. "It's our first one without my husband." She was trying not to dwell on it, but the memories haunted her, especially late at night, which had become her least favorite time of day. Her worries loomed large at that hour.

"Your children's father?" He was curious about her, and sensed heartaches she was too polite to mention.

"No, he died twenty years ago, after we divorced. He had moved to Texas with a new wife and they didn't see much of him, but he was still their father. I remarried sixteen years ago, to a wonderful man. He died in an accident this summer. It's been a big adjustment." In more ways than she was willing to disclose to him. "There have been some complications with the estate." Two greedy, nasty stepdaughters, and nothing for the widow. She was still angry at Andrew about it at times. It was hard not to be, for dying, and for not taking care of what he should have. If he had, everything would have been different. She wouldn't have had to work and she wouldn't be facing jail. But, on the other hand, she had met Ed Chin and was going to have the thrill of starting a business with him. She tried to maintain a glass-half-full outlook, except in the wee hours when she was terrified of running out of money and going to prison. "It's been a difficult year," she acknowledged, topped off by her recent arrest for trafficking in stolen goods. "You really never know what's going to happen in life. The last six months have taught me that."

"That's true in a good way too," he reminded her. "You never know what fantastic event or person is going to come along and change your luck and life forever. Is your daughter going to be there for dinner, by the way? I had a nice conversation with her, when you were . . . being detained." He tried to find a gentle way to express it without saying "when you were in jail."

He knew how shaken she still was by it, and frightened of the future. The possibility of prison was horrifying. And once or twice she wondered if she had the right to start a business with Ed. What if she was convicted and went to prison? She didn't want to leave him in the lurch, or miss the opportunity he was offering her.

She brought it up with Ed that night, when they were talking on the phone about their plans. He had texted her all evening before that, every time he had an idea or a name to share with her. They'd been trying to come up with a name for their business and were leaning toward Sydney Chin. It was distinctive, and she wanted it to have an Asian feeling to it, out of deference to him and his family, who were making their new venture possible. She was grateful for their willingness to include her in the plan, despite her current problems.

"What if I go to prison? Have you thought of that?" she asked him seriously. Steve had told her it was a real possibility if things went badly for her at the trial. And he assumed there would be one. There was too much evidence against her for the charges to be dismissed. Paul Zeller was a powerful man, and had covered himself well. He had begun lying to everyone, and the press, from the moment it happened. He had spoken to the U.S. attorney, who had made it clear they were not going to go easy on her, and they wanted to question her in depth about Paul Zeller.

"You can't just sit there for the next year, waiting for the other shoe to drop," Ed admonished her. "You have to go on living. I don't think they'll convict you, but if they do, we'll deal with it when it happens. I'm not going to miss out on building something really important with you because Paul Zeller is an asshole and we're scared. I've waited my whole life to do this. And I want to do it with you." He had profound respect for her after working with her. In fact, he'd been waiting seven years to start his own venture, since he graduated from design school.

"Does your family know about the case against me?" She hoped he'd been honest with them about her arrest.

"I told them what happened. They were very sorry to hear about it, but it didn't scare them off. They checked out your lawyer again, by the way, and he has an excellent reputation."

"I like him." She was grateful to Ed and his family for that as well. "He's coming to dinner on Christmas Eve too. He's smart and seems like a really nice guy." And then she thought of something. He never talked about it much, and was alone most of the time, and working, but she thought he might like to bring someone with him to dinner, so she asked him.

"You're sweet to ask. I've seen someone a few times, but

there are no major heartthrobs in my life. I don't have time for that. I'm too busy to engage in a relationship and do it justice. Maybe in a few years when we get our business off the ground, but not now. Thanks anyway."

"You sound like Sabrina. She says exactly the same thing. And Sophie has a boyfriend, officially anyway, but they hardly see each other and he's very eccentric. Fashion isn't fertile ground for romance. No one has the energy or the time."

"How did you manage to design and date and marry Andrew?" He had wondered about that for a while.

"It was a race against time every day, with work, him, and two little girls. He convinced me to give it up when we got married. He wanted me free to travel with him. And not working gave me a chance to be with my kids. I missed working for a few years, but then I was glad I'd done it. I enjoyed the time I could spend with him and my girls. Your family life is very different when you're working full-time. There's never enough of you to go around, and do a good job at work too."

"Well, just make sure you don't do that again," Ed said, sounding worried. "I mean get married and quit your job with me."

"You have nothing to worry about. I'm not planning to get married again, and I don't have young kids at home anymore," she reminded him. "My girls don't have time to see me either. They work as hard as we do, and Sabrina is crazy. She loves what she does more than she's ever loved a man."

"That's how I feel about it," he said comfortably.

"And I'll never give up my work again for a man," Sydney said with determination. She couldn't imagine being with another man now. She'd had what she considered the perfect relationship and a great marriage with Andrew. It was only now that he was gone that everything had fallen apart and cast a shadow on her memories. But when he was alive, she'd been happy. They had rarely argued, were kind to each other, and shared many of the same interests, and he'd been wonderful to her girls. But after the way it had ended, she never wanted to be dependent on a man again.

"Just make sure you stick to that," Ed warned her. "If Prince Charming comes along after we start the business, tell him you're a working woman, and you won't give it up."

"I promise," she said fervently, and meant it.

They said good night to each other then, and she knew they'd be texting and talking constantly in the coming days and months. They had a lot of decisions to make, and she already had some ideas for sketches and designs for their show in the fall. She wanted to do a predominantly white collection, since the clothes they would be showing to the trade would be in stores for the following summer.

*

The guests arrived on Christmas Eve at seven-thirty. Sydney offered them a choice between hot toddies and eggnog laced with rum. It was one of their Christmas traditions. The apartment looked pretty with the Christmas decorations she'd bought, and there were candles lit everywhere. There was just enough seating for the six of them, with some effort, and it was very cozy. Sydney was wearing a long plaid wool skirt and a red sweater, which she'd worn on Christmas before and had brought with her, with her hair straight down her back. Sabrina came in a short black cocktail dress of her own design, which showed off her long, sexy legs. Her dark hair was shining and she'd worn it down like her mother. She was wearing bright red lipstick and high heels and looked beautiful as she hugged her mother. She was the first to arrive and had brought two bottles of good French wine. She was in a celebratory mood about her new job. She had only been employed there for a week, and already loved it. Her previous boss's impulsive reaction to fire her, over the knockoffs of her designs by Lady Louise, had proved to be an extraordinary blessing. She had leapt in at full speed at her new job and was designing additions to their collection for February's Fashion Week, she was working harder than ever and had never been happier.

"Who else is coming, Mom?" she asked, as she followed her mother over to the kitchen counter. She could smell a turkey in the oven, and she peeked at the vegetables on the stove. Sydney had been working on the meal all day with her only cookbook, and it had turned out well. She had made all their favorites. The dishes that came with the apartment weren't pretty, but she had managed to set a nice table anyway, with candles, a few gold angels, and some pinecones. The whole apartment was fragrant and smelled like the holidays.

"I told you I invited Ed Chin," whom she and Sophie had met once. "Sophie is bringing Grayson, making a rare cameo appearance." They both laughed at that. He was phobic about families and commitment, and said he hated holidays but had agreed to come after Sophie had begged him to for weeks. He was a talented graphic designer, and an unusual person. He had lost his parents as a child and had grown up in foster care, and had moved around a lot. He and Sophie loved each other, but he didn't want marriage, children, or long-term commitment. Sydney thought Sophie was young enough to put up with his limitations, but she didn't think the relationship would go far. They had been dating for a year, and anytime he thought the relationship was getting too serious, he stopped seeing her for a while, and then wandered back when things had cooled off. Her mother and sister were surprised she was still with him, but Sophie insisted he was a good guy, and saw virtues in him that others didn't. He was a prickly porcupine at times.

"And I invited my lawyer, Steve Weinstein. He said he

didn't have any plans. And, Sabrina," she said, looking seriously at her older daughter, "I want you to know how grateful I am for your arranging my bail and paying his retainer. I intend to repay you as soon as I can." She was planning to sell a piece of jewelry if she had to, although she didn't have many and had been trying to hang on to everything she could, to sell in the future if she needed to. But this was one of those times. She had depleted Sabrina's savings, and she wasn't going to let it stay that way for long.

"I don't need the money right now, Mom. And there was no way I was going to let you stay in jail, or not have a decent lawyer. Do you think he's okay?" She had liked him when they spoke, and he seemed competent.

"I think he's very good, and Ed's family checked him out." She knew that didn't mean he would be able to get her off. There were variables in the case and, as Steve had told her, once a matter went to trial, the results were unpredictable. It wasn't going to be a shoo-in, but it wasn't a lost cause either. And hopefully they would find damning evidence on Paul Zeller before they went to trial.

They were still talking about it when Ed Chin rang the buzzer, and when he came in the door he greeted Sabrina, pleased to see her. He congratulated her on her new job, and they launched into animated conversation immediately. He admired her dress, she admitted that the design was one of hers, and he told her he loved it. Ed had worn jeans, a black turtleneck, a black cashmere jacket, and suede loafers, and looked as chic as Sabrina. He had the wardrobe and the style to wear it, and had all his clothes made at his tailor in Hong Kong whenever he went home. They were talking about her new job and the people he knew there, when Sophie and Grayson arrived.

Grayson walked into the apartment looking nervous in jeans and a sweatshirt he'd had since he was at the Rhode Island School of Design, where he'd gotten a full scholarship and had graduated eight years before. He was thirty, had brown hair, was sporting five days of beard stubble, and wore battered high-topped sneakers with holes in them. He glanced around the room and spoke to no one in particular as he cautiously accepted a cup of eggnog.

"I don't normally do holidays, but Sophie insisted," he said as Sydney smiled warmly at him and kissed her younger daughter. Sophie was wearing a black leather miniskirt, a black sweater, black tights, and high-heeled black suede boots that reached her thighs. She looked sexy and young, and more casual than her sister, and had a more voluptuous figure. Her whole style was younger and less sophisticated than Sabrina's. She wore her hair wild and loose and long in a mane of curls she'd had since she was a child.

"We're glad you could come," Sydney told Grayson graciously, and managed to keep a straight face when the eggnog coated his mustache and turned it white. Then the doorbell rang again and it was Steve, carrying a big baker's box and a bottle of good California wine. His offerings were gratefully received, and when Sydney peeked inside the box as she set it down, she saw that it was a beautiful yule log for dessert. She'd been planning to serve Christmas pudding, and instantly decided to serve both and thanked him. She introduced all the young people to each other as they came in. And the chatter of conversation reached a comfortable level, except for Grayson, who sat quietly on the couch, watching the others. If nothing else, he always seemed odd, and Sophie explained that he was shy. Ed commented on his sweatshirt when he sat down next to him, and said he had always wanted to go to RISD, but hadn't been accepted, and had gone to design school in London instead. Grayson relaxed a little after that, and it amused Sydney to realize that of the six people in the room, five of them were designers, in one form or another, and four of the six were in fashion.

"You're the only sane grown-up here, not in fashion or design," she teased Steve, and she liked being able to count herself among the designers again. It gave form and purpose to her life, aside from feeding her and helping to pay her rent for the past five months.

"It's definitely intimidating," he admitted. "I changed shirts four times, and jackets twice before deciding on an appropriate outfit. Having dinner with a bunch of fashion designers definitely puts the heat on." In the end, he had opted for a blue collared shirt, a tweed jacket, jeans, and brown suede oxfords that were very stylish.

"You did just fine," Sydney complimented him, impressed by how nice he looked. He was more handsome than she'd realized in court, when she'd been distracted by more serious preoccupations than how he dressed.

"I just wore my old school sweatshirt," Grayson said, looking nervous again, as he helped himself to more eggnog, and Sophie watched him. She didn't want him to get drunk because he was ill at ease with people.

They made it to the table at nine, when the turkey was done, and Steve opened the wine and poured it. They were drinking Sabrina's bottles first. Sydney had seated Sabrina next to Steve, and she was on his other side. And she put Ed on Sabrina's other side, with Sophie and Grayson between Ed and herself, and the conversation at dinner flourished, aided by the excellent wine Sabrina had provided. Steve complimented her on it.

Steve's yule log was a big hit for dessert, with the Christmas pudding, which Sydney poured brandy over and lit. And they all talked about how they had spent Christmas as children. Sophie and Sabrina's warm description of their family traditions brought tears to their mother's eyes. Ed said that his family had always celebrated Christmas and Chinese New Year's, and gave big dinner parties with family and friends for both events. "My family loves a party!" he said, and everybody laughed.

"We celebrated Chanukah when I was a kid, but pretty loosely," Steve commented. "My parents let me have a Christmas tree too, because my friends did. They always envied me because Chanukah lasts for eight days, but they got all their presents at once, which I thought was cooler. And I'm happy to be with you," he added. "My family is all away this year, and I'd be sitting in my apartment feeling sorry for myself tonight if I weren't here, so thank you, Sydney, for inviting me, and to all of you for having me." He raised his glass and smiled at his new client.

"I'm an atheist," Grayson announced. "I don't believe in Christmas," he said, and there was silence at the table for a minute, "but I'm having a good time, thank you," he added, as everyone exhaled, and he raised his glass too.

Sophie suggested charades after dinner, and after several glasses of wine, Grayson was the best one at it, and could guess nearly anything before anyone else could, and his pantomimes were hilarious and made them all laugh. And although she hadn't expected it to be that way, Sydney thought it was one of the best Christmases she'd had in years, despite Andrew's absence. The atmosphere was warm and cozy, and it was a special night among friends who genuinely liked each other, and were glad to be together.

She noticed that Steve and Sabrina had engaged in conversation repeatedly, when she wasn't talking to Ed about fashion. Ed and Sydney talked a little about the new business they were starting. And no one had the bad taste to mention her recent legal difficulties or the threat of an upcoming trial. They had put it aside for the night, and so had Sydney. She was just enjoying everyone. No one made a move to leave until after one in the morning, and when Sabrina stood up, Steve offered to take her home, since he didn't live far from her. They all said goodbye reluctantly, and Ed stayed for a few minutes after the others left.

"What a lovely evening you gave all of us," he complimented her, as he sipped the last of his wine. "And I think you may have started something tonight." He looked at her mischievously and guessed that she had done it on purpose.

"Steve and Sabrina?" He nodded, and they both laughed. "I thought that might work. At least I hoped so. I like him. And poor Grayson looked like he was going to fall apart when he walked in, but he rallied. I think the eggnog helped. He's a sweet kid and a very good designer. He just had a lousy childhood, and has a lot of issues."

"I liked him," Ed said easily. "I liked all of them, and your daughters are fantastic. I could have talked to them all night."

"They're good women. I'm very proud of them."

He offered to help her clean up and do the dishes, and she told him she'd do it in the morning and he didn't have to, and he left a few minutes later. She sat alone on the couch after he was gone and thought about the evening.

It had been perfect and just what she wanted it to be, for all of them. Even Grayson had joined in the fun with good humor. They had managed to blend traditions, and the lack of them, between Christians, a Jew, a Buddhist, and an atheist, and shared a warm and wonderful evening, which was what Christmas was all about. And she hoped that wherever he was, Andrew was at peace too.

Chapter 10

On Christmas Day, the morning after her dinner party, Sydney got up early to do the dishes and clean up, and thought again about how warm and congenial it had been the night before. And as she scrubbed the pan the turkey had roasted in, she realized that she hadn't heard from Veronica or any of her old friends over the holidays, but she didn't miss them. She was totally absorbed in her new life. Sydney hadn't heard from Veronica after their last conversation. She had only been interested in delivering bad news, and Sydney was no longer willing to hear it, which spoiled it for Veronica.

None of her other friends had called her to see how she was, or invite her to their holiday parties. It was as though they felt it was too awkward now to acknowledge her, particularly since the news had spread like wildfire that she had no money left, and her arrest had been in the papers. It was disappointing to observe how important Andrew's money had been to them. In the past six months, she felt like the forgotten woman. She hadn't called them either and felt strange doing so, and now that her arrest had hit the fashion press, she was afraid to talk to anyone, and didn't want to discuss it with them. But her friends from their married days certainly hadn't been loyal or attentive. They had valued the lifestyle she'd shared with Andrew, but apparently not her friendship.

Steve called her as she was putting the last rinsed dish in the dishwasher, and thanked her profusely for dinner.

"Thank *you* for the delicious wine and that gorgeous yule log," she said warmly.

"You made the evening lovely for all of us," he said kindly. "I wanted to ask you something, it's a little awkward. I don't normally do this with clients." She wondered what was coming, and hoped her matchmaking had worked. It sounded like it, and had looked that way the night before. "Would you mind if I call Sabrina? She's a fantastic woman, and she looks just like you except for the dark hair. I don't normally date my clients' daughters, but in this case, I'd like to make an exception, if you agree." He was obviously nervous as he put the question to her, and Sydney forced herself to seem casual when she answered, but at her end she was beaming from ear to ear. She had thought he was perfect for her daughter, and she hoped that Sabrina liked him too.

"I have no problem with it whatsoever," she assured him. "I thought you'd get along. She's awfully busy, though, and when Fashion Week happens twice a year, she disappears."

"I think I can manage. I have a few things to do too." He was planning to suggest lunch to her, and go easy with it. "Is she involved with anyone? I don't want to step on any toes."

"Yes, her work. 24/7," Sydney said, and he laughed.

"I like a woman who works hard. It makes me feel less guilty when I have to."

Sydney gave him Sabrina's number, and then he said they should get together in the coming weeks to talk about the detective he wanted to hire to do some snooping around on Paul Zeller. There had been no word about the grand jury hearing yet.

"Will a detective be hideously expensive?" Sydney asked, sounding worried. She was afraid to run up a lot of bills she couldn't afford, and Sabrina had paid enough for bail and his fee.

"It's not cheap," he said honestly, "but it could give us just what we need to get the case against you dismissed, or win at a trial."

"Then it's worth it." She made an appointment with him for early January, and wished him a merry Christmas again. And after they hung up, she wondered how fast he'd call Sabrina, or if he'd wait until the new year and play it cool.

Sabrina called her half an hour later, sounding pleased. "You'll never guess who called me," she said, surprised, while her mother feigned ignorance.

"Let's see, Brad Pitt . . . Harrison Ford . . . Leonardo DiCaprio?" Sabrina laughed at her mother.

"Yes, obviously. But after they called, Steve Weinstein called me half an hour ago. He invited me to lunch on Sunday. And he asked if I had plans on New Year's Eve. I guess he just broke up with someone, and he's at loose ends. I was going to do some work that night. But he suggested dinner and a movie. That sounds about right for someone I don't know that well. What are you doing on New Year's Eve?" she asked, concerned for her mother. She didn't want her to be lonely, and she didn't seem to have a social life these days. She and her sister were both aware of it. It was a big change from the active life she and Andrew had shared when they were married. They were always going to some dinner party in Connecticut, cocktail party in New York, black-tie benefit at a museum, or out to dinner at their favorite restaurants. And now all of that seemed to be gone, and she was sure her mother missed it.

"I'm staying home with a good book," Sydney said about New Year's Eve. "And I might do some work too. But you're too young to do that at twenty-seven. You should go out with Steve."

"I said I would." Sabrina sounded pleased. "He's good company and seems like a nice person. He's very bright, and has a lot of interests."

"He strikes me that way too." And hopefully he's a

brilliant lawyer, Sydney thought to herself. "I thought Grayson did very well last night," Sydney said generously.

"The poor guy is such a ball of nerves. I always have the feeling that if I say the wrong thing, he'll run out of the room. But he was very funny at charades, and you were right about Ed Chin. I love him. I was leery about meeting him at first because he worked for that sausage factory, but I see now that he's a serious person. He was smart to quit. Zeller is going to take everyone down with him, just like he did to you." Sydney didn't disagree.

"Well, have fun with Steve. Don't get him too distracted so he can still win my case." It was beginning to feel like there was no case to win. Everything had gone back to normal, she was home again, and her four days in jail seemed like a bad dream. But sooner or later, she knew the case would rear its ugly head again, like a snake, and she would have to deal with it.

As she had said she would, Sydney stayed home on New Year's Eve. She watched some old movies, and did some sketches. Ed called her from a party at midnight. But she didn't want to be anywhere this year, except at home. She knew she'd probably go out on New Year's Eve again one day, but it didn't feel right this year, so soon after Andrew's death and everything that had happened since.

Sophie called her at midnight to wish her a happy New Year and said that Grayson was asleep. They had stayed home too, and Sophie had watched the ball in Times Square on TV, which seemed a little too sedate to her mother.

Sabrina called her the next day and said she and Steve had gone to dinner in the Village, and instead of the movies, they went skating at Rockefeller Center underneath the giant Christmas tree, and had sat in the bar for hours afterward, drinking champagne and getting to know each other. Sabrina said it had been the perfect New Year's Eve. Sydney thought it sounded like a great beginning.

After the first of the year, she and Ed got busy with their plans for the business, and tried to define what they wanted their clothes to look like and be noted for. Great fabrics, interesting designs, subtle textures, a look that was structured and serious, but not severe, and now and then had a surprise wisp of softness. They wanted their clothes to be what every woman wanted to wear, and affordable, but not dirt-cheap either, like Lady Louise. There were still a lot of things they needed to work out and decide on, and people they wanted to hire.

In the second week of January, she met with Steve Weinstein again about her case, as they had arranged. He talked to her about the detective he wanted to hire and had used before. And he told her that he wanted to use a local operative in Beijing whom they could send to the manufacturer to see what they were willing to say about Paul Zeller. Steve wanted the detective to turn over every stone until they found the one they needed. He was sure it was there. They just had to find it. Steve agreed to cap the detective's work at a certain price that they both thought was reasonable, and said he would be willing to front the money for the detective, and she could repay him later, which was a relief to her. The money was flowing like water for her court case, and she didn't want the faucet open too wide, so she didn't drown paying for it.

When Sydney met with Steve, they didn't talk about Sabrina. She didn't want to mix her business and her daughter's romance, but she was very curious if they were seeing each other. With Fashion Week only weeks away in New York, she knew that Sabrina must be buried until it was over. And Sophie was just as busy with her line. She had just won an award for the best designs for young juniors she was thrilled, and Sydney was pleased for her. She had found her perfect niche. Her clothes had a fresh, youthful look that was fun and pretty, and didn't make teenagers look like hookers.

A week after Sydney's meeting with Steve, they went to see the deputy U.S. attorney in charge of her case, and he questioned her intensely about Paul Zeller. They acted as though she should know more than she did, and leaned on her heavily. But Sydney insisted truthfully that she knew no more than she had told them. Paul had not confided in her about stolen goods or any illegal activities. And she said again that she had believed the stolen purses were merely copies, though very good ones. The U.S. attorney was not pleased. The grand jury had convened by then, and based on the evidence available to them, the indictment had been confirmed and the case was going forward and proceeding to trial. There was no way out.

In February, she went to Sabrina's first fashion show for her new company, and Sophie's presentation. The fashion shows were always dramatic, with hordes of beautiful models, and for the most part spectacular clothes by great designers. Sydney always loved going, for the clothes and to see her daughter's work. She went with Ed to see Sabrina's new line, and they commented at length about the clothes as the models went down the runway. Halfway through, she nudged him with her elbow.

"What?" He was surprised if she meant she liked the dress that had just walked past him. He thought it was chic but not exceptional, and so did she. But she was looking toward the front row of seats on the other side of the runway, almost facing them. She hadn't noticed him before. It was her lawyer, Steve. She smiled at Ed and raised an eyebrow. Steve hadn't seen them, and they went over to say hello to him after the show. He looked mildly embarrassed, as though they had caught him doing something he shouldn't.

"I've never been to a fashion show before," he confessed. "Sabrina invited me."

"It's fun for you to see," Sydney encouraged him. "These shows are always crazy, and they spend a fortune producing them. It's half about the spectacle and half about the clothes."

"I like what she does," he said honestly.

"We do too," Ed added for Sydney and himself.

They drifted apart then, as Ed greeted several people, Sydney stayed with him, and Steve went backstage to congratulate Sabrina. Her mother knew what a crush it would be backstage, and she didn't want to fight the crowds. She was going to call Sabrina later.

They were on their way back toward the entrance of a tent pitched in Central Park for the event. All the important magazine editors sat in the front rows, like Anna Wintour and Grace Coddington, with her flaming red hair a lot like Sophie's. And squeezing toward the exit, jostled by the crowd, Sydney suddenly found herself nose to nose with Kyra, her stepdaughter. She was the last person she wanted to meet. And there was no avoiding her, as they were pressed together by the crowd.

"Nice to see you," Sydney said coolly, but nevertheless politely. Kyra was her stepdaughter, after all, and she said it for Andrew's sake, since she was his daughter. Sydney knew she came to Fashion Week events often and ordered clothes for the following season.

"Did they let you out of jail to see Sabrina's show?" Kyra said viciously, and for a moment, Sydney was speechless and didn't know what to say. There was no way to get away from her. The mob around them held them in place like cement. Sydney didn't answer her, but she felt as if her stepdaughter had punched her in the solar plexus and knocked the air right out of her. She couldn't think of a single appropriate response. She turned her head away, and was relieved when the crowd finally moved forward and she could get away.

"What did that woman say to you?" Ed asked her when they were on the path, hurrying away. "You went sheet-white."

"It was one of my nasty stepdaughters. She made a rude reference to jail."

"You should have said something," he scolded her. "I'd have clobbered her with my umbrella." It had been raining all day. "What a bitch."

"Yes, she is," she agreed. But Kyra had really taken the wind out of her sails and spoiled the day for her, and Ed was sorry to see it.

"Don't give them power over you," he said to her later when they were back in their office in Chelsea, which had really taken shape. "No one can take away who you are," he reminded her. She knew it was true. But they had taken her home since Andrew's death, and even some of her self-confidence and her faith in human nature. It was difficult not to be affected by everything that had changed.

In April, Ed and Sydney did a small, select presentation for an elite group to show a preview of what they would be offering when they introduced their new line at Fashion Week in September. It was a taste of what was to come, and they chose their audience carefully, some of the more important editors, a few major buyers, and select members of the fashion press. Sydney was nervous about it, but Ed was more confident. They did it at their Chelsea location, and served champagne and hors d'oeuvres. They used their favorite models to show the clothes. The idea of a preview was new, and Sydney was afraid it would hurt them if they got bad reviews before they even started. She'd been able to focus on it totally since her next court appearance had been continued until May, which was a relief for her.

Ed's parents and one of his uncles came from Hong Kong to show support, and Sydney loved seeing them again. She invited her daughters, and introduced them to the Chins. Both she and Ed had family members present to bolster them. There were ten looks in the show, and Sydney had worked relentlessly with the fit models, the patternmakers, and their sewers to get everything just right. Neither she nor Ed got to bed the night before, working right up until the time of the presentation.

"Ready?" Ed asked her, before their VIP guests arrived, and she nodded, feeling breathless. It was terrifying. They had combined their talent, followed their dream, and were now introducing their love child to the world.

They had invited sixty very influential people in the world of fashion. There was valet parking outside. Waiters circulated with flutes of champagne, and there was a table offering American caviar in the corner. They even had more guests than they'd expected. Two of the editors had brought friends, several journalists called and asked to come at the last minute, and the Chins had brought their banker from Hong Kong, who had business in New York that week. His name was Robert Townsend. He was British and had arrived with them. Ed had introduced Sydney to him, but she had been too nervous to pay attention, and had gone backstage again to check on the girls, who were prancing like show horses in their outfits, and knew it was a major event.

Sydney's heart felt like a drumroll when everyone took their seats and the music began. The lighting was perfect, the music was just right with a sound system they'd rented for the occasion, and everyone sat riveted as the models came out.

There was intense concentration in the room, and all eyes were focused on the girls, as the elite of the industry waited to give their approval, or not, to the two designers who had created Sydney Chin four months before.

The girls came out at a good pace. They had rehearsed countless times, and when the last girl emerged in a spectacular evening gown, in contrast to the more casual but elegant daytime clothes, everyone stood up and there was thunderous applause from the small crowd.

"Fantastic . . . beautiful . . . absolutely tops . . ." Praise for them was flying around the room when the lights came on, and all the *Vogue* editors were smiling when they left. They had been very supportive of them, as they often were with young designers, and Sydney came under that heading now too, since the line was new, and she had been away from the upper end of the industry for so long. Her brief time at Lady Louise didn't count, except to pay her rent. The line for them bearing her name had not been introduced before her unfortunate arrest.

Ed came to hug her as she emerged from backstage, people were milling around the room, and more champagne was poured. Ed's parents had sent them cases of Cristal as a gift.

"I'm not among the cognoscenti of fashion, but that was a beautiful show," Robert Townsend said to Sydney when he saw her again. Her knees were still shaking, she'd been so stressed. She had put her heart and soul into what she had designed for the presentation, and she and Ed had been working on it tirelessly for months. They were going to include a few of the pieces in their show during Fashion Week, but most of it had been for this particular event, to give people a preview of their combined talents and line. "You must be very proud," Townsend said.

"Just relieved," she said honestly. "I was scared to death." He couldn't imagine it. She was such a pro, and Ed had told them in Hong Kong months earlier about her history as a top designer twenty years before. "Every show is like the first time," she said breathlessly, as she accepted a flute of Cristal from a waiter and looked up at him. He seemed very tall, although she wasn't short, but she was wearing flat shoes. He looked about fifty years old, with a thick head of dark hair and an impeccable haircut, with gray at his temples and deep blue eyes, almost the same color as hers. She was wearing black jeans and a black T-shirt, and black suede ballerina shoes. Ed had been wearing similar black jeans and T-shirt when they stepped onto the runway, holding hands, and quickly took a bow.

"We're very proud of Ed in Hong Kong," Bob Townsend said with a warm smile. "We just wish he'd come home more often. He'll be too busy now, for a while anyway."

"We'll show the whole collection here in September," she explained, "but we might do a show there sometime," as a charity event, or in deference to his hometown.

"You should come and see us too," he said politely.

"I was there with Ed last year. It's an amazing city."

"It is," he agreed, watching her closely. He thought she was a beautiful woman with startling, deep, sad eyes. He could see that life had not been easy for her, despite her gracious manner and warm way of speaking with people. "I grew up in London, but I fell in love with Hong Kong the first time I saw it. I've lived in several cities in Asia, Shanghai, Tokyo, but Hong Kong owns my heart." She smiled at what he said. "I can't imagine leaving it. I travel a lot, but I'm always happy to get back." Ed's parents joined them then, and they chatted for a few more minutes, and then she moved on to their other guests. It was nearly nine when the last one left, still congratulating them. Ed was having dinner with his family that night at 21 and had invited her to join them, but she said she was exhausted and looked a mess.

"So do I, so what?" Ed said, beaming at her. "We're stars now," he said grandly, and they both laughed, knowing that it could have just as easily gone the other way and been a bomb. Steve and Sabrina had left by then, and had a dinner party to go to, and Sophie had to go home and work. Ed insisted that Sydney couldn't just go back to her apartment after their tour de force. She finally agreed to join them, and took a cab with Ed to the restaurant, and they chatted on the way uptown, as they both started to unwind. Sydney had eaten and slept so little in the past twenty-four hours that she was feeling the effects of a single glass of champagne, and said she felt drunk.

"If I fall asleep at the table, kick me," she warned him. "I feel like I could sleep for a week."

"Me too." The pressure was off, and the night had been

a victory for them. "I saw you talking to Bob Townsend after the show. He's a great guy. He's not like most bankers. He was married to one of the most famous Chinese writers. They got divorced years ago. She moved to London and left him with four kids. He was married to a famous Chinese actress briefly after that. He's not as serious as he looks." Ed laughed.

"Sounds like a player," she commented with a yawn. She could hardly stay awake.

"Not really. I grew up with his kids. If I were straight, I'd marry his oldest daughter in a hot minute," he said, grinning. "And his son is a writer. They're a talented, enterprising bunch. He's a big art collector, and he represents some of the really big money in Hong Kong. He comes here a lot."

"So he said." They had reached the restaurant by then, and got out of the taxi. Ed's parents had reserved the private room and had invited several friends to join them. Everyone congratulated Ed and Sydney again as soon as they walked in and gave them a round of applause. Sydney felt like she had won an Oscar or a CFDA Fashion Award. Their first presentation had definitely been a success. And when they sat down at the dinner in their designated seats, she found herself next to Bob Townsend. He seemed intriguing now that she knew more about him. And at least she knew something about his children from Ed.

"Ed told me your son is a writer," she said as they waited for the preordered dinner to arrive, with all of 21's specialties. She hadn't been there in a long time and had forgotten how much she liked it. The atmosphere in the private room was relaxed and congenial.

"He's trying to be," Bob said with a wry smile. "He just finished his first novel. One of my daughters is a painter in Shanghai. My youngest is in medical school in England, and my oldest daughter is a chef at one of the best French restaurants in Hong Kong. She studied at Cordon Bleu in Paris." He smiled with pride as he went down the list, and she could see how much he loved his kids. She suspected they must have had a special bond if he brought them up alone.

"That's quite a variety of talents," she said, thinking about it. He had obviously encouraged them to pursue their dreams, however different. And if so, it seemed admirable to her.

"Were those your daughters at the show?" he asked her. "One of them looks just like you. You could have been sisters." She knew he meant Sabrina. Sophie looked entirely different with her wild mane of red curls.

"They were there. They're both designers. I guess I gave them the fashion bug when they were little. I used to take them to haute couture shows in Paris. I was working as a designer when they were growing up, before I remarried."

"And after you did?" He was interested in what she had

to say, and the woman behind the talent. Ed had spoken highly of her.

"I retired. I just came back into the industry last year." He could sense that there was more to the story.

"You're divorced?" Ed hadn't said if she was married or not.

"Widowed." She tried to make it seem matter-of-fact and not pathetic. She was slowly getting used to the word and the sound of it on her lips to describe herself. It always felt as though she was talking about someone else. How could she be a widow at forty-nine? But she was.

"I'm sorry," he said, and she nodded, not wanting to go into it. "It's good that you went back to work," he commented sensibly. "My wife and I got divorced when our children were very young, and she left Hong Kong. They used to spend summers and holidays with her. They were with me the rest of the time. I felt sorry for myself for a while, a long while, and then I got busy again. We lived in Tokyo for five years, Shanghai for two, we went back to England for a year, and then we came back to Hong Kong. Moving around like that opened a whole world to them, and to me too. The downside of course is that now they feel the world is their oyster, and they live all over the place. At least I have two in Hong Kong now. My two oldest. Both my younger daughters have acute wanderlust. We all do. I would have liked to spend a year in Paris with them when they were younger, but I don't have business dealings there. My work takes me between London, Asia, and New York. It's not a bad assortment of cities. I'm here about every six weeks, sometimes every month." He was an important figure in international finance, Ed had told her, mostly with immensely wealthy Chinese clients.

"My husband was an investment banker, but not internationally. We went to Paris a lot, though. I love it. I'm selling our apartment there now," she said, trying not to sound sad about it.

"What a pity. You don't think you'll go there anymore?" he asked cautiously, not wanting to pry.

"Too many memories," she said succinctly, and he didn't pursue the subject, but nodded that he understood. He wondered if she'd feel differently with time.

"Most of us don't see it that way, but there are chapters in our lives," he said quietly. "We want to believe that the same characters will be in the story forever. But it rarely seems to work out that way. Some characters leave the story, others come along. It keeps it lively and surprising, don't you think?" He looked sympathetic as he said it.

"I've never thought of it that way. I guess I expected the story to stay the same forever. It's easier that way."

"We don't often get to make that choice. Fate does it for us." He smiled wisely. "I'm fifty-four years old, I've been married twice, to two very interesting, unusual women. I didn't plan it that way, but looking at it now, I might have been bored if the story hadn't changed radically from time to time."

"I've been married twice too," she admitted. "My first marriage wasn't destined to last forever. My second could have, and should have." She was still holding on to the shreds of her marriage to Andrew, although there was so little left of what they'd shared. And she no longer felt like the same person that she was then.

"Apparently it wasn't meant to last then, if it didn't," he said philosophically. "That's easy for me to say. And some changes are much harder than others. I seem to learn most of my lessons the hard way," he added, laughing at himself. "My children keep me honest. Whenever I feel sorry for myself, they remind me of how much fun I've had, boot me in the butt, and tell me to get on with it. And they're quite right usually. And when I'm sad over what I lost, I often find that things look better in the rearview mirror than they really were, in my case anyway." After the last eight months, she knew he had a point. She had loved Andrew, but the mess he had left her in had tarnished some of her memories of him. "So what are your plans now?" he asked, changing the subject. "Huge success with Edward in your new business, obviously. I think we got a glimpse of the future tonight. You have good times to look forward to," he said with certainty. He was a strong and positive person, and she liked that about him.

"I'm so happy we started the business. It's a fantastic

opportunity for me. I love being back in fashion, and designing with him," she said warmly with a smile.

"He's clearly enjoying it too. You're a wonderful combination artistically," he complimented her, and meant it.

"I love the collaboration. We complement each other's work. He softens mine, and I toughen his up a little." It was about fabrics, structure, and style. Ed could never resist a flowing fabric, or something that would float if draped right. She liked stronger shapes and cleaner lines. They had managed to incorporate both in the work they'd done so far.

"Would you ever want to have your own line? Just you, not a collaboration?" he asked her, curious, as their meal arrived and they started eating. He had chosen the filet mignon, and she was having steak tartare. The other options were lobster and a vegetarian entree.

"I hope not," she said in answer to his question. "I want to design with Ed for a long, long time. This is just the beginning." He nodded, and she thought of what he'd said before, that there were chapters in life. But this was a new story for her, with Ed as a business partner. "How long will you be in New York?" she asked him.

"A few days. A week at most. I'm going to San Francisco after this, to meet with some venture capitalists. And then back to Hong Kong. But I'll be back in a month or two."

She was seated next to one of Ed's uncles on her other side, Phillip, the one who had referred her to Steve

Weinstein, and she thanked him again in a low voice while they chatted, and Bob Townsend turned his attention to the person on his left.

"I hope everything worked out," Phillip said to her about her court case. "That sounded like a very nasty experience," he said, sorry for her.

"It was, it is. We're still working on it," she said, and they changed the subject.

It turned out to be a delightful evening, and ended around midnight. She left Ed and the others on the sidewalk, and after thanking his parents, she said good night to Bob and told him she'd enjoyed talking to him, and then took a cab back to her apartment. She could barely make it to her bedroom, lay down on the bed, and fell asleep with her clothes on. It had been a perfect night. It was official. The firm of Sydney Chin had been born.

Chapter 11

Bob Townsend called Sydney at the office the next day and invited her to lunch. She hesitated, thanked him, and said she had to call him back in a few minutes.

Ed heard the exchange when he walked into her office, and Sydney was looking nervous when she hung up.

"That was Bob Townsend," she volunteered without his asking. "He invited me to lunch."

"And? The problem is?" He looked pleased to hear it. Bob was one of his favorite people in Hong Kong, and a great guy, as he had told her the night before.

"I don't think I should go. I'm sure he's just asking me to be nice, and friendly. But if he has any interest in me at all, I think it's a bad idea." She looked determined as she said it.

"Would you like to explain that to me? You're forty-nine years old. Are we supposed to put you on a barge and set fire to you, to honor your late husband? I think that's gone a little out of fashion. We're starting a new business that's taking off, and he's a good man. Why don't you live a little instead of working all the time?"

"It's not about that." Although still feeling married to Andrew was a part of it, the problem was greater, as she saw it. "Six months from now I could be in prison for a long time. I don't think I have the right to drag anyone into this with me."

"Great, and what about me?" Ed said lightheartedly. "We own a business together. And I don't think you really believe what you just said about going to prison. If you did, you wouldn't have started Sydney Chin with me."

"I couldn't resist you. But Steve says prison is still a possibility. I don't think I should be dating right now. And I don't want to explain it to him. It sounds so sordid, and so sinister. 'Trafficking in stolen goods.' It makes me sound like some kind of gun moll, or a gangster." Ed shook his head at what she said.

"So don't tell him if you don't want to. Just go to lunch, for heaven's sake. You have to eat, although you don't do that often either. I order you to have lunch with him. He's not going to propose, so you won't leave him broken-hearted while you serve life imprisonment. He just wants to share a meal with you. It sounds pretty tame to me. And you'll have fun with him. I always do."

She thought about it for a few minutes after Ed went back to his office, and she decided that maybe she was being overly dramatic, and Ed was right. So she called Bob back and agreed to meet him in the West Village for lunch. She hadn't dressed for a date with anyone, and she was wearing jeans, a pink cashmere sweater, a navy blazer, and flat shoes, and she looked relaxed and young when she met him at the restaurant. He was already waiting at the table and was pleased to see her, as he stood up to greet her. In some ways, he was very British and extremely polite. Ed's whole family was too. She liked that about them. Their manners were impeccable. Bob looked just as handsome and well dressed as he had the evening before. He was wearing a business suit and Hermès tie for his meetings.

"Thank you for having lunch with me on such short notice," he said as they sat down. "I was hoping to see you again. I really enjoyed sitting next to you last night," Bob said with obvious admiration, "and I hope I didn't come across as too pious. I've never been widowed, and I don't know what it's like. I'm sure it's difficult to adjust to. I've only been divorced, and there's always a certain relief to that. No marriage is perfect. But people acquire a patina of perfection in our minds when they die. Maybe your husband has too. Or maybe he really was perfect." He was being generous about it and was afraid he might have upset her, but she looked happy to see him.

"We had a very, very good marriage, but no, he wasn't perfect, even in hindsight. And he did some things I discovered at the end that have made life very difficult for me now," she said honestly. He was easy to talk to.

Being European, Bob assumed he must have left a mistress she'd found out about after he died, who was giving her a hard time now, or the realization had broken her heart. Perhaps he'd even died in another woman's arms. Stranger things had happened to make a husband look bad after his death, and cast an ugly light on the marriage.

"I assume you mean another woman," he said cautiously, and she smiled and sighed.

"Two of them, actually." Bob raised an eyebrow at that. Her late husband had obviously been a busy man, he thought, as Sydney went on when their food arrived. "We were married for sixteen years. We had a very cut-and-dried prenuptial agreement. We waived all community property rights, whatever he paid for belonged to him, and he paid for everything, our house, art, lifestyle. He was a very generous man. But somehow he never thought to update his will once we were married, or temper our prenup over the years. He was young. He died at fifty-six. He was in good health. He must have thought he had time, which he should have. He had a motorcycle accident and died instantly, with the last will he'd written before he ever met me still in force. He had twin daughters who hated me with a passion from the first time they laid eyes on me. They got everything, the house, the art, everything. They gave me thirty days to get out of our home, and the contents of the house went with it. I got my wardrobe and what was in our grocery account, and a pied-à-terre in Paris he'd given me as a gift, which I'm trying to sell now.

So from one minute to the next, I had nothing, barely enough to eat and pay rent. He would never have wanted that to happen, but he had done nothing to prevent it. His twins have it all, and they were ecstatic that I got nothing. So that's the story. He should have been more responsible about writing up a new will, at some point. A major oversight that has changed my life forever. But I got a job, met Ed, and he saved me, and now we have a business together. So I guess things work out in the end, just as you said."

She didn't seem bitter about it, or angry, which amazed him. She could have been. He could only imagine how difficult the last months must have been, with no money, getting thrown out of their home and losing everything. "You couldn't negotiate with his daughters for the house?"

"They would have burned me at the stake if they could have. They've always hated me, with the help of their very unpleasant mother. To be honest, sometimes I'm angry about it now. I have very mixed feelings about the situation."

"I wouldn't," he said clearly, as they ate their salads. "I'd want to strangle them. In fact, I want to do it for you. What sort of girls are they to put you out of your home in thirty days? That's barbaric. How old are they?"

"Thirty-three, but they're very spoiled, nasty girls."

"I'll say. They sound like raving bitches to me." He

looked at her with new admiration, realizing what she'd been up against in the months since her husband's death, and how heartbreaking and terrifying it must have been for her. "Is the boat back on even keel now?" It was a good image, and she smiled.

"The *Titanic* isn't going down. Although I thought it would for a while. I'm managing, and if the business is a success, all will be fine. I'm working again. It's just a very big change from the life we led while I was married. But as you said, nothing lasts forever. I just didn't expect it all to end so soon, and so suddenly. I never thought something like that could happen."

"Fortunately, you're young enough to right the ship again," he said, and she nodded with a serious expression.

"So that's my sad story." But she looked like she was doing extremely well. They talked of other things then, and the time at lunch flew by. He hated to leave her, but he said he had a meeting on Wall Street, and asked for the check after two hours. He wanted to tell her that he had enormous admiration for all that she'd survived, and so bravely, and her spirit was still whole and intact. But he didn't want to embarrass her, so he didn't mention it.

She thanked him for lunch, and they left each other outside the restaurant. He promised to call her the next time he was in New York. She went back to the office then, and he took a cab to Wall Street. Ed was waiting for her and saw her come in.

"So how was it?" he asked, curious about the lunch, and what had happened. He liked the idea of two people he loved being together, and hadn't thought of it until he saw them talking to each other the night before. Bob and Sydney together suddenly appealed to him immensely.

"It was perfect," she said matter-of-factly. "He proposed. I accepted. Our lawyers are drawing up the marriage contracts. They'll send them over by end of business today." He looked shocked for a minute and then burst out laughing.

"Did you tell him about your court case?" Ed wanted to know about that too, and what she had decided to say, if anything.

"No, I didn't. I told him I lost everything to my stepdaughters when Andrew died. I figured that was enough Poor Pitiful Pearl for one meeting. I'll tell him about life imprisonment next time, if there is one. You were right. I had a good time. He's a really good guy. I'll have lunch with him again if he asks me."

"I'm sure he will." And Ed knew there was nothing pitiful about her. That was one of the amazing things about her. She had bounced back. She was a survivor.

She went back to work then, and sent Bob an email to thank him. It was nice having a new friend.

In May, Sydney had another court appearance, the one that had been postponed in April, in the lengthy process that led up to trial. It was a formality, but it brought the whole situation back to her again. The rest of the time she was busy with life and her new business and could put it out of her mind. But now she had to face the possibility that she could go to prison if she lost. It was hard to guess how it would turn out. The detective they hired had discovered nothing incriminating about Paul Zeller. He had covered his tracks well. At the hearing, they had questioned her again about Paul's activities, and she had told them again that she knew nothing. She wasn't in his confidence, didn't know him well, and hardly saw him once she took the job. But they didn't seem to believe her.

She was sitting in a small conference room with Steve Weinstein after her appearance, discussing what would happen next, when the assistant U.S. attorney stuck his head in the door and asked to speak to Steve. Steve left the room to consult with him, and came back twenty minutes later. He looked at Sydney seriously and sat down across from her.

"They want to offer you a deal. That means they're tired of the case, but they're not willing to let it go. A trial will be costly for both sides, a huge amount of work to prepare, and they'd rather make a deal with you and avoid a trial."

"What kind of a deal?" She was suspicious, and he explained it to her.

"They're offering you the opportunity to plead guilty to

a lesser charge. They haven't determined what that is yet, but it would still be a felony charge. Maybe grand theft larceny, something less onerous than trafficking in stolen goods. And they're offering you a year in prison in exchange for your pleading guilty, and telling them whatever you know about Zeller." She looked shocked as he said it. "You'd probably get out in nine months."

"I've already told them everything I know about him. And you're telling me that I'd plead guilty to felony charges, so I'd have a criminal record, and I'd serve nine months to a year in prison? What kind of deal is that?"

"Not a great one," he admitted honestly. "I couldn't get better terms from him than that. They're still determined to make an example of you. But if we go to trial, it could end up a lot worse. The jury could convict you, and the judge could give you five to ten years. That's a *lot* worse than nine months to a year."

"But I'm not guilty," she said with a look of despair.

"Unfortunately, sometimes that's beside the point. The problem we have is that as far as they're concerned, they caught you red-handed, and your signature is all over everything. You have no witnesses to prove you weren't in cahoots with the seller. Other than Ed's testimony, we have no concrete evidence that you were acting on Zeller's orders, and Ed wasn't present at every conversation you had with him. Your employer is playing innocent and blaming you for everything, and even implying that you might have double-crossed him and taken a kickback from the manufacturer for moving stolen goods. With the evidence against you as it stands now, a trial could go very badly. You might be acquitted, but if they believe the evidence, it's not likely. By accepting a plea bargain, you limit the damage and you know ahead of time what your sentence will be. I know a year sounds terrible to you, but I'm scared of a five-year sentence or worse, if we lose."

"Do you think we will lose?" she asked, panicked again. She didn't want to plead guilty if she wasn't, and have a criminal record for something she didn't do.

"Anything is possible," Steve told her again. "I can't guarantee anything once we go to trial. A jury is always a wild card. And the judge can be too, for sentencing."

"What would you do?" she asked him, searching his eyes for what he really thought.

"Honestly, I'm a gambler. I would turn down their deal for now, and see if they give us a better one closer to the trial. The deal they're offering isn't good enough yet. I think they want to show us how tough they are. I would wait a little longer. And let's get the detective on it again. If we get something on Zeller, it will be worth it, whatever it costs." She agreed with what he said, and he went to turn the plea bargain down and was back in five minutes. She had been sitting in the conference room, waiting for him, feeling extremely anxious. The prospect of going to prison for five years, or ten, or even one year, was devastating.

"Okay, we're done," he said, and gathered up his things. A few minutes later, they left the courthouse together. She had her heart in her shoes and she looked it.

She went home directly after court, hoping she had done the right thing turning down the plea bargain, and contemplating what her life would be like if she went to prison. It was still a nightmare, and she still had to face trial for a crime she didn't commit, and certainly not knowingly. She had imported the bags for Paul, precisely according to his orders, but had had no idea they were stolen and doctored with false linings and added shoulder straps. She realized now that the quality of the leather should have tipped her off, but it didn't. She had trusted Paul and his sources completely. She felt stupid now more than guilty, and above all terrified for the future and the results at a trial, but not enough to accept a bad plea bargain. And Steve seemed to agree with her, although he was worried.

They were going to try the detective again. It was their only hope of implicating Paul Zeller and getting her off the hook.

She was still depressed the next day when she went to the office and told Ed what had happened.

"I think you did the right thing about the plea bargain,"

he reassured her. "You don't want to go to jail for a crime you didn't commit."

"That's what I think." Her daughters agreed with her too. She had told them the night before when they called to check in. Sabrina had already heard about it from Steve. They had been seeing each other since Christmas. They were both busy, but managing to spend time together, and their relationship was flourishing.

Two days after the hearing and the plea offer she had turned down, Bob Townsend called her. He was in New York for a few days and invited her to lunch again. But this time, she turned him down without hesitating, and she told Ed Chin about it.

"I can't, Ed. I'm looking at going to prison if things go wrong. I can't do that to anyone. I don't want to get to know him or date anyone until I know what's going to happen, or till after I've been acquitted."

"So you're supposed to live in a vacuum until then? How does that seem fair to you?" The thought of it made him feel profoundly upset for her.

"It's fair to him. I don't have the right to inflict my problems on someone else."

"I'm in it with you," he said simply. "And I'm not complaining. Maybe you should tell him the truth, and let him decide if he wants to see you when he comes to town. My guess is he'll want to anyway. Don't carry this all alone,

Syd. That's not right for you." The trial was set for September, exactly during Fashion Week when they were doing their first fashion show, which was the final irony, but Steve didn't want to change the trial date. At least not yet. She had no idea how she was going to manage a trial and their first collection, but somehow she'd have to.

Bob called her again that afternoon and suggested dinner instead of lunch, if that worked better for her, and she said it did, which wasn't really true. She was free for both, but her refusal was about the sword hanging over her head that he knew nothing about. She was planning to tell him, as Ed had suggested, but she wasn't looking forward to it.

She invited him to her apartment for a drink, and they were going to a French restaurant in the neighborhood afterward. She wasn't sure if she should tell him at the beginning or the end of dinner. She was going to play it by ear once she saw him.

She could see that he was a little startled at the size of her apartment, while she made light of it and joked about living in a shoebox. From everything he'd seen of her so far, he could sense what her life had been like before, without her going into detail. The kind of clothes she wore, the occasional gold bracelet, the Hermès Kelly bag she'd worn when they had lunch, her whole demeanor, she had gone from the lap of luxury to a tiny apartment, with most of the possessions she had left piled up in boxes.

But even the picture frames she had scattered were beautiful. She had led a life of quality, and she had lost it due to her husband's negligence. It made him angry for her, even if she was gracious about it.

She poured him a scotch and soda, and they sat and talked for a while and he told her what he'd been doing since he'd last seen her. He'd been to Dubai and Saudi Arabia, Shanghai to see his daughter, and at home in Hong Kong, and she told him how establishing the business was going. When they had finished the exchange, he looked at her for a long moment. He had a sense of her that he couldn't explain, and she felt it too.

"Something's bothering you, Sydney. Do you want to tell me what it is? And why you keep balking about seeing me?" He was sure there was a reason, and she hesitated for a long moment before she answered.

"There's something I haven't told you, about everything that's happened since my husband died. I needed a job, so I took one at a company that my kids said was owned by a scumbag. It wasn't all bad, because I met Ed there and I wouldn't have met him otherwise. And the scumbag was extremely kind to me at first. He gave me a job even though I hadn't designed in nearly two decades. He said he wanted to give me my own signature line, which sounded fantastic and is a big deal in fashion. And Ed taught me a lot about the business as it is today, to bring me up to date. We went to China together. It seemed like a great opportunity. But it's essentially a knockoff house. The theories are good, the way the owner explains it. He says he wants to bring high fashion to the masses, and in many instances he does, and the stuff looks great. They copy other designers a lot, and he's careful about not going too far, and changing it just enough, but they have a bad reputation for copying anyway. It's not noble but they do meet a need in the market, and people eat up their stuff. But I discovered the hard way that their practices aren't always legal.

"He showed me some sample bags that looked terrific. They seemed like high-quality leather. There was something familiar about them, although not completely, and we were buying them so cheap we could sell them for next to nothing. He put me in charge of purchasing them, and told me he'd give me a signature line and a percentage of the profits, which was very appealing. He sent me to China to buy the bags. I signed all the requisition, import, and order forms, and he had me sign all the customs documents. I shipped them, and he had me pick them up at customs in New York, to clear them with the broker.

"I'll spare you the gory details, but all two hundred handbags were stolen. They were by a famous designer, and slightly modified to change them—not in production but after the fact. They had false linings to conceal their real brand. They were flat-out stolen. I had no idea. I went to clear them through customs, and got arrested as soon as I showed up. My name and signature is on everything, and I've been charged with trafficking stolen goods. My employer claims he had no idea they were stolen, and has even implied that I was on the take from the shipper and manufacturer to bring them in. I go to trial in September, and if I can't prove I'm innocent, I could go to prison. They offered me a deal two days ago, but it involves my pleading guilty to a felony, and agreeing to a year in prison for something I didn't do, and didn't know. I'm innocent, so I turned down the deal."

Tears burned her eyes as she said it, and she never took her eyes off his. "We've got detectives looking for evidence of my boss's guilt, but so far we've got nothing. So I may really go to prison, possibly for five to ten years if a jury finds me guilty. I don't want to pull you into it, make you feel sorry for me, or start something I can't finish until I'm sixty when I get out. Until this is over, I have no right to date anyone. I don't want to do that to you. This is why Ed quit where we were working when he saw what they did to me, and why we wound up starting our own business, thanks to the Chins. And Phillip Chin very kindly found my attorney.

"Now you know everything," she said simply. For a long time, he didn't speak, and just sat on the couch, looking at her and thinking about what she'd said. He didn't know how to even begin to tell her what he was feeling, as he took her hand in his and held it. Then she saw a slow, gentle smile spread across his face, and wasn't sure what that meant.

"I promise you, Sydney, if you go to prison, I will bring you oranges, and a cake with a file in it. That is the most horrific story I have ever heard, and the man you worked for should be hanged, or horsewhipped. I cannot believe that your innocence will not shine through, or that you won't find the evidence you need to implicate him. But I want you to know that whatever happens, I don't think less of you. I don't believe for a moment that you're guilty. And it makes me sick to think of you going through this, and the agony you've undoubtedly suffered because of it. But I am not for one moment going to wait ten years to see you and take you out to dinner. And whatever happens, happens. You can't stop living because of this, and you have to keep believing in some kind of justice."

She nodded as tears filled her eyes. "I'm trying to. It gets pretty scary sometimes. The four days I spent in jail were the most terrifying of my life. I can't even imagine what ten years would be like, let alone one." She choked on a sob as she said it.

"I don't think that will ever happen," he said quietly. "But you have to put it in perspective. Think of prisoners of war, and people in concentration camps. You can live through whatever you have to. You'll find the strength you need if it comes to that. But I don't think it ever will. I think good will prevail here. I firmly believe that." He couldn't imagine all that she'd been through in less than a year. As he thought about it, he leaned over and put an arm around her and pulled her close to him. "We're not going to worry about it now. Work on your business, keep busy, create your clothing line. Do what the lawyer says. And when you go to trial, we'll deal with it. You are surrounded by people who love you." Although they both knew that the treatment she had met at her stepdaughters' hands hadn't been just, or loving, or fair.

"I've let everyone down," she said, with her voice breaking. "It's already been in the fashion press and all over the Internet. They are making an example of me. Can you conceive how my children will feel if I go to prison?"

"They'll survive it, but I believe none of you will have to. You just have to take this one day at a time, until it's finally behind you. And, Sydney, I want you to know that I think you are a very brave woman. Thank you for telling me." It had taken courage too to tell him, and he admired her honesty.

"It didn't feel right not telling you, but I didn't want you to hate me for it either."

"I don't hate you, but your ex-boss is a different matter. What a sonofabitch this guy is to set you up, let you take the risks, and then take the fall for him. If there is justice in this world, he's going to be a very, very unhappy person after this. His whole world may come crumbling down." It was an appealing prospect but there was no sign of it so far. His world was intact, and she might be going to prison.

They walked to the nearby bistro then, and held hands as he commented on all that she had told him.

"Between your husband dying, your stepdaughters, and this monster you worked for, I can't imagine how you've gotten through this year and stayed sane."

"I don't know either. But good things happened too. Ed, the business. My kids, I have a good lawyer, meeting you." She smiled at him and he put an arm around her shoulders again.

"It's going to be all right, Sydney. I don't know how, but I just feel it."

"I hope you're right," she said in a sober voice, and he was quiet too. He was shuddering inwardly at what it would be like for her if she was convicted and sent to prison. It just couldn't happen. He wished it with his whole being. And then they went into the restaurant and sat down. Much to her surprise, in spite of her serious confessions to him, they had a lovely evening, laughing and talking, and didn't mention the trial again.

Chapter 12

It was the first really hot weekend of the summer, a broiling hot Sunday in June, and Sydney was catching up on her reading. She had a stack of *Women's Wear Dailys* to get through, the Sunday *Times,* a copy of *The Wall Street Journal,* and the *New York Post.* She knew she couldn't read all of them, but she had to keep up with *Women's Wear Daily* for work, and she picked up the *New York Post* just for fun, and first turned to the gossip column on Page Six. She scanned it for anyone familiar and stopped halfway down the page, riveted.

"Heiress Kellie Wells Madison, heir to the fortune of her father, Andrew Wells of the investment banking firm of the same name, is being divorced by her husband, Geoff Madison. The man-about-town recently seen with two well-known actresses and a brand-new divorcée left the family home six weeks ago, a source close to the couple assures us. He's allegedly suing her for a $100 million settlement and spousal support. House rich and cash poor (she and her twin sister, Kyra, now own the family estate), Kellie is selling the exceptional Connecticut home and extensive grounds for a mere $70 million, in order to give her twin her share and satisfy Geoff's demands in the divorce . . . and do we hear wedding bells in the distance for Geoff? We think so. Sorry, Kellie. Hope someone buys the house soon!"

Sydney read the piece three times to make sure she got it right, and felt her stomach turn over while she did. They were selling the house that she and Andrew had loved so much, and done so much to improve. First they threw her out, and now they were selling it a year after his death, to pay off Kellie's cheating greedy gigolo husband. She knew Andrew would have been sick about it too.

She called Sabrina immediately. She was in the Hamptons with Steve for the weekend, but she answered her cell when she saw her mother's name come up.

"I just read last Thursday's edition of the *Post,* Page Six," she said as soon as she heard Sabrina's voice. "See if you can Google it. Kellie is selling the house. Geoff is divorcing her, and she needs the money. He wants a hundred-million-dollar settlement and spousal support, and they're intimating that he's marrying someone else. The guy's a pro." Sabrina wasn't sure how to react to the news, except that in a way she felt that they didn't deserve to keep the house, but she knew that whatever happened, it would upset her mother. She had loved the house. But Sabrina also loved the idea that Geoff was dumping one of the twins.

"It serves her right," Sabrina gloated. "But I'm sorry about the house, Mom."

"So am I," she said sadly. "Andrew would be heart-broken." But Sabrina was more so that the girls had thrown her mother out, and she was still angry at Andrew for not protecting her mother from that and his rotten daughters. "I can't imagine they'll get that kind of money for it," Sydney continued.

"It depends on who buys it. They will if it's some Russian oligarch, or new Chinese money. Look at the bright side, even after they sell it, if they get their price, she'll still owe Geoff another sixty or seventy million dollars. Kellie must be mortified that he's leaving her for someone else." They both knew that Kyra wouldn't care about selling the house. She hated living in the country, and would probably rather have the money.

"I guess it's what Sophie said before. Karma," Sydney said, mourning the house again. "And Veronica said they poured a fortune into it in the remodel." Not that any part of it had needed to be redone. It had been in pristine shape when Sydney had turned it over to Kellie.

"Try not to think about it," Sabrina told her. "It won't change anything now." They talked for a few more minutes, and afterward, Sabrina called Sophie to tell her. She and Grayson were lying on the roof of her building in bathing suits, frying. He hated the beach and didn't like the country. He felt safer in the city. Sophie couldn't believe the story when Sabrina sent it to her from her iPhone.

"How's Mom taking it?" Sophie asked, worried.

"She sounds sad. It's such a waste. They throw her out, so they can move in supposedly, ruin her life, and sell it a year later. Geoff is such a greedy little bastard. But the whole thing serves Kellie right."

"She must be ready to kill him," Sophie said in amusement. "Where are you, by the way?"

"Sag Harbor, with Steve," she said happily.

"Say hi to him for me," Sophie said wistfully. She wished she could get Grayson to the Hamptons. They'd had dinner a few times with Steve and Sabrina, but with Grayson's social anxiety, he didn't like going out to dinner either. Sophie was trying to help him work through it. But it was hard sometimes being with someone so badly scarred by his childhood. She felt more like his therapist than his girlfriend at times. And they missed out on so many things that would have been fun. Sabrina had been telling her for months that she ought to break up with him, but Sophie felt sorry for him and didn't want to hurt him. But seeing her sister with Steve made her realize what she was missing.

Sydney put the *Post* aside to show it to her daughters, and worked through the stack of *WWD*s that she had neglected all week. And like clockwork, halfway through her reading, Veronica called.

"How *are* you?" Veronica said cheerfully. "I've been meaning to call you all week."

"I'll bet you have," Sydney said ironically. "Probably since Thursday," she said, glancing at the *New York Post* on the coffee table.

"Why? Did something happen on Thursday? Did you get that problem with the stolen bags worked out?" she asked innocently, hoping for a juicy tidbit.

"That's all taken care of," Sydney lied to her. She wasn't going to give her the satisfaction of telling her she was going to trial. Veronica was a gossipmonger. And Sydney had heard from none of her other friends in a year, and no longer cared. She had gotten over it. "I started a new clothing line with a friend six months ago."

"That's *so* exciting!" she said, pretending that she gave a damn, which Sydney knew she didn't. "That's so wonderful that you've gotten back into designing. Who's the friend?"

"No one you know. He's from Hong Kong." Veronica's ears picked up at that. She smelled money.

"I thought you'd want to know the house is on the market. For seventy million. I doubt they'll get it."

"I heard about it. They might get their price from the right buyer."

"They screwed it up with the remodel," Veronica said dismissively. "Geoff's divorcing her."

"I know that too. I read it in the *Post*. I guess you did

too. What would we do without Page Six to keep us informed?" Veronica liked showing that she was in the know.

"I just thought you'd want to hear. I know how you loved that house."

"Actually, I still do," Sydney said honestly. "And tell me something, were you hoping to make me feel better or worse telling me that they've put the house on the market?"

"I thought you should know, that's all." Veronica sounded instantly defensive.

"I tell you what, let's make a deal. When something really bad happens to me and I'm really down about it, I'll call you. That way you'll have the jump on everyone else and can tell them the gossip. You don't need to call me with bad news to make me feel bad, because I read it in the papers, just like you do. How does that sound to you? You don't have to call me anymore, Veronica. I don't think we have anything left to say to each other, do you?" She felt a weight lift off her heart as she said it.

"I don't know why you're being so nasty about it. I just thought you'd rather hear it from a friend first, instead of reading it in the papers."

"Theoretically, that's true. I would rather hear it from a friend. But I don't think you qualify these days, do you? When was the last time you called just to say hi, and see how I am? I can't remember the last time. I don't need a bad news bulletin, Veronica, so you can revel in my miseries and pretend to be sympathetic. To tell you the truth, that's gotten really old. And I'm more interested in good news these days. Maybe you should try calling Kellie. I'm sure she has a lot to say about Geoff and the divorce. My life is pretty boring now. No one has died. I'm not getting divorced. I think my new venture is going to do very well. We might even make some decent money. So you can stop the news bulletins now. I'm over it. Thanks for calling."

Without waiting to hear her answer, Sydney hung up and felt great when she did. She was just sorry she hadn't done it sooner. And at least if she went to prison in September, Veronica wouldn't be able to call her to find out how she was doing, and spread the gossip among the neighbors. Sydney sat on the couch, smiling to herself. She was back in fighting mode, and she wasn't going to let someone like Veronica pull her down. She didn't want people like that in her life anymore.

Sydney had recently turned fifty but had refused to celebrate it. She wasn't in the mood for celebrations these days either, with the trial looming closer, but she had allowed her daughters to take her to a quiet dinner. She was much happier with them than phony friends.

She went back to reading *Women's Wear* then, and had finished all of them by the end of the afternoon. The apartment was still stifling, and she lay on her bed, when the phone rang. It was Bob Townsend calling her from

Hong Kong. He called about once a week now, just to catch up on what they were both doing, and find out how she was. He said he was coming back to New York in a few weeks and he wanted to know if she would be there. She and Ed weren't going anywhere that summer. They had too much work to do before September.

He was going to visit friends in the south of France before that, and his daughter in England, and then he'd see her.

"Any news from Steve?" he asked.

"Nothing. I think Paul covered his tracks completely," Sydney said in a subdued tone.

"It's not over yet. Wait and see what happens." He still believed that evidence would turn up to exonerate her. She thought it was wishful thinking, but his unshakable faith encouraged her.

She told him about Kellie selling the house and her mega-million-dollar divorce. He could hear that she was sad about the house, and he didn't blame her. It had been her home, and with her exquisite taste he was sure it had been beautiful and a painful contrast with her uncomfortably small apartment.

"See you in a few weeks then," he said as he hung up, and she thought about him for a long time after he called. Starting a relationship with him didn't make a lot of sense. He lived in Hong Kong, and she lived in New York, but she was very tempted nonetheless. No man had appealed to her as much since Andrew. Bob was very kind to her. He had said several times that he wanted her to meet his children, which she wasn't enthused about. Kellie and Kyra had cured her forever from wanting to create a relationship with other people's children, whatever their age, even if Bob's would be infinitely better behaved and kinder people, if they were anything like their father.

She worked on some sketches that night, and was back at work in the morning. The arctic temperature they kept their air-conditioning on in the office was sheer heaven and kept her working day and night.

Chapter 13

As life had a way of doing sometimes, all the stars and planets converged on Sydney's life at the same time in September. The trial was set to start during Fashion Week, the day after their show. It was going to be utterly insane, showing their collection at a major venue. They had thirty-eight models lined up to wear the clothes. The day before, they were giving a party to launch their new line.

And the morning after the show, she was going to trial for trafficking and attempting to import stolen goods.

Bob had come to see her briefly in July and August, although the city had been blistering hot, and he planned to be at their show in September, as did Ed's parents. Bob had asked her if he could attend the trial, and she had reluctantly agreed. It was embarrassing, but she was grateful for the support. Her daughters would be there too. And to make life even more complicated, Ed had just gotten involved in a new romance with a senior at Parsons who had interned with them that summer, and was going to help them backstage with the show. Sydney felt as though her head was spinning with everything she had to do. She had hired an assistant, but much of it she had to do herself.

They were still putting the last touches on the collection. They had embroideries that hadn't arrived yet from Lesage in Paris, who did all the embroidery for haute couture. There was one fabric from Italy for their grand finale evening gown that was trapped in customs, while their seamstresses and patternmaker were chomping at the bit to make the dress in time.

Bob had arranged his schedule to fly in three days before the show. He was going to spend a week in town, depending on what happened at the trial. If she needed him to stay longer, he had said he would. They had grown extremely close since she met him in April at their first presentation, but she hadn't slept with him yet, and he hadn't pressed her. She needed time to get used to the idea, and she still felt wrong about it if she went to prison. She didn't expect him to remain loyal or faithful to her if she was incarcerated, which was a worst-case scenario but nonetheless possible, according to Steve, who didn't like fostering false illusions in his clients. He was busy preparing for the trial, and Sabrina was just as busy with her show.

Bob was going to be staying at a hotel in the mid-Sixties, and he and Sydney had dinner the night he arrived. They were just leaving the restaurant when she got a call from Steve.

"I need to see you in the morning," he said tersely. "How early can you get to my office?"

"You tell me when you want me. I'll be there," she said. "Is something wrong?"

"Not at all. Why don't you come in at eight?" He wanted to see her before a court appearance for another client. They had already gone over the material for the trial, and she was well prepared. She had needed to do it before Fashion Week started. After that, she wouldn't have a minute to herself. She told Bob about the call while he walked her home. The jet lag was starting to catch up with him. She was exhausted too, and living on adrenaline, but she was happy he was there. She had come to rely on him more than she wanted to, and was grateful to have him with her.

"Did he say why he wants to see you?" He made a point of sounding neutral about it and not concerned, so he didn't feed her worries.

"No, he didn't. More prep, I guess."

"Do you want me to come with you?" he offered. "I'll be up at dawn with jet lag anyway."

"I hate to drag you out at that hour." But she liked the idea.

"I'll pick you up at seven-thirty." He had hired a car and driver for the week, which he thought might help her too, and encouraged her to use them when she needed to. He was always trying to make things easier for her.

When they got to her building, he kissed her good night, and looked half asleep. He watched her walk in, and then got in his car and rode back to the hotel. He was practically asleep on his feet.

She was trying to keep her mind on the collection and the show, so she didn't think about the trial that would start the day after. They had done everything they could, and no further evidence had turned up. She had spent a fortune on detectives for nothing. Bob kept reminding her that truth was the best defense, and she had honesty and innocence on her side. She hoped he was right.

Bob picked her up promptly at seven-thirty the next morning, impeccably groomed as always, freshly shaven, and in one of his immaculately tailored custom-made suits. She was wearing a black linen dress in the Indian summer heat. They talked quietly in the car on the way downtown, and reached Steve's office at precisely eight o'clock. She tried to read his expression when they walked into his office, but he didn't give them any clues or information until they sat down. He cut to the chase and ended their suspense as to why he had wanted them to come in.

"We have a statement from the manufacturer. And copies of several emails from Zeller that prove that he knew they were stolen goods. He knew they were from Prada, and they discussed how to disguise the markings on the inside and alter the shoulder straps. He needed someone to be responsible so he wouldn't be on the front line, and you were the right person at the right time for him, available to go, so he sent you. We can prove it now." He was smiling from ear to ear as Bob also broke into a smile and Sydney stared at Steve in disbelief. Their big break had come at the eleventh hour, days before the trial. Bob was right.

"Why did the supplier decide to come forward now?"

"Zeller burned him on a deal a few weeks ago, and had already refused to pay for the shipment they confiscated. The guy is pissed. He lost a lot of money on the first deal, and even more on the second one. Zeller is still bringing in stolen goods. He's sending them to a middleman now. We can prove that too. The guy in the middle probably doesn't even know he's receiving stolen goods."

"So am I off the hook? That's it? It's over?" She was elated, and Steve got serious again.

"The judge has to accept the evidence. I've got a meeting with the assistant U.S. attorney on the case this afternoon, to show him what we've got. Their case against you should collapse like a soufflé after this." Steve looked confident, but he didn't want to promise her anything yet. Judges could be unpredictable, and the U.S. attorney wouldn't be happy to give up the case after all the work they'd put into it. But they could prosecute Zeller now. He was the real criminal in the story, not Sydney. "I'll call you after the meeting. Where will you be?"

"At my office, running around like a lunatic." She had

gotten a text late the night before. The Italian fabric they were waiting for had been released from customs, and their sewers were desperate to start on it. The embroideries from Paris were due at noon.

"Well, this is certainly good news," Bob added to the conversation.

"I'll call you later," Steve said after they had read the statement and the emails. There was no question. Zeller had known, and the statement was very damning, as were the emails. Steve was sure Zeller had deleted them off his computer, but government techies could retrieve them, no matter how well buried they were.

The atmosphere in the car on the way uptown was considerably lighter and more cheerful than on the way down.

"You should be out of it by tonight," Bob said optimistically. And she was sure he was right. Now she could think about the show without being distracted and worried about the trial.

But when Steve called Sydney that afternoon, he didn't have good news. "The U.S. attorney accepts that the statement and emails prove that Zeller knew the bags were stolen, but there's nothing to prove that you didn't, except your word for it. And Zeller already gave them a statement trying to absolve himself, saying that you knew. It's your word against his."

"Shit. Now what?"

"They're going to give it to the judge and get back to us. I'll call you when I hear something." But there was no further word from him that night. Bob was upset for her when she told him what Steve had said. They were pushing their case against her right to the very end. The trial was three days away.

She and Ed worked until two in the morning. She didn't have time to stop for dinner or to see Bob. They were still fitting garments on the models, while the sewers made minute corrections for each girl. Bob told her not to worry about him, and do what she had to do.

The next day was even more frantic, and they had the party that night. They had taken over a private room in a posh new restaurant, and were expecting a hundred guests, the cream of the fashion world. Everyone was scrambling for an invitation to their party, and Sydney was at the venue until the last minute, making sure that everything was perfect. She rushed home to change, and Steve called her just as she was flying out the door.

"They're holding us to trial," he said, sounding discouraged. "And they're taking the evidence against Zeller to the grand jury. The judge won't issue a warrant for him until they approve it." The wheels of justice were hard and slow. And the trial was thirty-six hours away. "There's no firm evidence you didn't know," he reminded her again, "and your signature is on the import documents. Zeller is on the hook now, with the new evidence we have. But you still are too. A jury will have to decide if you knew or not." Tears filled her eyes as he said it, and she hung up a moment later.

Sydney got to the party just as the first guests were arriving, and she saw Ed's parents there. He arrived shortly after, wearing an impeccably tailored black suit with a black T-shirt and alligator sneakers, with his long black hair in a knot at the nape of his neck. He looked beautiful, and so did Bob when he walked in, in a dark blue pinstriped suit with a white handkerchief in his pocket, a crisp white shirt, and a navy Hermès tie. Sydney was wearing a black cocktail dress she had designed herself. The party was an instant success as the champagne flowed and everyone wished them luck. The editor of *Vogue* had sent them an enormous orchid that afternoon.

It was halfway through the party before she got a minute to talk to Bob, and told him what Steve had said. He looked unhappy about it, but there was nothing they could do now. He felt certain the judge would dismiss the case against her when they got to court. He was probably just a stickler for form. And at least Paul Zeller would be arrested now, after the grand jury had heard the evidence.

The party went on till midnight, although it was only supposed to be for cocktails. And Ed, Bob, and Sydney finally left before the last guests. Ed and Sydney returned to the office to work through the night on the last details, and Bob went back to the hotel to sleep.

"Will you be all right? You must be exhausted," he said, and she was touched by his concern, but laughed.

"This is what Fashion Week is like," she reassured him, and she knew that her daughters were doing the same thing where they worked. They didn't even have time to call each other all week, but sent a few texts between fittings and meetings.

Sydney went back to her apartment at four A.M., and Ed left the office an hour later. They were both back at work, looking ragged but determined, at eight. Sydney had never known a designer to work as hard as he did. But their dream was being born. It had been ten months in the making, longer than a baby, and a lot more stressful, but Sydney felt as though everything was aligning just as they hoped. The models looked beautiful when they finally got them dressed at six o'clock. The show was due to start at seven, and Ed wanted it to be on time, which rarely happened. But at seven-fifteen precisely, the first model pounded down the runway in the highest heels Bob had ever seen. He had a seat in the front row, next to Ed's parents. Sabrina and Sophie had seats two rows back, watching proudly.

There was applause for almost every model, and a cheer when the most famous supermodel in the business came out on the runway as a surprise wearing the last dress, and she flirted and frolicked down the runway, and pouted at the press in the fabulous emerald green satin gown they had made from the fabric that came in so late. The entire collection was perfection, and forty minutes after it started, the last model was out, the whole group took a final tour down the runway, and Ed and Sydney came out from backstage and took a quick bow. They both looked exhausted and disheveled, but victory was theirs. Sydney Chin had been launched, and in grand style.

Ed and Sydney were nearly mobbed backstage. Bob eventually found them, and Sabrina and Sophie were right behind him. He had already met her girls, and they liked him, but their mother insisted they weren't dating, they were just friends, despite the fact that they either talked or texted night and day, and he was with her whenever possible.

Sydney stayed backstage for hours to see everything packed up. She wanted to make sure that nothing was left behind. It was all being taken back to their offices that night and set up on racks. A dozen models would be in attendance the next day when the buyers came to place their orders. The collection would be on display for them for the following week. But Sydney wouldn't be there. She would be at the federal courthouse for the trial that hadn't been canceled. Her daughters were going to be with her, and Bob and Ed had promised to come too. It seemed less ominous to Sydney now with the evidence against Paul Zeller that had surfaced, which he knew nothing about yet. He would have no idea that he was on the hot seat until the grand jury issued the indictment and the judge signed the warrant, and officers showed up at his home or office to arrest him. For the moment, he still thought he was safe.

When Bob and Sydney arrived at the courthouse the next morning, Steve was waiting for them with a grim expression.

"They're not giving an inch," he said. "They still want more information from you about Zeller." Sydney looked devastated. "They say there's no evidence that you weren't in cahoots with Zeller on this, or making a deal of your own, and your signing the documents is sufficient evidence to warrant a trial and probably convict you." She looked ready to cry, as Steve led her into the courtroom and she took the defendant's chair at a long table next to Steve. The courtroom looked like a movie set, and when the judge walked in, in his robes, he was a sour old man. The bailiff shouted "All rise," and everyone in the entire room stood up.

There had been no time to savor their victory of the night before. She was on trial, and still at risk of going to prison, because the U.S. attorney wouldn't let go of the case.

She tried to glance over her shoulder to see Bob, for reassurance, and Steve whispered to her not to, as the judge announced they would be selecting the jury. Forty jurors were led into the room by a deputy sheriff and told to sit down. The twelve final jurors would be chosen from the larger pool, with one or more alternates in case one got sick. Both attorneys had peremptory challenges, and the judge addressed the jurors and explained what the case was about. She still couldn't believe the trial was going forward, as she sat watching the proceedings. They had an unreal quality to them, and she had that under-water feeling she'd had for weeks after Andrew died.

They sat there for three hours while potential jurors were led on and off the stand, questioned, and some of them released. And then the judge called for a two-hour recess so everyone could eat lunch, and Sydney was about to leave the courtroom with Steve when the federal prosecutor asked to speak to him. Steve told Sydney to wait in her seat, and he'd be back. He suspected what was coming but didn't want to raise her hopes. They had taken this right to the end.

Sabrina and Sophie approached her after everyone left the courtroom, and so did Bob and Ed. The four of them had been sitting together in the front row.

"What's happening?" Sophie whispered.

"I have no idea," Sydney whispered back. Steve was gone for almost an hour and none of them moved, waiting for him. He looked serious when he finally returned and suggested they go outside to talk.

They stood in a huddle in a corner of the hallway while he explained.

"Okay, we're getting there. They want to make a deal. They won't dismiss the case. Their point is that you could have been in on it, and we can't prove you weren't. Zeller threw you under the bus right in the beginning, by accusing you of that. According to the prosecutor, you were at customs picking up stolen bags, and every single form had your name and signature on it, which is bad evidence they have against you, so they're not going to dismiss. They want to offer you a deal for a plea bargain."

"And go to prison?" Sydney looked terrified all over again and Bob squeezed her hand.

"They want you to plead to a misdemeanor, possibly a lesser charge of perjury on customs documents since the bags weren't listed as stolen, obviously. They'll figure out some bogus misdemeanor for you to plead to, and a misdemeanor isn't going to look very serious on your records," he tried to reassure her. "They want to keep the pressure on you to tell them more about Zeller's illegal operations, if you know anything. No prison time. They wanted to keep it as a felony, but I refused. They want six months' house arrest with an electronic bracelet, and two years' probation. That's the deal. What you'd essentially be pleading guilty to is lying on customs documents, not importing stolen goods. They'll only agree to dismiss if you tell them more about Zeller's illegal activities. Failing that, they're making an example of you to a moderate degree." Their offer was the best they could hope for.

"Six months' house arrest? And how can I tell them something I don't know! I never knew anything about his illegal activities and still don't." Sydney looked distressed, but Bob looked relieved. She hadn't thought it through yet. Six months' house arrest and a misdemeanor was a gift. "How can I do my job locked in my apartment if I can't go to work?" she said frantically, stressed and shaken by all of it.

"We'll set up a monitor, you can Skype. Your assistant can run designs back and forth. We can bring you fabrics and fit models," Ed said reasonably. "It's not a big deal. We can make that work. It's only for six months. That's a hell of a lot better than five years in prison," he reminded her, and Steve nodded agreement.

"It's a good deal, Sydney. Pleading to a misdemeanor won't hurt you. There won't be ramifications later. You can even get it expunged a few years down the road. I'd much rather see you stuck in your apartment with an anklet than in federal prison. If we go to trial, we have that risk. You don't know what kind of jury you're going to get, or if they'll be sympathetic. Zeller is going to take the fall for this now. He'll get prison time for sure. I don't want you to, and he'll try to take you down with him if you go to trial," Steve said firmly. "I can't force you to take the deal, but I strongly recommend it to you, as your attorney. It's a slap on the wrist. In some instances, they let people go to work, even while under house arrest, but this judge is a stickler, and very old-school, and I couldn't get him to agree to it. But even stuck at home for six months, I think it's a good deal and you should do it." But she had been hoping for no slap at all, especially once they found the evidence against Zeller. She stood quietly for a moment, thinking about it, and looked from her daughters to Ed, to Bob.

"Take it, Mom," Sabrina pleaded with her. "Nothing bad will happen to you at home. You could get killed in prison. And we can see you any time at home."

"Do I get to leave the apartment at all?" she asked Steve.

"Only for medical reasons, to go to a doctor or a hospital, or for a death in the family." It was a tiny apartment to spend six months in, but it was better than a cell, and she knew it too. She looked at Steve and nodded. It was going to be uncomfortable, but not frightening or dangerous. If she had to receive a sentence, it was the best she could do, although it still didn't seem fair that they were charging her and punishing her when she was innocent.

"Okay, I'll do it," she said seriously, and they all patted her shoulder and her arm, and Sophie had tears running down her cheeks.

"I love you, Mom," Sophie said between sobs of relief, hugging her.

"Thank God you don't have to go to prison," Sabrina said quietly. They all looked relieved.

"We'll get state-of-the-art computers set up in your apartment, and a giant screen with two-way video. You'll love it!" Ed said, and they all laughed. "You can watch movies on it at night." And she smiled too.

"Thank you, Steve," she said somberly, realizing the fate she had escaped. It had come very, very close, and his insisting on their reducing it to a misdemeanor had been a major legal victory for her. He had fought hard for it, and he had sensed that they didn't want the time and expense of a trial. It was a bogus case, but they could have made it stick if they chose to. He was just glad they didn't.

"I'll go tell them now. You can't leave yet."

"When would it start?" Sydney asked him.

"Probably right away. I may be able to get you a few days' grace, if there are things you need to do for work. But you won't be able to leave your apartment after this." She nodded that she understood.

"You'd better all come and see me," she said to the group after Steve went to tell the prosecutor that she was willing to plead. They all promised that they would. He was back much faster this time, and he was smiling.

"We have a deal," he said to her. "I'll need you to come with me to sign some papers. They agreed to let you start on Monday, after you fill out the rest of the paperwork. You don't have to wait," he said to the others. "Sometimes this can be slow." Ed decided to leave with Sabrina and Sophie, and Bob said he'd stay with her. Sydney promised Ed she'd be back at the office as soon as she was finished. Suddenly she wanted to get out and walk while she still could. It was hard to imagine being confined to a tiny apartment for six months, unable to go anywhere or get fresh air. But she realized how lucky she had been. It could have been so much worse, and almost was.

She followed Steve through a doorway, with Bob right behind her. The federal prosecutor was waiting for them, and told her she had made a wise decision.

It took her half an hour to sign the papers, she thanked Steve again, and she and Bob walked down the courthouse steps. He put an arm around her, then pulled her into his arms and kissed her hard on the mouth, and when he stopped, she saw that there were tears in his eyes.

"Thank God you didn't go to prison," was all he could say, and, hand in hand, they got into his rented town car. "At least I'll know where you are all the time," he teased her. "And I'll come to visit as often as I can." It was a long way from Hong Kong, but she was sure he would. And as they drove uptown, she thought about it, and knew her lucky stars had been in perfect alignment and fully operative that day.

Chapter 14

Bob and Sydney stopped for lunch on the way uptown, and he could see the tension slowly easing from her face. The nightmare had taken ten months to resolve, almost a year. She had carried with her the fear of going to prison for all that time.

"I never thought something like that could happen to me," she said to him over lunch. That and Andrew's death had taught her irreversibly how life could change in the blink of an eye, without warning. Suddenly everything you knew and counted on could be taken away, and was gone. Your freedom, your health, the people you loved, your money, your peace of mind. It was a frightening thought.

"It's over now," he said calmly, "or it will be soon. We'll figure out things to do when we're in the apartment," he teased her, and she laughed.

"It's going to be strange being trapped like that." But not as strange as prison, she knew.

They went back to her office after lunch, and she was stunned by the number of buyers there, filling out orders for what they wanted from the collection they'd shown the night before. Ed was beaming as he circulated in the crowd, and Sydney joined him for a while. Bob left to make some calls from his hotel. And she packed up her office, and took all the drawing equipment she'd need at home. Ed promised to have their IT people there on Monday to set up a computer system with a large monitor that would function as a two-way video screen. She needed more than just her iPad and laptop at home now. She was trying to think of everything, and Ed gave her a big hug. He was as relieved as she was that they weren't sending her away, and she hadn't had to go through a trial.

"You had me scared for a while," he admitted. They both remembered the night she had almost committed suicide, although they never talked about it. But it was a memory that still made him shudder. He hoped the bad times were behind her now.

"I'm going to miss seeing you here every day," he said wistfully, "but I'll see you on the monitor," and then he laughed.

"Come and visit me. It's going to be weird not being able to go out. I'll get a lot done, stuck at home," she promised. They had to start working on the next collection soon, and she already had some ideas she wanted to discuss with him.

Bob came back for her at six o'clock, and Sydney left

the office regretfully. They stopped at a drugstore on the way home. There were things she wanted to buy before her incarceration, and she wanted to go shopping on Saturday, and take a walk in Central Park. She wanted to drink it all in before she had to be sequestered from the world to pay for a sin she hadn't been aware of committing. She had acted in good faith and innocence, and had been duped.

"I hope they throw the book at Zeller," Bob said, as they got back to her apartment. They had picked up some food at the nearby deli. She was too tired to go out. When they walked into the apartment, she let herself collapse on the couch next to him and leaned her head on his shoulder.

"Thank you for being there with me," she said in a soft voice as he leaned over and kissed her more fervently than he had dared to till then, and she responded just as passionately. They had waited a long time for this, and now she wasn't worried about leaving him to go to prison. She felt free to follow her heart.

Without saying anything or asking permission, he began to undress her, and a few minutes later they rushed to her bedroom, as they laughed and she pulled him into her bed beside her. They were both naked by then, and the tides could no longer be stopped. Their desire for each other was overwhelming and insatiable, until they finally lay spent in each other's arms, barely able to catch their breath.

"That was worth waiting for," he said, stunned by the power of their lovemaking, and she smiled and looked up at him.

"I wanted you so much, but I didn't think it was fair till we knew what would happen."

"I love you, Sydney. I'm glad we went through this together. I would have hated your facing it alone."

"So would I." It had all been so much more tolerable since he'd been in her life. And this seemed a respectful amount of time since Andrew had died. It had been fourteen months. Her life with him seemed so far away now, and all their familiar landmarks were gone, their home, the apartment in Paris, the art they had bought together, the things they had loved that belonged to his daughters now. She wondered what would happen to all of it when they sold the house. But it didn't matter now. She didn't need the material objects of their marriage. She had their memories. And now she had Bob, and she belonged to him.

They lay in bed quietly together for a long time, and they made love again, and then they dozed in each other's arms for a while. It was nearly midnight when they got up and went to get something to eat in the kitchen.

"I can't imagine a life without you," he said with deep feeling in his voice.

"Me either," she said gently, but the idea frightened her. What if he died, like Andrew? She couldn't bear losing him too, or anyone again. But if they stayed together and lived to be very old, one of them would go first and leave the other lost and heartbroken. It was inevitable, and more than she could stand to think about.

"I wish I could stay in New York," he said longingly. But his business was in Hong Kong. She had been thinking of going back with Ed to see Bob. But she'd have to wait. She was going to be a prisoner in her apartment for six long months. "It'll go quickly," he reassured her, and she hoped he was right. "I want you to meet my children," he said, and she looked cautious at that.

"I'm not very popular with other people's children, judging by my stepdaughters," she said hesitantly, and he laughed.

"They sound crazy to me. You'd be everybody's dream stepmother."

"Apparently not." She smiled ruefully at the memory of Kellie and Kyra and how hateful they had been. There had been very few good times with them.

"My children didn't like my second wife," he admitted, "but they were younger then, and she was a child herself. She wanted all my attention, and was jealous of them. I knew it wouldn't last, but I was besotted with her. The marriage only lasted for six months. She ended up marrying a Chinese movie star. I have no idea what happened to her. It was a long time ago. The kids have been very good about the ladies in my life ever since. And they're going to love you." He seemed sure of it, but she wasn't. She loved him, of that she was certain, but the twins had scared her off other people's children.

"It must have been hard when you had to bring four of them up yourself," she said sympathetically.

"We had a lot of fun," he said, smiling at her. "And now you and I are going to have a lot of fun. There are so many things I want to do with you," he said dreamily, as they sat at the kitchen counter and ate what they'd bought at the deli. She looked thoughtful then.

"I hope I don't get fat sitting around the apartment." She was worried and he laughed.

"Hardly. You could do with a little weight." She was almost too thin, as was Sabrina. It was their body type, but neither of them ate much. And Sydney had been stressed for months, more than a year now.

They sat and talked in the living room, and then went back to bed at two o'clock. They drifted off to sleep talking, and when they woke up the next morning, the sun was streaming into the room. It was a beautiful day, and Sydney wanted to get out and walk while she could. She was frowning when she made them both coffee, and looked around the room.

"Do you suppose I have room for a treadmill?" He laughed at the thought.

"If you hang it off the ceiling." There wasn't an inch of spare floor space in the living room or bedroom.

"I'll need to get exercise."

"You'll have to run in place," he said practically. But these were small problems to have now, compared to what she would have encountered in prison.

They shared a bath, and left the apartment an hour later, casually dressed for the warm fall weather, and headed for the park. Everything looked beautiful to her now. The world had become a gentler place overnight. It was the culmination of a terrible year, but now it was spring in her heart, and he was as much in love as she was. They wandered over to Madison Avenue afterward and looked in all the shops, and he had an idea when they strolled past a jeweler and insisted they go inside. She didn't want him to buy her anything, or something foolish and expensive, but he knew exactly what he wanted. He chose a wide band of white gold with pavé diamonds on the front. He could easily afford it, and he asked for it in her size. He slipped it on her finger and it was beautiful.

"Now don't get nervous," he teased her. "It's not an engagement ring, it's an 'I love you band.' If you're going to wear an ugly anklet for six months, you might as well have something pretty on your finger. And this one won't confine you. I just want you to remember when I'm not around that I love you." He had correctly sensed that she was uneasy about getting tied down again. It had proven disastrous after Andrew was gone. She didn't want to be disappointed later, but Bob had a very nonthreatening way of dealing with her and loving her and said all the right things. She was admiring her new ring as they left the store.

"I love it." She smiled excitedly at him. They walked a long way, and wandered into Barneys for a few things she needed, and then they walked back to her apartment. They were going to Sabrina's for dinner that night.

She ordered in sushi, and Steve made pasta and salad for those who wanted it. Sophie came too, but Grayson stayed home. She said he was working on a big assignment, and they all knew that he rarely went out. But the others more than made up for it. Bob had fun with them. He and Steve hit it off, and he loved Sydney's girls, who were warm and welcoming to him. They were grateful for his being there for their mother, and both girls noticed her new ring as soon as she walked in.

"What's that?" Sophie whispered when they were in the kitchen. "Is it an engagement ring?" Sydney shook her head, and she realized that she would always remember that he gave it to her after the first time they made love. It really was an "I love you" ring, which made it even more special to her. There had been no luxuries in her life for a while now. She kept looking at it all through the evening and then smiled at him.

They spent Sunday together and went to church. She had a lot to be thankful for. And they went to a movie and ate popcorn and kissed like teenagers, and then they raced home and made love again.

"I think I'm addicted to you," he said afterward.

"Good. I want you to miss me," she said, and traced her tongue along his neck until he shuddered with delight, and they made love again. He was leaving for Hong Kong in the morning, and she wanted him to remember their last night since they didn't know when he'd be back again. He had moved his things from the hotel to her apartment that morning, so he could go directly to the airport the next day.

She got up with him at six o'clock and made him breakfast while he showered, and before he left the apartment, he held her naked in his arms and looked into her eyes and told her he loved her.

"I'll be back soon," he promised, and she knew he would.

She was waving from the window when he got in the car and drove away. She looked at her ring after that, and he called her five minutes later.

"I already miss you."

"So do I," she said, feeling tender toward him.

He called her again before the plane took off, and after that she went downtown to meet Steve at the courthouse again to get her anklet and have them put it on. She was relieved when he told her that Sabrina's apartment was no longer in jeopardy, since the case was resolved. Sydney still owed her $5,000 for bail and $25,000 for what she had paid Steve in the beginning. She also owed him the cost of the detectives he'd paid for, which he hadn't billed Sydney for yet. And she owed him another $25,000 for his time and accomplishing the plea bargain. In all, she owed him about $35,000, including the detective fees, and she owed Sabrina $30,000, and she was anxious to pay it back, but she couldn't yet. She still needed to sell the apartment in Paris. No one had bought it so far, but the rent she was getting for it was helpful every month. And she was getting a generous salary from Ed to pay her day-to-day expenses. Her finances were less dire than they had been, although she still had to pay for the court case, which had cost her a lot.

They put the electronic bracelet around her ankle and locked it into place in court. It was a waterproof band with a small box attached, which worked on the same principle as a GPS, and would track her whereabouts at all times. She was to call the monitoring service when she got home and they would activate it. And from then on, they would know exactly where she was, and an alarm would go off if she left the apartment. She would be monitored twenty-four hours a day. It was ugly and cumbersome, but they told her she'd get used to it. And since it was her Don't Go to Jail card, she didn't complain.

The IT people Ed sent over arrived as soon as she got home, and they had her fully set up by five o'clock, and she laughed when she saw Ed on the giant screen, and he said he could see her perfectly.

She reorganized everything in the living room that night, and turned it into a workspace and design studio. Ed had sent over a big tabletop for her to work on, and she turned her dining table into a desk. It would take some rearranging if she had people in for dinner, but she had everything she needed now to work, and she could eat at the counter, or even on the coffee table when she was alone. She was lonely without Bob in the apartment. It had been wonderful having him there with her for a week.

And that night, Sophie told her about a ballet teacher she could work with by Skype. Sydney called her and set that up too. She was going to take class three times a week, right from her apartment. She had decided to turn the next six months into work and health time. She was going to eat healthy meals since she couldn't get out and walk, do ballet on Skype, and use the months ahead as a positive project, not incarceration. And she'd have more time to work since she wasn't going out.

The most exciting news was that Ed told her the orders from their collection were fantastic, and they had many more appointments with buyers set up for the next two weeks. Their new business was very much up and running, and his family was pleased too. He said he missed her in the office, and he teased her about being a virtual partner now since he could only see her on the screen. But he was planning to come over in a day or two and start working on new designs with her.

She had missed Sabrina's and Sophie's shows, but she saw them on Vogue.com. There was almost nothing she couldn't do from the apartment except go out and get fresh air. She even had a list of grocery services that would deliver food, and restaurants that sent meals.

Steve called her after a few days to see how it was going, and she said she was busy working, which didn't surprise him. She had a good attitude about life. It was only late at night, after she'd been cooped up all day, that she would look out the window at times and wish she could go out. She knew that if she broke the rules, she'd spend the remaining time in jail.

Steve told her that a federal agent would be coming to see her, to take her statement about Paul Zeller. He brought a court stenographer with him when he showed up, and Sydney dictated the facts as it had all happened and told him all she knew, and she heard nothing after that. A week later, Steve said he didn't think Paul had been arrested yet, which seemed odd to her, with the evidence they had gathered. But Steve explained to her that the findings of the grand jury were kept secret, and they wouldn't know anything about the process until an arrest was made. Sydney hoped it would be soon. He deserved it, and whatever they did to him, he had coming. Of that she was sure.

Chapter 15

Paul was sitting at his desk going over buying reports and manufacturing bills, with spreadsheets all over his desk to refer to, when his assistant told him on the intercom that there was someone there to see him. She didn't say who, and didn't dare, since the four FBI agents who had shown up had told her not to. She was silent as they walked into his office and told him he was under arrest for money laundering and the importation of stolen items. They read him his rights and snapped handcuffs on him before he could object, and he stared at them in disbelief.

"This is ridiculous!" he said in an angry tone. "That little witch put you up to this, didn't she? She's the guilty one, I'm not. This is a grave mistake." He was shouting at them, and they weren't impressed, as they told him to walk out of his office. He tried to take a swing at the agent closest to him, using the handcuffs as a weapon, and with a single blow they dropped him to the ground, and he lay there, winded.

"Come on, get up," the senior agent said to him. "Let's

get going." Paul struggled to his feet, his dignity badly ruffled.

"I want to call my lawyer," he said, sounding frightened.

"You can do that from downtown."

"Where am I going?" He wasn't moving till they told him, and the four agents eyed each other, wondering if they'd have to carry him out. They would prefer not to, and had assumed he'd be polite and subdued.

"You're going to federal jail for now, until your arraignment." The grand jury had already indicted him and approved the warrant for his arrest, which had been signed by a federal judge that morning. It was two weeks after Sydney had begun her house arrest.

"I have nothing to do with this, nothing, do you hear me?" he shouted at them. "This is all that woman's doing. She's the smuggler here. I had no idea what she was buying."

"That's not up to us, sir. You'll have to discuss that with the judge."

"Call my lawyer," he shouted to his assistant, who could see him through the open doorway. "Tell him they're arresting me, and taking me to federal jail."

"Are we going to take you out of here in shackles and leg irons, or are you going to walk?" the second officer asked him. "It's up to you. I don't care either way. It might look a little more dignified to your employees if you walk out under your own steam." They were giving him one last chance before they trussed him up like a turkey and carried him out, and Paul was beginning to get that message. Reluctantly, he followed the lead man out of the room, with an agent on either side of him, and one behind him. Several people had heard the ruckus by then, and two of them picked up their iPhones and took videos of him. Others took stills and posted them on Instagram and Twitter.

"Stop that!" he shouted at them. "Take their cellphones away," he told the agents, who ignored him and kept walking alongside him. They escorted him out of the building and pushed him into a waiting FBI car, and by then Paul was shouting at them again, screaming obscenities and calling them names. The employees continued watching him, and a few minutes later the two FBI cars drove away. It was all dispersed over the Internet within seconds. By the next day it was on the front page of the *Post* and *The New York Times,* and the article had been reprinted in *WWD.* Sydney saw the coverage on the news that day, and watched him on YouTube, and she called the girls. She felt vindicated now that he was in jail. And she was comfortably at home in her apartment, however small, drinking coffee and working as usual. She had settled into a routine.

The newspaper articles about Paul explained the charges against him and mentioned her too. But the item about her was simple and clean. It said only that she had been charged with a misdemeanor and was under short-term house arrest, and that was it. She realized again then that Steve had gotten her a great deal with the plea bargain. It sounded like she'd been given a ticket for jay-walking and had gotten a small slap on the wrist. But the stories about Paul were more shocking. More evidence had surfaced that he'd been importing and selling stolen goods for years, the charges were more severe, and the penalties were liable to be too. They said that he could get from ten to twenty years in prison. It was serious business.

Steve called her about it that day. "He's in jail now," he reported to her. "And the bail is going to be pretty high." They had the goods on Paul and were prosecuting him to the limit, and rightfully so. It was karma again, as Sydney said to Ed.

A follow-up article a week later said that his business was up for sale, and his wife was filing for divorce. It was a clean sweep. Sydney knew it wouldn't go to trial for quite a while, but sooner or later Paul would have to pay for what he did. And Bob was pleased about it too. The good guys were winning.

Sydney was reading the papers more closely now than she used to. She wanted to stay abreast of what was happening in the world. And occasional gossip was a good distraction too. She loved reading Page Six in the *Post* and saw a week later that Kellie's husband, Geoff Madison, had upped the ante and wanted the whole house, not just her half of it. Apparently he intended to sell it. Three days later, she saw a sad little item that Kyra had been drunk and disorderly at a nightclub, and subsequently charged with possession of a controlled substance with intent to sell, which meant she had a lot of it. So she was in trouble too. With their newly enlarged fortunes, they were being exploited and indulging themselves, not living well.

Kellie's and Kyra's lives were falling apart, perhaps because of what they'd done to her, and in spite of all that they'd inherited. She said as much to Bob, who didn't disagree.

Almost three weeks to the day from when he'd last been there, Bob Townsend flew back to New York to see her. He said he'd been in Switzerland on business, and it wasn't a long flight to New York. He had rung her doorbell and there he was. He swept her into his arms the moment he saw her, and spun her around, almost knocking something over. The place was crammed to the rafters with furniture and equipment now. But she had everything she needed, and she loved the two-way screen to the office. She felt like she was right there with them and could talk to Ed face-to-face anytime, or show him a new design.

"You know," Bob said as Sydney fixed him lunch after he arrived. He put his feet on the coffee table, and relaxed after the flight. "You're the only jailbird I visit," he teased her. "In fact, you're the only jailbird I've ever been in love with."

"Very funny," she said as she handed him a sandwich and some potato chips. He was happy to see that she was in good spirits.

They wound up in bed as soon as he finished his sandwich, and he reminded her to turn the video screen off so no one would hear them. Sydney could hardly wait, and he was as anxious as she was. He told her he had missed her desperately while he was away.

They lay in bed, relaxing, in the afterglow of lovemaking. He told her all about what he'd been doing. Although they talked every day, they always had more to say. It was October by then, and cold outside, and she was cozy in her apartment, which had become the haven where he rested from the rigors of the world when he was with her.

A week after Bob left New York, Sydney read that Paul Zeller was out on five hundred thousand dollars' bail, his trial still months away. His business had been bought by Chinese investors. It had happened very quickly. He had apparently wanted to sell before he went to prison, possibly to pay for his divorce and criminal defense. She had lost her freedom as a result of what he'd done. And so would he, but he had lost his wife and his business too. Ed's not trusting Paul entirely and warnings about him had proven to be well founded. It still terrified her to think about what might have happened to her without the attorney Ed had found her, the evidence their detective had been able to unearth about Paul, and if Steve hadn't been able to make the deal he did. Without Steve's help, Sydney felt she would have gone to prison for sure.

After a month of being confined to her apartment, she was feeling crowded and had cabin fever. She missed her freedom, but Ed was keeping her busy. They were both hard at work designing, and showed each other their progress several times a day. And the orders for their first collection were continuing to pour in. It had been a huge success. In addition to the two-way screen, which was proving invaluable, he came to see her several times a week. Couriers were bringing her fabric samples so she could see the textures and colors, and they made constant joint decisions. He had asked her about adding a bathing suit line, and she thought it was too soon. And they were both delighted that they worked well together and respected each other's decisions.

"How's your romance going, by the way?" she asked him one Friday afternoon, when they were talking on the big screen. Bob was in town but out at a meeting with a client, and Ed was alone in his office. On weekends, she missed the buzz of activity at the office. It was nice seeing people on the monitor and the enormous screen which covered one wall.

"Kevin is a good guy," Ed said with a sigh, confiding in

her about the young man he was dating. Most of the time he was extremely private and kept his love life to himself. "He's young, though. He's still in design school."

"How old is he?" He looked mature and close to Ed's age, although she knew he was in his last year at Parsons.

"Twenty-two. But still. I feel it at times. But he's very serious, his father died when he was a kid, and he helped his mother raise his three younger siblings. He's been working since he was fifteen."

"Are we going to hire him when he graduates?" She was curious about Ed's intentions, and suspected he didn't know himself yet. They'd only been seeing each other for a few months.

"Maybe. I would discuss it with you first, obviously. He's got a nice hand at designing, but he's more interested in the business end. He's in the economics and business section, and he wants to go to grad school eventually and get an MBA, after he works for a few years."

"At least he won't be trying to compete with you, and he understands the industry," Sydney commented, and Ed nodded pensively. He had considered all of that himself and hadn't come to any major conclusions. He was just enjoying their time together. He had recently turned thirty, and he wasn't sure about the eight-year gap between them, and whether it bothered him enough to worry about. Most of the time it didn't, particularly when they were alone.

"What about you?" he asked her, venturing into waters they didn't usually discuss, as she just had. They were both very private people, and usually didn't talk about their personal lives. They confined their conversations and dealings with each other primarily to work-related subjects. Fabrics, designs, colors, what textile factories to use, how various employees were fitting in, deadlines, press, embroiderers, sewers, patternmakers, and all the complicated minute components of their business, and occasionally a good laugh to ease the tension after a long day at work. In many ways, they were very similar, despite the differences in their ages, life experience, and culture. They lived and breathed fashion, worked incredibly hard, and were perfectionists in all they did. Neither of them ever stopped until their work was done. But he could also see, whenever they were together, how happy she was with Bob. She was less worldly than most of the women Bob usually went out with, and she was far more serious about her work. "How's it going with Bob?" Ed asked cautiously. It seemed to have gotten very serious very quickly, in part due to the pressures on her before the trial.

"Amazingly well," she said with a smile. "I never expected something like this to happen. I didn't even want to date after Andrew died. I don't know where it will go, living eight thousand miles apart. Long-distance relationships are hard to sustain."

"He travels a lot, though," Ed said thoughtfully, "and

he's coming to New York more than he used to. Nowadays, you can work from almost anywhere in the world." She laughed when he said it.

"True, the two-way screen is working well for us." It had been a genius idea on his part. They had cameras all over the office now, so she could switch to almost any room, could watch their fittings on models, and talk to the on-site patternmakers and sewers while they worked. They did a lot of their finish work there where they could oversee it. The main production was being done at Ed's family's factories in China, which was essential to cost. They had a tremendous advantage being able to use his family's facilities at an extraordinarily low rate. "But I'm not sure how well two-way screens work for romance," she added, and he laughed.

"He's crazy about you, Syd. He talks about you whenever I see him. I think he's really in love with you."

"And I love him. I just can't figure out how this would look for the long haul."

"Maybe don't think about it for now. That's what I'm telling myself with Kevin. You don't need all the answers immediately. See how it goes."

"Do you want to come for Thanksgiving, by the way? You can bring Kevin of course," she added.

"I'd like that. I don't think he wants to go home. And I can't go with him. His mom doesn't want his siblings to know he's gay. She thinks it's contagious." He smiled when he said it. He'd been there before, with other people's parents and families who refused to face the truth. It made everything that much harder. He always said how understanding his own parents were about it.

"Sounds complicated," she said, and Ed nodded. "My apartment is a mess," she added as she looked around. She was enjoying chatting with him. "I'm starting to look like a hoarder. I have everything I need here and all my work supplies, but you can hardly move. I'll use my design table for Thanksgiving dinner. I think I'm going to get a bigger apartment when I can get out. Nothing fancy, but a little more breathing room, especially with Bob here so much." The business had taken off with a bang and was doing well, and her salary more than covered her meager expenses, but she constantly thought about wanting to pay Sabrina back for her legal fees before she did anything else. It was her first priority now.

"He has a fabulous apartment in Hong Kong, you'd love it," Ed told her. "It's kind of a bachelor pad, with a second apartment below for his kids when they're around. I don't think any of them live there now. The one who cooks and the artist have pretty simple tastes, and his daughter in medical school is in England, and his son the writer lives in a garret somewhere. None of them are showy people, but the place is fantastic."

"What are the kids like?" They were having a good visit

and letting their hair down about private matters, which was rare, and she'd wanted to ask him for a long time.

"They're normal, kind, fun. I went to school with the oldest one, the chef. I think Bob got married pretty young the first time. He always seemed like a young dad when we were growing up. I thought mine were older because they're my parents. His kids are just good people. He always encouraged them to pursue the work they wanted." She could tell that from their varied professions, but she was worried about how they'd react to her. Andrew's twins had set an ugly precedent, and scarred her. "You'll like them," he tried to reassure her, understanding why she was worried. "They're not like your stepdaughters." The stepmonsters, as Sophie and Sabrina called them.

"Hitler and Stalin were like the twins. I just don't want to get into some big battle with any man's family again. I don't need the headache." And she had paid a high price for Andrew putting her at their mercy.

"His kids are all very independent. And they've seen a lot of women come and go," Ed said, smiling.

"I'm not sure that's reassuring." She laughed at his comment. Bob had said as much himself, and that this was entirely different, with her.

"He's a serious person and a good father." Andrew had been too, but his daughters had behaved atrociously, with their mother's tutelage. "You'll have to come back to Hong Kong to meet them," he said.

"Well, for the moment, it's not a pressing problem. He can just tell them I'm in jail until next spring." She was developing a sense of humor about it, now that she knew nothing worse would happen. It was just a challenging time she had to get through. "What about you? Are you going to take Kevin to Hong Kong?"

"Maybe someday. Not now. That's a big statement. I'm not there yet." They were dating, not living together. "He met my parents during Fashion Week. That's enough for the time being. But thank you for including him on Thanksgiving. I assume the girls are coming."

"Of course." Sydney had been wondering if Steve would invite Sabrina to go to Boston with him, to his family, but so far he hadn't. "You're the godfather of Sabrina's romance too," she reminded Ed, since he'd found Steve for Sydney when she needed a criminal lawyer. And he had introduced her to Bob. "You're pretty good at this."

"Except for myself," he chuckled. "I just hit on our interns." But she knew from him and an earlier admission that this was a first for him. He had been diligent about not dating anyone where he worked, and never someone who worked directly for him. Until Kevin. It was too awkward if the relationship went wrong.

"What are you doing this weekend?" she asked him.

"We're going to stay with friends in Connecticut, to see the changing of the leaves. They got married last year, and just adopted a baby. I'm not sure that's the model I want to show Kevin. It'll probably cure both of us from domestic life by the end of the weekend." Ed always said he wasn't looking to get married, and might want children one day but not for a long time. And she knew it was the first serious relationship he'd had since the lover who'd committed suicide years before. He'd been careful not to get too deeply involved ever since. But Kevin, with his innocence and natural sweetness, had made it through his wall of barbed wire.

"It sounds like fun," Sydney said wistfully about his weekend. "I think I'm going to pitch a tent in Central Park after all this. I never realized how much I'd miss being outdoors, or walking down the street."

"It's not forever," he reminded her gently.

"I know, and I'm grateful to be here and not the alternative." She had thought of putting up a chart with the numbers of days for six months, and then decided it would be depressing and make the time go slower, while she waited every day to cross off one more day. A month had gone by already. All she had to do was get through another five. "Well, have a good weekend," she said as they wound up the call. It was getting late, and Ed had to get home and pack for the weekend.

"Say hi to Bob," Ed said, and as he did, she heard his key in the lock, and he came through the door, carrying packages. He had picked up groceries on the way home, so they could cook dinner, instead of ordering in, which they did a lot, from restaurants all over town when he was there. By now, she had a long list of favorite food and meal delivery services she used constantly.

"Hi, Ed!" Bob said, and waved at the screen. "How's everything?"

"Great. Lots of orders. How long will you be in town?"

"About a week if I can swing it. Five days otherwise. Do you want to come over for dinner?" he asked as Sydney kissed him and he smiled.

"I'd love to, but I'm going away for the weekend. Maybe Monday if you're still here."

"I will be. Have a good weekend." All three of them waved and said goodbye then, as Bob took off his coat and Sydney unpacked the groceries. She loved seeing him at the end of the day, and cuddling up with him at night to talk, and relax, and drink wine. It was a wonderful contrast to the long nights she worked into the wee hours when she was alone. She was sleeping less now and working even longer hours, since she couldn't go out. Instead of being lazy, being trapped at home was making her work harder.

"How was your day?" she asked, as she poured him a glass of red wine and handed it to him.

"Good," he said, smiling at her gratefully. "Except for a call from my oldest daughter, Francesca. She quit her job without telling me, sank herself in debt up to her ears, also without asking her father, and she's opening her own restaurant. She had a great job, at the best restaurant in Hong Kong, with three Michelin stars. Now she wants to open a bistro, which won't show off her talents and is almost a sure way to lose money. I think her boyfriend talked her into it." He looked worried and frustrated, as he glanced up at Sydney. "Usually they ask my advice, but in the end, they always do what they want anyway."

"Maybe we did too at their age. My parents hated my first husband. They thought he was lazy and a user and they were right. And they had both died by the time I married Andrew, so they never saw me get it right." But they would have been upset by the last year too, when she lost everything and was confined to her apartment with an electronic bracelet around her ankle from the court. "I guess we're never too old to screw up," she said with a sigh and a rueful smile.

"Your only crime was being naïve," he reminded her. "Paul Zeller knew what he was doing. He probably spotted you for an easy mark when he hired you, and had a plan in mind then, and you were convenient for him," he said wisely. He was a good judge of human nature, better than she was. He was more businesslike and less trusting.

"I was so grateful for the job, when the employment agencies told me no one would hire me after being out of the game for so long. And Paul was so kind to me on the plane."

"Bad guys are almost always nice, too nice, otherwise

how would they get away with it?" he said sensibly, and she nodded.

"What are you going to do about your daughter?" she asked him. She could see that it was troubling him.

"Try and talk her out of it, but she'll do what she wants. I don't like the boyfriend, and she knows it. He's another lazy charmer. She works so much, she never meets anyone, and she's easy prey for guys like him. He's a part-time bartender. The rest of the time he does nothing and sponges off her. The only guys she meets are the ones who work in her kitchen," he said unhappily, and then he smiled at her. "I guess that's what I did too. I fell in love with the wrong woman. My first wife, Helen, was brilliant and I was enamored with her mind. I never asked myself if she'd be a good wife or a good mother. And I don't think she did either. I wanted a lot of kids, and she went along with it. Five years later she figured out that she hated being married and had no maternal instincts, so she took off. The only one who was surprised was me. And I married my second wife, Brigid, because she had a great body, and I felt like a star when I was with her. She figured that one out in six months, while I was still buying her jewelry and bikinis." He was able to laugh at himself, but he hadn't then. He had been shocked, humiliated, and brokenhearted, and readily admitted it now, and already had to Sydney. "The two women couldn't have been more different. Helen and I are good friends these days. I don't even know where Brigid is, she seems to have faded from the skies. Someone told me she's in India making cheap movies, which is probably likely. But the two women were opposite extremes."

"So were Patrick and Andrew. Patrick was totally irresponsible, and Andrew was the most responsible man I'd ever met." Until his oversight at the end. Bob thought that if he'd been truly responsible, she wouldn't have been living in an apartment the size of a birdcage for a canary, barely able to scrape by, and he knew she was well aware of it herself, so he didn't want to add to it and criticize her late husband.

"I'm going to talk to Francesca when I get home. At least if she lets me lend her the money, she won't wind up drowning in debt. But she's very independent. She doesn't want anything from me. She shouldn't have quit her job."

"I was afraid when Sabrina wouldn't go back to her old job after they fired her because of me. I thought they'd paralyze her with a noncompete if she quit. And it turned out even better in the end. I'm sure Francesca will land on her feet too, if she's anything like her father." She smiled at him.

"I had no idea I'd worry about them this much at their ages. It was so much easier when they were younger." Although his son, Dorian, had gotten into drugs for a year in college and gone to rehab, but he hadn't had a problem since. He had told Sydney about that too. "It takes courage to have kids. I love my kids, but I wouldn't have the guts to do it again, or have more. I worry now that I'm doing it all wrong and giving them bad advice based on my own mistakes and my own fears. Every time my son goes out with some hot babe, I think of Brigid and tell him to run. He pointed out recently that I only approve of his going out with unattractive women and if he found one with a mustache who was butt ugly, I'd be thrilled." He chuckled then as he looked at Sydney. "I thought about it, and he's right. You're the only beautiful woman who doesn't scare me." She knew from Ed that he'd had a lot of beautiful women in his life since Brigid but had never taken any of them seriously. He was considered something of a man-about-town and a catch in Hong Kong.

"You have nothing to fear from me," she reassured him, and kissed him, "except my bad cooking. The only meals I know how to make are turkey on Christmas and Thanksgiving, and tacos," she admitted, and he laughed.

"Sounds good to me. And I have a solution for that," he said, as he set down his glass of wine. "I'm cooking dinner."

"You don't trust me," she said, pretending to be insulted. She wasn't known for her culinary skill, and had already demonstrated it to him on several occasions.

"In the kitchen, not really. You're the only person I've ever met who can burn pasta," he teased her, and she chuckled.

"You may have a point, but wait till you eat my turkey," she conceded, and they cooked dinner together. He made them excellent steaks, and she made the salad, which was all she ever ate anyway. She was thin because she wasn't a big eater and watched her weight, as did her daughters. Fashion was a harsh mistress, and the people who worked in it cruel judges. Designers were expected to be as thin as the models, and most of them were. Ed was too. Bob hadn't seen a normal-sized person in the business since he'd started dating her, and his daughter in Shanghai, the artist, was no better. The chef and the medical student had more normal eating habits. But Bob was lean too, very athletic, and stayed trim. He claimed it was because he didn't like airline food and spent most of his life on planes, but she knew he worked out with a trainer in Hong Kong, and swam at his club whenever he could, or when he stayed at a hotel with a pool.

Sydney was working out a lot now. The ballet teacher she met with on Skype that Sophie had recommended was proving to be a hard taskmaster. She had several models as clients, and women who traveled a lot and couldn't attend class in person. She had a booming business with individual sessions on Skype, and Sydney could already see changes in her thin body. It made her feel healthy to do something while she was confined to the apartment and couldn't even go for a walk. And running in place was too boring.

She and Bob watched a movie that night and went to bed early. He went for a run the next morning when he got up, and came back with a bag of croissants and brioches filled with chocolate.

"That's not fair!" she complained. She had just gotten out of the shower and was drying her hair, wearing pink jeans and a pink sweater, and looked like a breath of spring despite the wintry weather outside. "You go for a run, and I sit here getting fat and you tempt me with croissants? You must like chubby women," she accused him, but ate one of the chocolate buns while she did, and he laughed. He was a good sport about being stuck in the apartment with her. When she wasn't working, they played Scrabble and cards, and liar's dice, and she was ecstatic when she beat him. And sometimes they just lay around and read. He always bought her a stack of books when he was in town, or she ordered the latest bestsellers on the Internet while he was traveling. They were adjusting well to their confined life, and he insisted he didn't mind. With Sydney, everything was fun. And when he wasn't around, she was working.

Ed came to dinner on Monday, as he had promised, without Kevin, since he had a late class and a midterm the next day. Sydney showed him some new drawings she'd worked on, and Ed made some suggestions, which she liked. They always enhanced each other's work, tossing ideas back and forth. And he'd had good news that day. A chain of stores in Asia had placed an enormous order.

"You should open a store in Hong Kong," Bob suggested during dinner. They were balancing plates of Mexican food on their knees because she had work spread out on the design table. Sydney had made tacos, and Bob conceded they were excellent.

"I've thought of it," Ed said seriously. "I'm not sure if we should open one here first. A lot of big designers are setting up flagships in Beijing, but if we do something in Asia, I'd rather do Hong Kong," he said thoughtfully. He and Sydney had talked about it, but agreed they weren't ready. For the moment they were doing well with department store sales in the States, without taking on the overhead and buildout costs of a retail store of their own in New York, although it was among their midterm plans, just not yet.

"Well, I think Hong Kong would be a great idea," Bob said, smiling at them both. "Though I'll admit, I'm not without ulterior motives." He was trying to find a way to get Sydney to Hong Kong on a regular basis once she was free, other than just to see him. He knew that her work ruled her life, and he'd never get her there without it, or not often. But they had time to figure it out, and for the next five months it was a moot point.

Ed stayed late that night, enjoying long conversations

with them over dinner, and called to thank her the next morning.

"You two are so good together," he commented.

"We are," she agreed. "Maybe because we're not together all the time. It keeps the romance fresh."

"I worry about that with Kevin. He wants to move in, but maybe we'd get bored with each other. It's too soon anyway."

"How was the weekend, by the way?" She had forgotten to ask the night before.

"Oh my God, they're completely hysterical. I think they take the poor kid to the emergency room every day to make sure he's still breathing. They have monitors with video screens all over the house. I was a nervous wreck by the time we left. They thought he had a fever and called the doctor three times on Sunday. I think they just had too many cashmere sweaters and blankets on him. I am definitely not ready for that." She laughed, the idea of two gay men fussing frantically over a baby was sweet, but sounded intense, as most new parents were. She wondered sometimes when Sabrina and Sophie would want children, or if they ever would. They were so consumed by their work, there was no room for a baby in either of their lives. She didn't think the thought had even crossed their minds, and she didn't feel ready to be a grandmother yet either, at fifty. When Kellie had had children, she had hoped it would soften her and improve her relationship

Danielle Steel

with her, but it hadn't. If anything, she was nastier, except with her father, and wouldn't let Sydney near her kids. Nothing had changed.

She and Ed talked about business for a few minutes, and they set up a face-to-face design meeting later in the week. And Bob left on Wednesday. He had to get back to Hong Kong for board meetings, and he was anxious to see his daughter and try to talk her out of making a mistake with her bistro and crushing debt.

Bob promised to come back in four weeks this time. He had a lot to do until then, and he was going to try to be with her for Thanksgiving, since he knew it meant a lot to her. They'd be talking on FaceTime every day, but that wasn't the same. The apartment seemed empty and sad to her when he left. It was too quiet that night without him, as she lay in bed alone. She got up and made herself a cup of chamomile tea, and sat looking out the window at the quiet street. He was on the plane by then, and she thought about how entwined their lives had become and hoped it was a good idea. It was so easy to love him, and they were a good fit. But then what? How far could it go, with him living in Hong Kong and she in New York? They each had children who took up their attention and energy, even if they were grown. They had their own demanding careers, and in the long run living on two different continents would take dedication and work. But she loved him now. They got along seamlessly. She wondered what would

286

happen, and as she stood looking out the window, it started to snow. She couldn't see into the future and she didn't have the answers, as a thick white blanket silently covered New York. She opened the window wide despite the cold and stuck her hand out, so she could feel it, as the snowflakes fell into her palm, and she thought about the man she had come to love, and the day she was longing for when she could finally walk down the street next to him again.

Chapter 16

Sydney and Ed worked hard in November, honing their designs for the new collection they'd be presenting during Fashion Week in February, and they were making good progress. They selected the fabrics together and special-ordered a number of them, custom-made just for them with interesting textures and designs. They were developing their own very distinctive style, and both of them felt that they were stretching farther than they ever had creatively, and that their respective work enhanced each other's. They were a great team.

She and Bob talked whenever they could about everything, their work, their lives, their fears, their dreams, their children. He was discouraged that he hadn't been able to sway his daughter from opening her own bistro, and she was going ahead with her plans, taking on heavy debt, and was refusing her father's help. Other than that, his children were doing well, and they were all coming home to him for Christmas. He was still intending to join Sydney in New York for Thanksgiving. The time apart was weighing on both of them, and Sydney was sad at times. The nights were long and lonely, except when she worked, and the apartment seemed increasingly confining. She had been incarcerated for more than two months by the time he arrived for Thanksgiving in New York. And the months ahead, of not being able to go out, seemed long. The weather had been bad, but it didn't make a difference. She would have given anything to walk through the rain, and even sleet or snow.

She was waiting up for him anxiously the night he arrived, the day before Thanksgiving, and rushed into his arms the minute he came through the door. He held her close to him, feeling the silk of her hair, unable to speak for an instant.

"God, how I've missed you, Sydney." The last month had seemed a thousand years long to both of them. He'd had a heavy workload in Hong Kong, and had made several short trips in Asia. For Sydney, the tension was mounting before their next show, with the usual production problems, fabric disasters, and delays, which were all par for the course in her business. She and Ed were spending hours on their two-way screen to resolve problems, and he was coming by almost every day as Fashion Week approached. It was just under twelve weeks away, but some of the textile mills and factories would be closed during the holidays, so there would be delays with deliveries.

It was an enormous relief to see Bob again, and to be

able to hold and touch each other, and make love, without interruptions, difficult time differences, and the demands of their busy lives. They felt as though they knew everything about each other. He had even walked around his apartment in Hong Kong, holding his computer so she could see everything. The apartment was beautiful, the art impressive, and the views magnificent. His taste was very different from Andrew's, more modern, and in some ways more like hers. He couldn't wait for her to visit one day, and she was planning to, sometime after she was released in March, which seemed light-years away.

They stayed up late the night he arrived, and she crept out of bed at six in the morning to start the preparations for the meal, and saw that it was snowing again. Afterward, she stood in her bedroom for a minute, smiling at the sight of him sound asleep in her bed, naked from their lovemaking the night before. His eyes were closed and his hair was tousled, he was a beautiful sight, and then she heard the low rumble of his morning voice, which made her stomach do double flips every time. She was more in love with him than ever. And their time apart only brought them closer together.

"Get your ass back into bed," he said, without opening his eyes, sounding sexy and irresistible. She dropped her robe on the floor, slid in next to him, and pressed her body against his, as he turned toward her and kissed her, and she could feel his passion hard against her. "I love you, woman," he said, opening his eyes, and they smiled at each other. "You're beautiful in the morning," he said, admiring her for an instant.

"You're crazy, but I love you," she whispered, and he began making love to her, and then fell asleep in her arms again afterward. He was tired from the trip, but happy to be back with her in her bed. He would have flown twice as far to be with her.

He was up and moving around the apartment at noon, while she tended to the turkey, basting it, in her pink cashmere bathrobe and bare feet. She had brought the robe with her from her old house and couldn't have afforded to buy one like it now. It was a favorite, especially in the drafty apartment. When there was a cold wind outside, it was chilly. But she was never cold in Bob's arms. And he was wearing a silk robe he had brought with him and looked very distinguished despite his unbrushed hair and needing a shave.

"What time are the guests coming?" he asked, as she handed him a cup of coffee from the fancy cappuccino machine he had bought her, so she didn't miss going to Starbucks every day for a vanilla latte with cinnamon and nonfat froth. She had become an expert at making them herself.

"They're invited at five, I thought we'd eat around six or six-thirty."

He nodded. He had never spent Thanksgiving in the

States before, although American friends in Hong Kong had invited him to their Thanksgiving celebrations on many occasions. But this was the real thing. "The usual crew?" he asked her, and she nodded.

"Sabrina and Steve," who were a regular fixture together now, and wonderful to see together. They were a perfect match, and had been inseparable for the year since she'd been arrested. He was the silver lining in the ordeal for Sabrina, and for Sydney as well, seeing how happy they were. He had moved into her apartment that summer, and it was going well. "Sophie and Grayson. The two of us, and Ed is bringing Kevin, which I gather is a big deal. He's never shared holidays with anyone before, so this is a major statement for him, but Ed said he feels ready and Kevin was thrilled." He was only a few years younger than Sophie, so he'd fit in, and they all had fashion design in common.

"Do we dress up?" Bob asked, and she smiled at him.

"Actually, I like you just the way you are," she said with a look of mischief, "but you could wear a jacket and slacks. The young ones will wear jeans, Grayson, and probably Kevin." She had only seen Kevin in jeans and T-shirts so far, with sneakers, when he was working, or following Ed around. "You don't need to wear a tie."

"I have one if you prefer." She shook her head. She knew that Sabrina would probably wear something dressy, and Sophie casual chic and sexy from her own line. Sydney was planning to wear white slacks and a soft white silk blouse with big sleeves, which was brave while she was cooking. But everything would be done by then. She was preparing all the traditional favorites: brussels sprouts, creamed spinach, carrots, sweet potatoes with marshmallows, the turkey with stuffing, cranberry jelly, hot biscuits. And she'd had three pies delivered the day before: apple, mincemeat, and pumpkin, with ice cream. It was a lot to prepare in her tiny kitchen, and she was very proud of herself, but she was determined to make it memorable for all of them, and especially Bob and her children. She had a lot to be thankful for this year. Bob, her new business with Ed, and the fact that she wasn't in prison.

They spent a relaxing afternoon while she fussed in the kitchen, consulting her favorite cookbook every step of the way. It continued to snow, and by five o'clock when the guests were expected, everything was ready and she looked like she'd done nothing all afternoon, in her white slacks and pretty blouse. Bob opened the Château Margaux he had bought, so it could breathe, since she had no decanters to pour it into and they'd have to serve it from the bottle. She had left all her fine crystal in Connecticut, she explained, when he asked if she had any decanters, and he promised to buy her a couple before they entertained again, probably around Christmas, since he planned to be in Hong Kong with his children for the actual holiday. He seemed very proud to be with her, as people began arriving, and he made it clear that he was playing host.

Sabrina and Steve were the first to arrive and said it was freezing outside. She had worn snow boots, since it had been snowing all day, and there were several inches on the ground, and drifts that were deeper. They looked happy and she was wearing a short red dress, which was unlike her. Her mother complimented her on it, since she always wore black, and Steve was beaming at her, completely besotted. It was sweet to see and warmed her heart. Steve was exactly the kind of man Sydney had always hoped Sabrina would meet and fall in love with. Serious, solid, as hardworking as she was, and he adored her. She had high hopes for Sophie as well, but at twenty-five, she still seemed too young to settle down. She just wished she'd stop taking in wounded birds like Grayson and find someone more fun and who would take care of her.

Sophie arrived next and was alone.

"Where's Grayson?" her mother asked her. "Is he sick?" Sophie hesitated for a minute before she answered and looked awkward.

"He's not coming. We . . . we decided to call it a day a couple of weeks ago. He's a wonderful person, but his issues make everything really difficult." They all knew it was true, and though Sydney didn't say it, she was relieved. Now Sophie could find someone less troubled to spend time with. Her relationship with Grayson had been hard work, even though he was a good person.

"I think you made the right decision," she said gently.

"It was more his decision than mine," she admitted. Sabrina had known, but they hadn't told their mother yet. Sophie wanted to be sure first that they would stick with it, but she realized now too that it was the right thing. Grayson seemed relieved when she talked to him. He didn't want the pressure of a relationship. He said it was too much for him, even if he loved her, which he said he did. She loved him too, but he had become a heavy burden to carry with all his problems and quirks and scars.

The two girls chatted easily with Bob and Steve, and Ed arrived a few minutes later with Kevin. Sydney was impressed by how stylish Kevin was. He looked like a model in a slim black suit with a black sweater and boots.

"Did you dress him?" she whispered to Ed when he visited her in the kitchen area, where she was busy. Bob was pouring them all wine. Ed laughed at her question.

"No, he cleans up pretty good on his own. And looks like a grownup. He used to model."

"He's gorgeous," Sydney said, impressed. They made a good-looking couple, and in proper clothes the eight years between them were no longer noticeable. The other two men had dressed more traditionally, in blazers and gray flannel slacks. Sydney thought Bob looked particularly handsome and very British. He had a noticeably European style that she loved.

They sat down at the table at six-thirty. Sydney had covered her design table with a white linen cloth she had ordered online with matching napkins, and no one noticed the mismatched plates that had come with the apartment, with the abundance of food on them. Sabrina had lent her some bowls and platters the week before. They all complimented the food, and the turkey was delicious and not dry. She had even made gravy for it. The dinner was her masterpiece, and she had put a lot of effort into it.

"I stand corrected," Bob said in awe. "You're a fantastic cook!" She knew she wasn't but was pleased to hear it, the dinner was excellent, and she could see he was having a good time. He and Sabrina had engaged in a lively conversation, and they were all being warm and caring with Sophie, who looked a little forlorn without Grayson. He had been her pet project for a long time, but a difficult one at best. Sydney thought her life would be better without him, but she was sure Sophie would miss him, and knew she had cared about him and felt sorry for him. His early years had damaged him so badly, which was sad.

Bob kept the wine flowing generously throughout dinner, and after Sydney brought out the pies and ice cream, and Bob poured another round of wine, Sabrina looked around the small group nervously and exchanged a look with Steve. Bob spotted the silent glance between them, and guessed what was coming. Sydney was too busy dishing out the ice cream on everyone's pie to notice, until Sabrina said they had an announcement to make, and Sydney stopped what she was doing, rooted to the spot, and sat down.

"We're getting married," Sabrina blurted out, grinning at all of them, as Sydney stared at her. She knew she should have expected it, but she hadn't. No one in their world seemed to get married anymore. They just lived together or had babies unmarried. This was her fondest hope for her daughter, a wonderful husband to love and care for her. Sabrina looked ecstatic, and Steve kissed her and beamed like a big happy boy, and then turned apologetically to his future mother-in-law.

"I know I should have asked you first," he said in a low voice, looking contrite. "It just kind of slipped out a few days ago, at an engagement party we went to. Are you okay with it?" he asked Sydney, worried, and she gave him a big hug. It would have been nice to be asked, or forewarned, but she doubted that many people did that anymore, and she thought they were perfect for each other.

"I wholeheartedly approve. You both have my blessing," she said with damp eyes, looking very moved. "You make it worthwhile getting arrested and nearly going to prison, if Sabrina gets a terrific husband out of it," she said, and meant it, and everyone at the table laughed and congratulated them. Sabrina was twenty-eight years old, financially successful, and had a booming career, and so did he. He was ten years older than she was, and everything about their union seemed right to Sydney, and to Bob when they talked about it later.

Sabrina wanted to get married in June, and said they wanted a small wedding. It brought home to Sydney again the difficulties of her financial situation. Until a year and a half before, she could have given her an elaborate reception, and Andrew would have wanted to throw a lavish event for her, probably at their home. Now it would be a challenge to do anything except a simple, very restrained gathering, on a tiny budget. It made Sydney sad to think she would be cheating her daughter of her dream wedding. And she still owed her money from the court case. All her life and as a little girl, Sabrina had talked about wanting a big formal wedding, and now she didn't have that option. And Sydney didn't want Sabrina paying for her own wedding. It was a challenge she would have to figure out in the coming months. Bob could see that she was troubled about something, but couldn't figure out what since she liked the groom so much, and meant to ask her about it when they were alone.

For the rest of dinner, the conversation was all about the young couple and their plans. It was all very new, and the wedding was still seven months away, so nothing had been organized yet.

"We're doing the wedding dress, of course," Ed announced immediately, and Sabrina accepted with delight. "Will you have bridesmaids?" he asked her, and she said she hadn't decided yet, but she thought she only wanted Sophie as her maid of honor, and no other attendants. It was Sophie who had always said she wanted a simple wedding, or none at all. This was new for Sabrina, who had changed her tune radically, and Sydney suspected it was out of deference to her.

"We'll do her dress too," Ed said about Sophie. "And your mother's." He smiled at Sydney. "Oh, I *love* weddings!" he crowed with glee, clapping his hands, and they all laughed. "When can we start? I wanted to do a bride in our first collection, but we didn't have time. This is going to be fabulous!" He had designed bridal gowns at Dior, but hadn't had the chance to since. The decibel level at the table rose, and Bob brought out two bottles of champagne he had bought for him and Sydney, and the remainder of the evening turned into a celebration.

"Who's going to walk you down the aisle?" Ed asked her, obsessed with every aspect of the wedding. He said he had a fantastic new florist, he was suggesting venues, and Sabrina looked uncertain how to answer his question about who would walk her down the aisle. Now that Andrew was gone, there were no other important men in

Sabrina's life, except her future husband. Her own father was long gone, and she had no brother or male relatives of any kind.

"My mom, I guess," Sabrina said hesitantly. She was the only person she could think of with an adult role in her life, and Sydney looked deeply touched by the suggestion.

"I don't know if that will look right," Ed said, concerned with the fashion statement and the visual of two women walking down the aisle together.

"I'd be happy to, if you'd like me to," Bob said in a clear, calm voice, and Sabrina was startled, but not averse to it, as Sydney's eyes filled with tears again. Life had a way of giving them what they needed, even if from unexpected sources. She had no way of knowing if she and Bob would even be dating seven months from now, although she hoped so. But she was very moved by the offer, and Sabrina was too. He was a kind man.

"That might be very nice," Sabrina said quietly. "Thank you, Bob."

"I like the way that looks much better," Ed said as the self-appointed wedding planner, and they all laughed again. "And I like small weddings. You never get to talk to anyone at big weddings. It's just a giant cattle show, with everyone milling around. What kind of cake? What about chocolate with vanilla icing? They had a fabulous one at Jack and Tom's wedding. I can ask them who their baker was." He was on a roll, and Sydney leaned over and kissed her business partner on the cheek and couldn't resist teasing him.

"You make a fantastic mother of the bride, and wedding planner. I think we should start doing brides."

"I'd love it," he said honestly. "But no one would take us seriously. I'm not Vera Wang," he said, and everyone laughed. Sabrina had added an element of joy to Thanksgiving with her announcement, and Steve smiled for the rest of the night. He looked happy and proud.

They all had a little too much to drink, once Bob served the champagne to celebrate the engagement. But they all left in high spirits, and Sydney held her daughter tight for a minute and told her how happy she was for her. And she gave Steve a big hug when they left. They were taking Sophie with them and were going to drop her off at home.

"Well, what a special evening that turned out to be," Bob said, impressed. They'd all had a wonderful time. "It would be hard to top that. I picked the right year to start celebrating Thanksgiving with you." He kissed her and searched her eyes for a minute. "You're pleased about it?" He thought she was but still felt that something was bothering her.

"I am. I couldn't be happier. He's a terrific guy, and they love each other. You never know which marriages will work and which won't, but I think they'll be a great couple."

"You looked worried for a minute, at one point, or sad."

He wasn't sure which, and she hesitated, not sure if she should share her most private thoughts with him, to that degree, and she didn't want him to think she wanted his help.

"I can't give her the kind of wedding she's always wanted, even if she says she wants a small one now. She's wanted a big, elaborate wedding since she was a little girl. But I can't do that now, and I don't want her paying for it herself. I think she's keeping it small to be considerate of me." She felt like a failure again, not being able to make her daughter's dreams come true.

"May I help you?" he asked gently, and she shook her head.

"I can't let you do that. It wouldn't be right. But thank you." She smiled gratefully at him. "And thank you too for offering to walk her down the aisle. That was incredibly sweet of you." She was very moved by his kindness and generosity.

"I don't want to overstep any boundaries, but I'll do whatever you allow, and she wants," he said, and she could see that he meant it. "Maybe she's changed her mind about a big wedding," he said thoughtfully. But either way, there was no other choice. And even a small wedding would be a stretch. It would be a big help that Ed would make their dresses. Beautiful wedding gowns, and especially the kind Sabrina would want, cost a fortune.

Bob pulled Sydney into his arms then and held her for

a long moment. He knew she was too proper and too proud to accept any financial help from him, but he would have helped gladly. Just knowing that was a gift to her, and having him at her side at her daughter's wedding. Big or small, it was going to be a joyous event.

They cleaned up the debris from dinner the next day, and were both startled by how much wine they had consumed, but it had been a celebration, and no one had gotten sloppy or visibly drunk. The evening had been a big success. They had the apartment neat again by lunchtime. Bob was always a big help. The snow had continued all day and had brought the city to a dead stop with two feet of it on the ground, and they were happy to be indoors, reading and watching movies and playing games. They lived on the leftovers from dinner for three days. Ed sent her emails all weekend with possible wedding dress designs, which made her smile. He was ecstatic about the wedding and doing Sabrina's wedding gown.

On Monday, Sydney got back to work on the collection, and Bob flew to Hong Kong. He sent Sabrina and Steve a beautiful silver frame from Tiffany as an engagement present before he left town. He was coming back to New York with his children in a month, right after Christmas, to spend New Year's with Sydney, and he hoped to stay longer that time.

Sydney had a serious conversation with Sabrina on Monday about the wedding, and apologized for not being able to give her a huge event as she had always said she wanted.

"I don't want that anymore, Mom." She sounded sincere about it. "I've grown up. I don't want all that pomp and ceremony and show-off stuff. I just want you and Sophie, our close friends, and Steve's family. That's all we need. Please don't worry about it." Sydney felt a weight lift off her shoulders when Sabrina said it. She felt even happier about the wedding after that.

Sydney was working on Monday after the Thanksgiving weekend, when she got an email from her realtor in Paris. She'd had an offer for the apartment, and she said that her tenant was ready to vacate in the next month anyway, by the end of the year. The potential buyer wanted a quick sale for a respectable amount. It wasn't a fortune, but the price was fair. The buyer was Italian and wanted a pied-à-terre in Paris, and he wanted to take possession of it rapidly with a fast closing. The realtor said that if she accepted the offer, she could have the money in early January. And if she agreed to the amount, they could sign a *promesse de vente* right away, which she knew was a promise to sell, which established the amount of purchase and the terms and was a binding contract.

Instead of writing back, Sydney called her, to see if there was any possibility for negotiation to raise the price a little.

"I can try, but it's a good offer," she told her, and Sydney knew it was.

"It never hurts to try." The realtor agreed to contact the buyer and called her back an hour later. He had come up another fifty thousand dollars, which satisfied Sydney. "I'll take it," she said to the realtor, with a silent prayer of thanks. Now she could pay Sabrina back, pay Steve's bill, and host an intimate, beautiful wedding for her daughter with all the gracious touches that would make it memorable for them, but not over-the-top or showy.

"Congratulations, madame," the realtor said to her, sounding pleased herself. It was a charming apartment, but small and old-fashioned and hadn't been easy to sell.

"Thank you, God," Sydney said as she hung up the phone. The timing was perfect, and her financial needs had been met. And she would have enough to live on modestly for quite some time. Everything was falling into place at last. She had faced the worst, and come through it.

Chapter 17

Sydney called Sabrina first to tell her about the sale of the Paris apartment, because she was the most directly affected by it. Sydney was so relieved to be able to tell her she could pay her back now for Steve's fees and the five thousand she had paid to the bail bondsman in cash. The deed to her apartment had been returned by the bail bondsman as soon as Sydney was sentenced. And now she could pay Steve in full too. He had been patient about it, but it had weighed heavily on her, especially with what she owed Sabrina. In January, with the sale of the apartment, she would be able to pay it all.

"You don't need to worry about it, Mom," Sabrina reassured her. "I've been fine."

"Well, I haven't been. I've been worried sick about taking money from you. That's not the way it's supposed to be," and it never had been before. But getting arrested had turned her whole world upside down. The sale of the Paris apartment would set it to rights again, or start to, and put things back in the order they were meant to be, with a mother helping her daughter, not the reverse. She never wanted to be a burden on her children again.

"Are you okay about the apartment, Mom?" Sabrina knew how much she loved it, and how sad she must be to give it up. She was, but other priorities were more pressing now, and the sale of the apartment would help her achieve them.

"I'm sad. I can't pretend I'm not. But I'm glad in a way too. It was a place for Andrew and me. And now I can pay you back, which is more important to me. It was upsetting me terribly that I couldn't till now. And I can give you a beautiful wedding, however you want it to be. I want you to have your dream wedding with Steve. So start thinking about where you want to do it." She sounded jubilant when she said it. It had made her heart ache thinking that she couldn't do all that she wanted for her, when Sabrina had announced their engagement on Thanksgiving.

"I don't need a big wedding," she insisted again graciously. "And I can chip in too. You shouldn't have to pay for everything." She didn't want her mother to spend everything she had for her wedding, or too much, and she had told Steve she didn't need anything elaborate and expensive, and neither did he. They were going to save money for a house, and with their combined salaries, they could buy a nice one, or an apartment in the city until they had children. And they were in no hurry to have kids yet. Sabrina wanted to concentrate solely on her career for several more years. She wasn't ready to give that up at twenty-eight.

"I'm your mother and I love you," Sydney insisted. "And I'm paying for the wedding, you're not. So start thinking. We can do something really lovely. Maybe in a garden somewhere outside the city. People rent their homes for that." They could have done it in Connecticut of course, in the "old days," but there was no point thinking about that now. She didn't want to look to the past. She wanted to be happy for Sabrina and stay focused on the present. The past was dangerous ground for her, a minefield of memories that would blow her to bits and break her heart if she let it. She didn't want to go there anymore. The present was more important now, and moving forward. She still missed Andrew at times, but he had left her such dire problems to deal with that she had to switch her focus rapidly from grief to survival.

Sabrina promised to think about a location for the wedding, and she thanked her mother for her generosity.

Sydney called Bob when he arrived in Hong Kong, and told him about the Paris apartment. He was quiet for a minute, knowing that it was a double-edged sword for her, and bittersweet.

"Will you miss it terribly?" He knew how much the Paris apartment had meant to her. She had told him about it, and he could tell.

"Yes . . . no . . ." she said honestly. "I love it, but I

couldn't go back there now. It's part of another life, and it's giving me what I need now. I'm grateful for that. It'll give me a cushion to live on so things aren't so tight. I can pay back Sabrina for Steve's legal fees. And I can give her a lovely wedding." She sounded immensely relieved about that. "She's being very sensible about it. She even offered to help, but I won't let her. So to answer your question, I'm grateful for what selling the apartment will do for me, so I'm a lot less upset than I would have been otherwise." She was being matter-of-fact about it and he respected her for it. He admired her courage, her spunk, and her style. She had an extraordinary ability to bounce back from events that would have crushed others. They talked about it for a while longer, and he said he'd love to go to Paris with her one day, "when she was no longer wearing her anklet," as he put it. And then she went back to work.

She thought about the Paris apartment a few times that night, but reminded herself each time of the benefits she was deriving from the sale, which cheered her up. The realtor had emailed her the papers to sign on Tuesday. She had already signed them, scanned them, and emailed them back to her. All she wanted now was the money and to get on with her life. She had enough to keep her occupied without wallowing in the past.

But three days later, she felt like she'd been hit by a wrecking ball when she read that Russians had bought their house in Connecticut. She stared at the article and read it again and again, as tears rolled down her cheeks. The twins had gotten their asking price, but whatever the Russians had paid, they had gotten a piece of her heart. It was one thing to lose a pied-à-terre in Paris that had been a toy for them and a luxury, but selling the house that had been their home, with all of her most beloved belongings in it, tore her heart out.

She sat there and cried for an hour, as she looked out the window, thinking about it. And this time, Veronica didn't call her. She never did anymore after Sydney told her not to. But their beloved home going to strangers was almost too much. And even worse right on the heels of the Paris apartment. Now everything was gone, only eighteen months after Andrew's death, and so much of what they'd loved. No one could take the memories from her, but they had taken everything else.

Bob could hear that something was off when he called her that night, and at first she insisted that nothing was wrong when he asked. She didn't want to talk about it, and didn't think she could without crying.

"Tell me, Sydney, what happened?" He said it so gently that she started crying and couldn't stop, and then told him that the house had been sold, with all their memories and all their history, and everything that had been stolen from her by her stepdaughters. Bob felt terrible listening to her and didn't know what to say. He wanted to put his arms around her, and hated that he wasn't with her to do it. They had to content themselves with words for now, and the fact that they loved each other.

"I can't even imagine how hard this must be," he said tenderly. It was almost like a fire or a flood or a hurricane that had swept everything away. "I'm so sorry they took it all away from you. It was so wrong of them." And the part her husband had played wasn't right either, but Bob didn't say that to her. There was no point blaming Andrew now. He just wanted to console her. "It's easy for me to say," he said apologetically, "but you just have to go on and make a good new life." She knew it too, and was doing her best to do so.

"I've been trying," she said, crying harder, "and then I got arrested, and I wound up stuck in this stupid apartment." She sounded like a little kid, and he smiled and loved her all the more.

"I'll be there soon, in the stupid apartment with you," he said in a loving tone, and she laughed. She hadn't lost her sense of humor, but occasionally it all got to her. And the sale of the Connecticut house was a hard blow that struck at her heart. It was truly gone now, and would belong to someone else. She wasn't sure if that was better or worse than the twins owning it and Kellie living there.

They talked for a while after that, and Sydney sounded calmer and had regained her composure by the time they hung up.

"I'm sorry I got upset," she said to him sheepishly.

"Don't be ridiculous. That's what I'm here for. I'd have been in a straitjacket by now after all you've been through. Women are much stronger about these things than men. I stayed in bed for a week when Brigid left, and we didn't even like each other by then," he said, and made her smile. "I'd be upset about the house too," he said seriously. And it was hard having it happen at Christmas, when memories and losses were always more acute.

She thought about it again, late that night, looking out the window, and she missed Andrew fiercely for the first time in a while. She wasn't as angry at him anymore, she just wished that things were different, and he was still alive. But she knew that she was lucky to have Bob, even if their love was new and they didn't have much history yet. She was sorry they couldn't spend Christmas together. But they both needed to be with their children, and lived worlds apart. They still didn't know how they would manage it in the future. Neither of them could commute between Hong Kong and New York all the time, although some people did. And Bob was coming to see her regularly. But as long as she was still under house arrest, she couldn't travel too, to lighten the load on him. There was nothing they could do about it. She was grateful that he came to see her as often as he did. Coming to spend New Year's Eve with her would be her best Christmas gift from him.

Sophie visited her a lot on weekends now that she

didn't have a boyfriend. Sydney ordered dinner for them, and they watched movies together. She still missed Grayson, but knew the breakup was right. Sabrina was busy with work, Steve, and their plans for the future, although she hadn't organized the wedding yet. She hadn't had time.

Sydney had managed to do some Christmas shopping online. It felt strange shopping that way, but it was all she could manage, unable to get out of the apartment. The girls and Steve were planning to have Christmas Eve dinner with her, and Kevin and Ed. And the day after Christmas, Steve was taking Sabrina to Florida to meet his parents, and after that they were going to spend the weekend alone in Palm Beach for New Year's Eve. Sophie was going skiing in Vermont with friends. It all sounded like a nice break to Sydney, whose horizons were limited now by a two-room apartment, and a window that looked out on the street. But she was happy they were willing to spend Christmas with her, and she enjoyed the time she was spending with Sophie, before she started dating again.

Sydney and Ed sent a lot of designs back and forth to each other in the weeks before Christmas. They were going to be closed between Christmas and New Year's, and after that they'd have six weeks till their show. And she couldn't be there to help this time. Coincidentally, it was going to be on Valentine's Day, which seemed a little corny to her.

And the time was coming closer. They had most of the designs done and the samples in production, except for a few where, as usual, they were waiting for fabrics from abroad that had been delayed. But there was plenty of time to catch up. And Ed was still sending her sketches of wedding gowns for Sabrina whenever he had time. It was a happy event to look forward to. They'd had too many sad ones in recent years. But finally, the tides had turned.

She was working on some drawings when Steve called her three days before Christmas and chatted with her for a few minutes, while she wondered why he had called, and then he asked if he could come to see her.

"Is anything wrong?" she asked nervously. He never came to see her alone, and her court case was closed, as long as she didn't leave the apartment until the end of March, which was still three months away.

"Not at all," he answered her. "I just thought I'd drop by if you're not too busy working. I have a Christmas present for you, and I wanted to bring it over myself." She was confused by what he said.

"Aren't you spending Christmas Eve with us, Steve?"

"Of course. But I thought this might be useful for you for the holidays." She wondered if he was bringing her a Christmas tree. She had already ordered one that would be delivered the next day. She wasn't much in the Christmas spirit yet. The sale of the Connecticut house was still weighing on her. "What's a good time?" he asked, persistent about dropping off his mysterious gift.

"Well, I won't be out when you come," she said and laughed.

"I hope not. How's four o'clock?" She would be working, but could take a break anytime. She couldn't imagine what it was.

He arrived promptly at the dot of four, and she stopped sketching and buzzed him in. She glanced in the mirror and saw that her hair was a mess and she had no makeup on. She hadn't bothered with how she looked – she usually didn't when she worked from home. He was wearing a business suit and a heavy coat and looked like he'd been to court that day, which was the case. He took off his coat and sat down on the couch with her.

They chatted for a few minutes about nothing in particular, and she was more mystified than ever as to why he was there, and then finally he got to the point.

"I wanted to bring you up to date on Paul Zeller, and I thought I'd do it in person." She nodded, not sure why it mattered anymore. "He had a hearing this week, and they offered him a deal. Apparently, they've pulled a lot of information from his computers, and he's been buying stolen goods for years. This wasn't new. He's always managed to do it under the radar, without pinning it on someone else. But you came along at the right time, pure as snow, and I guess he couldn't resist using you and letting you take the fall if something went wrong. You were a great cover for him this time."

"And they're letting him go free?" She anticipated what he was going to say, and Steve shook his head.

"Hardly. He could get twenty or twenty-five years. They spelled it out to him. Money laundering, tax evasion, dealing in stolen goods. And it's hard to trace, but there is some belief that money from counterfeit and stolen fashion items pays for terrorism in some parts of the world. The feds take this very seriously. They shut down his business after he sold it. The government is going to take what they consider their due, and I was told his ex-wife will get the rest. So he's got nothing left. The U.S. attorney wanted him to get twenty years or more. But he's got an outstanding lawyer who schmoozed the U.S. attorney, and everyone from here to the pearly gates, so they offered him a damn good deal. Ten years in prison, five on probation. And his lawyer somehow managed to get it down to seven and five. He's damn lucky they offered him that deal, or he'd have been in prison for a hell of a long time. Zeller wanted to turn the deal down, but his lawyer wouldn't let him. They would have crucified him at trial, particularly if they put you on the stand, to tell how you got prosecuted because of him. It would also make the U.S. attorney's office look bad for being tough on you and making you an example. They tried to pressure you for information they now realize you never had. So Zeller took the deal, kicking and screaming all the way. He signed it yesterday, and they're shipping him off to the federal penitentiary today or tomorrow. No bail in the meantime. He's done."

She sat thinking about it for a few minutes, and then nodded and looked at Steve. She suddenly remembered that Paul had a son in St. Louis who was a pediatrician and she wondered how he had reacted to his father going to prison, and she felt bad for him. She thought of all the grief and trauma Paul Zeller had caused her, when she had been innocent all along, and they hadn't believed her, because Paul had lied.

"Thank you for telling me," she said quietly. "Is that the Christmas present you meant?" She was curious, and needed time to absorb what he had told her about Paul Zeller. At least now it was over. And they weren't after her anymore.

"It's part of it," Steve said, referring to his gift, as he reached into his pocket, pulled out a small scissor and held it up.

"What's that for?" She looked puzzled.

"Well, as your lawyer, I managed to keep you out of prison, but you got stuck in here for six months," he said, glancing around at the now vastly cluttered apartment, crowded with computer equipment and her giant screen to meet with Ed and follow the business on a daily basis. "And if that sonofabitch can get seven years instead of twenty-five, I figured they owe you one. I met with the judge this morning. You're done, Sydney. They reduced it to three months, with credit for time served, so it's over. They deactivated your anklet at four P.M. today. And they've reduced probation to a year, with permission to travel because of your work. The judge said you can keep your passport—just send your probation officer an email when you leave and get back. And as long as you have no further problems or convictions, the judge said he'd talk to us in six months or a year about terminating probation and expunging your record." She was staring at him in disbelief. "They were overzealous with you and they knew it. Now they're trying to get out of it as gracefully as they can."

"You did all that today?"

"I did. You're a free woman, Sydney. Now give me your leg, and let's get that goddamn thing off and I'll return it to the DA's office." He held out his hand as she looked at him in amazement, lifted her ankle, and he cut the plastic band that held it in place till it fell away, and he smiled at her. "Merry Christmas, Sydney," he said, as tears poured down her face and she hugged him and gazed around the room as though seeing it for the first time.

"Oh my God . . . I'm free . . . I'm free! Can I go out?" Like an animal that had been chained up for three months, it was as though she had forgotten what to do when someone took off the chain.

"You can do anything you want. You're free," he repeated. "It's over."

"Oh my God . . . oh my God!" she said, chortling with delight and clapping her hands. Ed called her just then, and she didn't pick up, which he knew meant she was either in the bathroom, the tub, or asleep. But she wasn't ready to talk to anyone. She just wanted to savor the moment with Steve. "Do the girls know?"

He shook his head. "I thought you should hear it first."

"You're a miracle worker, *thank you!*" she said, and hugged him again, and he got up to leave.

"Wait, I'll go out with you," she said excitedly. "I'll get my coat." She reached into the closet and haphazardly grabbed an old fur and put it on. She felt a little crazy, with messy hair, a pair of ballerina flats, and an old mink coat.

"It's freezing out there," he warned her, but she was smiling and giddy and almost looked drunk she was so excited.

"I don't care if I freeze to death. I haven't had fresh air in three months." Literally to the day. "I'll call the girls when I get back," she said, sounding distracted.

"Don't forget your keys," he reminded her. She grabbed them off a table near the door, where Bob had left them the last time he was there. She put them in her pocket and shut the door behind them, and a minute later they were on the street. She glanced around her at the traffic and the people, the tall buildings, the dogs being walked, and people carrying Christmas trees home, and listened to the horns blaring. She looked as though she had landed in heaven and couldn't believe her good luck. She hugged him again and he grinned at her. In Steve's opinion, she deserved every break she could get from now on. "Be careful crossing the street!" he shouted after her as she walked away, looking dazed, and she turned and waved with a big grin on her face.

"I love you! Merry Christmas!" she called out to him, and then she just kept walking with a huge smile. She walked twenty blocks heading toward downtown, and then she strolled back, smiling at people, relishing every smell and color and face and sound and light. She loved the noise, and seeing everyone in a rush to go somewhere. She was going to tell her children, but she had decided not to tell Bob. She was going to surprise him when he came for New Year's Eve. She was a free woman again! And just glad she was alive.

Chapter 18

When Sydney got home from her walk, she called both of her daughters and told them what had happened, and gave Steve all the credit for it. She thought he was a magician to have gotten her released three months early. The prospect of getting her record expunged, even of a misdemeanor, was good news too. The girls were ecstatic for her. She told them she wanted to change the venue for Christmas Eve. She wanted to take everyone to the Plaza for dinner. It would be wonderful to get out, and treat them all to a nice dinner in a restaurant for a change. Even ordinary activities were a gift now.

She called Bob then, because she could see that he had called her three times while she was out, and he was worried when she answered.

"Are you okay?"

"I'm so sorry. I was sleeping." She didn't want to tell him. She wanted to surprise him when he arrived. It was only five days away, if she could hold out, but it was hard not to say anything to him.

She got up early the next morning and dressed for

work. She hadn't told Ed either, and she walked into his office casually, wearing gray wool slacks and a gray sweater and spoke to him as though she'd never left. He stared at her as though he'd seen a ghost.

"Sydney? What are you doing here?" He was afraid she had broken the rules and just left her apartment and gone out. He was relieved when she told him what Steve had accomplished.

"Oh my God!" he said and ran around his desk to hug her, and he kept hugging her, he was so excited. Everyone in the office was thrilled.

He took her out to lunch and she told him about Christmas dinner at the Plaza. Every day was a celebration now. It felt like a miracle to her that she was free.

He startled her with a question over lunch. "My mother throws a charity event in Hong Kong every year, to benefit breast cancer research. It's a big deal to her. Her mother and sister died of it. Two thousand people attend, and they raise a lot of money. They always have some special event or happening to make it more exciting." He looked slightly embarrassed to be asking her. "She wants to know if we'd send the collection over after Fashion Week. They'd pay for transportation and insurance, and they'll pay to hire the models. I didn't know how you'd feel about it. To be honest, it's a pain in the ass and a lot of work. I thought you wouldn't be out of your apartment by then, and I didn't want to do it alone. But now that you're free, what do you think? It's good publicity, and for a good cause, but we don't have to if you don't want to. I can tell her no. I already told her I didn't think we could, if you weren't there too." Sydney didn't hesitate for a second after she'd listened.

"It's a very good cause, and good publicity for us, even if it's in Hong Kong. And she's your mother. If it weren't for them, we wouldn't have a business," she reminded him.

"True," he said, thinking about it, and his mother had been gracious enough not to point that out. "They're talking about March first. The timing could work. We'll have the collection here for two weeks after the show to take orders, or ten days at least, and then we'll ship it to Hong Kong. I can take Kevin to help, and we can hire people there, and use local models." He had already thought about the logistics, but hadn't wanted to do it without Sydney. "So what do you think?"

"I say yes," Sydney said firmly, smiling at him. She was in love with the world now that she was out of her apartment.

"She's going to love you forever." He was smiling at her. It was great to see her back at work, even though they had covered the three months remarkably well. Better than they'd hoped. "I'll send her an email. She'll be thrilled. And it'll be fun to be in Hong Kong with you again," he said, and then he laughed. "And you can meet Bob's kids while you're there."

She looked horrified at the prospect. "Forget it. Cancel the event," she teased him.

"You'll like them, I promise."

"That's not the issue. They'll probably hate me."

"Why should they? They're all adults."

"That doesn't always make a difference."

"He must be ecstatic that you're a free woman now."

"He doesn't know," she said conspiratorially. "I want to surprise him when he comes next week."

Ed smiled at the idea. "He's going to be one very happy guy," he said, and she grinned broadly.

"I hope so." She was a happy woman too.

The six of them had dinner at the Plaza at her invitation on Christmas Eve. Ed and Kevin, Steve and Sabrina, Sophie and Sydney. It was a beautiful meal and a festive evening. They toasted Sydney's freedom with champagne, and admired the engagement ring Steve had given Sabrina earlier that day. It sparkled on her finger. Sydney went to midnight mass at Saint Ignatius on Park Avenue on her own after the meal. It was a beautiful service. She went to see the tree at Rockefeller Center afterward, and stood looking at it with awe, and then she walked all the way home. She walked everywhere now. It felt so incredibly good to be back in the world. She took nothing for granted and enjoyed it all.

She had lit a candle for Andrew at church, thinking

about their life together and how much everything had changed. It was almost as though she'd been a different person then, one she had been just for him, and he had taken that person with him, or she had died with him. Now she was designing again, working, and part owner in a business, thanks to Ed. She had survived losing their home, being dead broke, giving up the apartment she loved in Paris, being arrested, and going to jail, however briefly. She had been stripped of everything she had based her identity on, and discovered that she was still a whole person, that she still believed in the same things and had the same values. The things that had meant so much to her when they were married meant less to her now. And having lost them, she had found herself, and was stronger than she'd ever been before. She had always thought it would kill her to lose Andrew, but it hadn't. She was sad about him, and she still missed him at times, but he had died and she had survived. And what was left of her, what she had become after all the losses, belonged to her and to Bob now. She had discovered herself after Andrew died. She had become a butterfly with strong wings, and Andrew was the cocoon she had shed in order to fly.

Bob's secretary had sent Sydney his itinerary by email, as she always did, so she would know his flight number if he was delayed. Sydney had spoken to her on the phone a few times, and she seemed like a nice woman. Sydney made note of his flight number and arrival time, and hired a town car to take her to the airport. She could afford a few more luxuries now with her salary and the money that would come from the Paris apartment sale in January. Her finances were no longer as terrifyingly tight as they had been at first, after Andrew died.

There was no traffic on the way to the airport. It was three days after Christmas and a lot of people weren't working. There was no snow on the ground, and she arrived at the airport half an hour early, and wandered around waiting for him. He had no idea she'd be there. She had managed to keep the secret, although it had been agonizing to do so, but she loved the idea of surprising him, with good news for a change.

She saw from the big board listing arrivals that his plane was on the ground, on its way to the gate. And then it said that the passengers were in customs. She stood just to the side of the doors he would come through, so she would see him before he saw her.

He was one of the first passengers out, since he always traveled first class, and he moved quickly toward the terminal exit, pulling his bag on wheels. He was expecting a car and driver to meet him, which she had canceled, since she had hired one herself.

She followed him for a few feet, and then walked right up behind him and tapped him on the shoulder. He turned to see who it was, and stopped in his tracks without saying a word. Like Ed, for an instant he was afraid she had escaped from the apartment, but she put her arms around him and kissed him, as he held her in his arms.

"It's okay," she said softly. "I'm free . . . they let me go." She had seen the worry in his eyes. He kissed her again then, and they stood for a long time in the airport with people walking around them, smiling, and then he looked at her intently.

"What happened? . . . Why didn't you tell me . . . when?"

They started walking toward the exit and she told him the whole story, about Zeller pleading guilty, and Steve talking to the U.S. attorney and the judge.

"And they'll expunge my record in six months or a year, if I don't get arrested again," she said as though it was a normal occurrence, and he laughed.

"I think you can manage that, don't you?" She nodded, and they settled into the back of the car and rode into the city. But he had an idea as soon as he walked into the apartment and looked at Sydney. The place looked a shambles now. All the computer equipment and screens were in the way. The coffee machine wasn't working, and they were coming to get the big screen and office equipment the day after New Year's. It made them both feel claustrophobic now being there. She wanted a new apartment, but hadn't had time yet to do anything about it in the short time she'd been free.

"Let's get out of here," he said, as he opened his computer. "Let's go someplace hot and sunny. How does St. Barts sound?" He had barely taken his coat off, and was already looking up the hotel he preferred there. He knew they could have a villa with their own pool. Sydney sat and smiled at him when he called them. They had a villa available, and he made reservations for the next day. It sounded like a dream to her.

They lay in bed talking that night, wide awake. She had packed, and he said he'd buy what he needed there at the local stores, since he had only brought clothes for New York. And she told him she was coming to Hong Kong in March.

"You have been busy!" He laughed and looked pleased.

"We're doing a fashion show for a big benefit Mrs. Chin does every year. We'll take the whole collection there after Fashion Week. It should be fun," she said, and he smiled.

"It will be 'fun' having you in Hong Kong. Actually, it will be fantastic." It was his fondest wish come true, to have her in Hong Kong with him. "How long will you stay?"

"A few days, a week, as long as we need to, to put on the benefit."

"Would you stay an extra week, just for us?" he asked her seriously, and she nodded. And then he told her about Christmas with his children. They had all come home and had spent a wonderful week together, before they went off with friends to do their own thing, and he had left for New York. He said they were curious about her, and he hadn't told them that she was incarcerated in her apartment, and didn't intend to. They didn't need to know. They fell asleep that night in each other's arms, and they couldn't wait to leave for St. Barts the next day.

They got up early the next morning and left for the airport. She had sent Ed a text telling him she was going away, and knew he'd be fine with it. They flew to St. Martin and switched to a tiny plane to get to St. Barts. The plane made her nervous, but the flight was short, and it was like being in heaven when they got to the hotel. The villa was fabulous, the location amazing, and having their own pool was a divine luxury. She had never felt so spoiled, even on trips with Andrew.

They dined in their room on some nights, and went to local restaurants on others. They swam naked in their pool, and explored the shops in the port. It felt like a honeymoon and a reward for her three-month house arrest all at the same time. They extended their stay, with Ed's blessing, and spent a week there, and hated to go back to New York. It was the most perfect vacation she'd ever been on.

"The first of many, I hope," he said when she thanked him profusely on the flight home.

He had to leave for London the next day, for a board

meeting, but he was coming back for their show during Fashion Week, and then she would be going to Hong Kong for the breast cancer benefit. He had already bought a table for ten and wanted to invite friends so she could meet them. She would be busy backstage for most of the evening, but she could come and sit with them when the fashion show was over.

They had one night together in New York before he left. She was still floating on a cloud from their vacation, and so was he. And he loved knowing that she would be coming to Hong Kong soon. They talked about it that night until they fell asleep. And she was half asleep when he left for the airport at six o'clock the next morning. He kissed her and then he was gone.

When she got to the office that morning, she knew that the month ahead would be frantic. They had to finish the collection, put on the show, pack it up, go to Hong Kong, and start on the new collection. And before things got too crazy, she wanted to find a new apartment, another furnished one, nothing elaborate or too expensive, but bigger than where she was. The one she was in felt like a jail cell to her now. She couldn't wait to move.

She found one the following weekend. It was a furnished commercial rental, like a hotel suite, but it was big enough, and nicer than the one she was giving up. She didn't want the expense of decorating or buying furniture, so she was satisfied with furnished rentals for the time being, until she felt financially stable again. They looked impersonal but it didn't matter to her.

Sophie helped her move.

It was a relief when she got the money from Paris. She could pay Sabrina off at last, and Steve, and put the rest in the bank. It was the most money she had seen in almost two years, and she felt secure for the first time in a long time.

They were both working on their shows when Sabrina called her on the weekend to tell her that she and Steve had just found the location they wanted for their wedding reception. It was an English club with wood paneling and fireplaces. It had elegant rooms, a library, and a beautiful garden, and looked like a home, which it had once been. It was formal, traditional, and serious and suited them. The club rented it out for weddings, and the price seemed reasonable to both of them when Sabrina and Sydney went to look at it. Sabrina and Steve were definite that they only wanted a hundred people at the wedding. They wanted it to be intimate, traditional, and discreet. They loved that the club had an old-fashioned feel to it. Only Sophie was disappointed that they didn't want to do it somewhere funkier and more fun, which would have been more her own style than her older sister's. Sophie was trying to talk Sabrina into letting her wear hot pink as the maid of honor instead of a pale blush peach that Ed and

Sabrina had agreed on. And Sydney was planning to wear taupe with bronze accessories.

Sydney put a deposit on the club immediately, so that problem was solved. The club had its own caterer, so she didn't have to find one. They'd found a church they liked. All they needed now was a wedding cake, Ed's florist, and a photographer. She and Ed were making the gowns for Sabrina, Sophie, and herself. It was all turning out to be much less complicated and stressful than she'd expected. Steve and Sabrina were very low-key and not demanding, and weren't looking to show off, despite Sabrina's high standards in fashion. She wanted her wedding to remain simple and very private. Steve was fine with the idea, and his parents had agreed. Sabrina had done most of the work and research herself and had her own ideas about everything.

So with the main issues for the wedding solved, and deposits where they needed them, Sydney could focus on the collection and take care of the remaining wedding details later. They had time. But the pressure was on for Fashion Week, and she was at work till midnight every night. Ed was often there even later.

She was taking a break one night, eating a salad at her desk, before working on the show some more, and picked up the *Post* and turned to Page Six as a diversion. The usual names were there—the cheaters, the hot romances, the new babies both in and out of wedlock, who had a new house or lost one in a divorce—when she saw Kyra's name jump out at her, and wondered what nastiness she and her sister were up to now. She knew that Kellie's divorce was costing her a fortune, and Geoff was already engaged to another woman. The mention of Kyra was brief, and struck Sydney as sad. It said that she was in rehab for an alcohol and substance abuse problem that had led to several recent arrests, and she had been sent to rehab by the court in lieu of jail. Sydney had had her own problems with the law, but it seemed a terrible waste that someone with so much in her favor and to protect her should be so lost.

Kyra was thirty-four years old now, had no children, had never been married, had had a slew of bad boyfriends, and her life was totally without merit or accomplishment. Sydney hoped that she could turn it around. She had never known her to have a drug problem before, but maybe with all she had inherited she had lost her grip and gone wild. Neither of the twins seemed to be using their father's fortune well. One was squandering it on a gigolo husband and a bad divorce, and the other one was deep into drugs. Sydney was relieved to be well away from them, and glad that she hadn't run into them in a long time, and hoped she never would again. Their history together didn't seem real anymore. Too much had happened since.

She said something about it to Sabrina when they

talked the next day, and she agreed about what a mess they both seemed to be and what miserable lives they led. They'd been so anxious to take everything away from her and then lost it themselves.

"I heard from someone the other day who knows her that Kellie does a lot of cocaine these days too, and Geoff is threatening to take the kids," Sabrina told her mother. "It's pathetic."

"At least he wants them," Sydney commented.

"He probably wants them for the child support she'll have to give him," Sabrina said cynically, and then added in a gentler tone, "I'm sorry about the house, Mom."

"So am I, but it doesn't matter anymore. It's past history." And the future was looking bright. Since its first show, Sydney Chin had been an astonishing success, and was exceeding all expectations and predictions. Ed had told her that his family was very pleased. They had increased her equity and given her a big raise and a huge bonus. There was a certain satisfaction in knowing that whatever she had now she had earned herself, it hadn't been given to her by someone else, and no one could take it away. She would never put herself in that position again.

Bob arrived in New York two days before the show, and took her to dinner the night before Valentine's Day. She was running crazed but had agreed to have dinner with him. But afterward she had to go back to work. He was staying with her at her new apartment, which they both agreed wasn't glamorous or beautiful, but was an improvement over the last one, which she had been thrilled to leave.

"Ready for the big day tomorrow?" Bob asked her across the table, and she looked instantly anxious.

"God, no. We have six dresses to finish sewing tonight. Our appliqués and embroideries just came in this afternoon, and one of our biggest models just canceled. She broke a leg skiing in Courchevel yesterday, and we don't have a replacement for her yet. She was due in tonight." He smiled as he listened. He knew it was the jargon of the trade, and standard Fashion Week panic. In the end, the dresses would be done, the models would be there, the sewing would be finished, and in Sydney and Ed's case, the reviews would be great. Sabrina was going through the same thing where she worked. And Sophie was just as busy, or almost, with her junior line. It was the norm in their world.

"Are you staying at work tonight?" he asked, and she nodded. There was something he wanted to ask her, but he didn't think this was the night. She was too tired and too stressed. And she would be in Hong Kong in less than two weeks. He could ask her then. He was happy to see that she always wore his ring and never took it off. She called it her lucky charm, and had become superstitious about it.

Bob kissed her when he dropped her back at the office, and went to her apartment to sleep. It amazed him how much he loved her. He had never felt that way about any woman before, and in spite of the crazy business she was in, they got along well. The only problem they had was where they both lived, but they seemed to have a system that worked for now, and managed to see each other every three or four weeks, mostly thanks to him, because he had to go to New York anyway for meetings with clients, though not as often as he went for her. But he couldn't go without seeing her for long.

He woke up for an instant when he felt her slip into bed at four in the morning, and then out again at six. By the time he woke up fully two hours later, she was long gone and hard at work.

Chapter 19

Predictably, their show was even better than the first one, and the reviews were fabulous. Sydney and Ed were ecstatic. They both went home to sleep after the show, and the following night, Ed, Kevin, Sydney, and Bob had dinner to celebrate at La Grenouille. Their show had been called the best one of the season, and people were talking about their possibly winning a CFDA Fashion Award, which would be a major coup. It was like winning an Oscar for an actor or producer. And the orders were already rolling in.

Bob stayed a few more days after the show, and then headed back to Hong Kong. He was already making plans for dinners with her and special outings, a casual evening with his children, and a cocktail party with his friends to introduce her to everyone. Sydney was nervous about it. He was so excited to have her meet everyone that she felt overwhelmed. She talked to Ed about it on the plane, after they settled into their seats. It had been a whirlwind two weeks, with busy days ahead in Hong Kong.

"I hope you have your plane karma under control," he

warned her, and she laughed nervously. She never totally forgot the terror of the flight that had almost crashed and then landed in Nova Scotia. It had been fateful for her since it was when she had met Paul.

"I hope so too," she said anxiously. "Bob acts like this is a homecoming instead of just a visit. I haven't even met his kids yet. And I'm not signing up for another bunch of kids who hate me."

"Stop worrying about it. They're sane. Those other two witches aren't, and never were." He thought about it for a minute then and asked her a question. "Would you ever live there?" She shook her head without hesitating.

"I'm married to you and the business," she said, and he smiled. Kevin was on the same flight with them, traveling in business as a gift from Ed. Since it was a long flight, she and Ed were in first, which Sydney was enjoying. It was one of the luxuries she had missed and had come back to her now.

"You don't have to be married. But you could live any-where, you know. We proved that when you were under house arrest. You can send your drawings in by computer. We can FaceTime. As long as you come back for Fashion Week twice a year. Our design team can handle the pre-collections. You don't *have* to live in New York if you don't want to."

"I *want* to," she said, sounding adamant about it. "I have two children there. And I'm never giving up my life for a man again, or being dependent on someone to take care of me. That's the lesson of the past two years. I never should have given up my career when I got married. It was a huge mistake."

"So don't give up your career. I don't want you to do that either." He looked worried at the thought. They had a booming business now that depended on both of them. "I'm just saying you could live anywhere, as long as you have a computer and fly to New York several times a year. You would probably have to spend about a month before each Fashion Week in September and February. It's workable if you want to. You could be flexible." Ed was trying to work it out for her, so she could spend time with Bob.

"I don't see how that can work," she said, frowning. "Besides, I'd be moving there for Bob. And that's too big a change to make just for a man. And then he dies or dumps me, and I'm screwed and have to start all over again. I just did that." She looked unnerved at the thought. She was traumatized by what had happened to her when Andrew died, and she didn't want to put her life in any man's hands again, even Bob's, whom Ed knew she loved. "I'm not going to give up my life, my career, or my city for anyone. He lives in Hong Kong. I live in New York."

"What if you could do both?" Ed asked her calmly.

She didn't answer for a long moment. "I don't know," she said quietly. "It scares me. Are you trying to marry me off?" she asked him with a grin. "Did Bob ask you to talk to me?"

"No, but I can see how much he loves you, and you can't expect him to do all the traveling forever. And these days, even in our business, you can live where you want to and do a lot by computer. I just thought I'd remind you of that, to think outside the box." It was a generous gesture on his part, and she was touched.

"Would you move to another city for Kevin?"

Ed looked startled at the question. He'd never thought about it with anyone. "I don't know," he said honestly. "It would depend on how much I love him, and the city. I might try it for a while to check it out." She didn't answer him, and sat staring out the window, thinking about it. Bob had proven himself for the last year, and been there for her. But moving to Hong Kong would be a lot to ask. Fortunately, he never had. It was a decision she didn't want to make.

They both watched movies and slept on the flight, and Ed went to visit Kevin in business a few times. When they got to Hong Kong, Bob was waiting for her at the airport. Ed and Kevin were staying with Ed's family, who had sent their Bentley and driver for them. Bob drove Sydney to his place in his Aston Martin. When they got there, his apartment was as beautiful as she remembered from the video he had sent her.

"Welcome home," Bob said as he kissed her, and they stood on the terrace and looked at the view of Hong Kong below. The apartment was like a movie set. He poured champagne for both of them, and handed her a glass. "I've waited eleven months to get you here," he said, looking happy. It felt like a dream to him having her with him in Hong Kong, and as she sipped the champagne, she couldn't help remembering that he had stuck with her through the worst months of her life, including preparations for a trial and the possibility of prison, and he had never let her down once. The years with Andrew had been easy, for both of them. But Bob had been through everything hard, including three months of incarceration in a miserable apartment. And now she was back in the lap of luxury again, but it wasn't hers, it was his. She was acutely aware of that now, and the risks. And she didn't want to do that again. "What are you doing tomorrow?" he asked, always respectful of her plans and the demands on her, and willing to adjust. That was new to her.

"I have to help Ed set up the show. It's the day after tomorrow," she reminded him. "We have to pick the models and have fittings with them. But it won't be as crazy as New York." It was a benefit, not New York Fashion Week with critics to impress.

"We'll have time to do everything after the benefit," he said easily. She was staying a week after the fashion show, just to be with him. And his life was so seductive, as long as she didn't think about meeting his children.

He had an enormous marble bathtub in a huge bathroom, and they soaked in it together before they went to bed. He poured her more champagne, and she was already half asleep before she climbed into his big comfortable bed and put her arms around him, with pure happiness in her eyes.

"I love you," she whispered, and fell asleep instantly, as he turned off the light and smiled. His life was perfect with her there.

Sydney woke up late the next morning. Bob had gone to the office and let her sleep. She had to rush to meet Ed at the hotel at noon to choose the models. There were a fleet of assistants he'd hired already unpacking the clothes, which had arrived in good order, and Kevin was directing two young assistants, while a dozen seamstresses waited to fit the clothes to the girls.

They had just finished choosing the models, when Ed's mother stopped by to thank them again for doing the show for the benefit. Sydney was struck again by how beautiful she was, and how young to have a son Ed's age. She and Sydney were almost the same age. He and his mother looked like brother and sister. She had exquisite skin, and she was incredibly chic. She wore French haute couture. Ed had learned all about fashion from her, and from going to couture shows with her as a child.

They were finished with what they had to do by six o'clock, when Bob came to pick Sydney up. He invited Ed to join them for dinner, but he said he had to have dinner with his parents. He and Sydney agreed to meet the next morning at nine to go over details before a dress rehearsal at ten. The models they had chosen were all pros. A few didn't speak English but Ed spoke to them in Mandarin. They were all beautiful girls and wore the clothes well.

"Half the room will be my relatives tomorrow night," Ed commented, laughing. "My parents have four tables for the family and two of friends."

"I have a table too," Bob said. He had invited his favorite people and closest friends, so Sydney could meet them. As they got into his car, he said they were having dinner at home that night. She was relieved to hear it, as she was tired and jet-lagged. It had been a long day, and she couldn't wait to relax and soak in his huge tub. "My kids are coming to dinner tonight," he said casually. Sydney sat up straight in the car with a look of terror, and he smiled. "Except for the one in medical school in England, of course. But Charlotte is coming in from Shanghai. They all want to meet you, Sydney," he said as he glanced at her. "Don't look like that. They're not going to eat you, I promise." But it was obvious she didn't believe him, based on past experience with the twins. She had hoped to wait a while to meet his children. But he wanted to get it over with quickly, so she could relax. He knew how worried she was about it. She had dreaded it for months. Her fears about his children were a huge stumbling block for her to commit to him.

"When are they coming?" she asked nervously.

He checked his watch. "In about half an hour. It's very casual. You don't have to change." She was wearing jeans. "I had a local restaurant cater it. So all you have to do is eat and relax." She felt like Daniel walking into the lion's den when they got to his apartment, and she went to put on a fresh blouse, brush her hair, and wash her face. She was brushing her teeth when the doorbell rang, and she wanted to throw up. She was sure it was them.

She walked anxiously into the living room and saw Bob with his arm around a spectacularly beautiful girl, prettier than any model they'd hired that day. She was wearing a chef's jacket, checked pants, and clogs, so Sydney guessed easily which one she was. And Bob was very proud when he introduced his oldest daughter, Francesca, to Sydney. She had a warm, open smile and looked instantly apologetic.

"I'm so sorry I'm a mess. I was helping a friend out at his restaurant, and I came right from work." She shook Sydney's hand politely. She looked almost like a Eurasian version of Sabrina, and they were about the same age.

"I came right from work too." Sydney smiled at her cautiously and felt foolish for being so worried. Francesca couldn't have been nicer or more gracious and modest. She had none of that nasty foxy-eyed "I'm going to eat you for dinner or stab you in the back" look of the hateful twins and their mother. Francesca was as gentle and friendly as her father.

"Your show tomorrow sounds amazing," Francesca said, visibly impressed. "Dad invited me, but I have to work. I had already signed on to fill in for a friend before he asked me. Besides," she said shyly, "I don't have decent clothes. I spend my life in the kitchen." She was totally unassuming, like her father, and much less sophisticated than Sydney had expected. She could have been anyone's daughter, not one of the most successful men in Hong Kong. They were talking quietly about the bistro she wanted to open when Bob's son, Dorian, walked in. He beamed the minute he saw Sydney, as though he had been waiting to meet her all his life. He had them all laughing half an hour later with the description of his recent visit to his sister in England and masquerading as a doctor so he could make rounds with her, and almost finding himself in a delivery room by mistake. He was funny and very welcoming to Sydney and wanted to know all about Sophie and Sabrina. He said they sounded very glamorous, and she assured him they were down-to-earth but with jobs in fashion, and worked very hard.

"I never wear the right thing," he said awkwardly. "Dad took me to some fancy event a few months ago. I lost my dress shoes somewhere so I had to wear sneakers, and he was very upset." He smiled at his father, who rolled his eyes at the memory of it.

"I was only upset because the shoes you lost happened to be mine, and I had lent them to you."

"Oh, that," Dorian said, and grinned guiltily at Sydney, who laughed. He was an adorable young guy, with an aura of mischief and innocence about him that was hard to resist.

And as they were talking, a little elf wandered in wearing what looked like pajama bottoms, a paint-splattered pink sweatshirt, and pink high-top sneakers. She apologized profusely for being late, and said her flight from Shanghai had been delayed. She had pink streaks in her hair.

"And they stole your clothes on the flight?" her father asked disapprovingly.

"No, these are mine. I was working on a painting till the last second before I left. But they did lose my bag. They're bringing it later." She was smaller than the others and looked a lot like her father, and reminded Sydney a bit of Sophie when she was younger. She had the same self-deprecating way about her, and surprised, innocent eyes, and a permanently childlike aura about her.

"My daughter Charlotte, otherwise known as Charlie,"

Bob said to Sydney, who was totally at ease by then, and smiled at her. She looked like a ragamuffin, but a totally endearing one, and had her pink-streaked hair in pigtails.

"She always dresses like that," Dorian explained to Sydney. "Your daughters in fashion would never approve of any of us, and my sister Aimee wears hospital pajamas all the time. We're a disreputable lot," he said, smiling broadly, and his sisters laughed.

"We're a mess sometimes too," Sydney said honestly. "Sometimes I wear my nightgown all day when I'm drawing, and so do my girls."

"At the office?" Charlotte looked impressed. "I go to the bank sometimes in my pajamas, and Dad gets mad. But I like painting in them." Bob glanced at Sydney ruefully, and she couldn't help laughing. They reminded her of Peter Pan's lost boys, and none of them seemed to care about clothes, which was fine with her. They were each charming in their own way, and she could see why Bob said they all had fun together.

"Actually, I wear my nightgowns at home, but I'd love to wear them to the office," she responded to Charlotte. They told her about the family dogs then, who had all misbehaved, and one ate an entire buffet of food before the guests came, which inspired more stories. She was enjoying them enormously when dinner was announced, and they walked into the dining room to see a beautiful spread set out on china and crystal, with gleaming silver and flowers on the table. Despite their mischievous tales and haphazard style, she saw that they all had beautiful manners, were kind and polite to her, and were close to each other and crazy about their father, who adored them. It was a family full of love and good feelings, and rather than excluding her, like the twins, they all welcomed her warmly into their midst. She felt totally comfortable with them.

The food from one of the best restaurants in town was delicious. Bob had planned it carefully for her and had gone all out. And the conversation during dinner was warm and funny. They teased each other and their father, but without malice, and seemed perfectly happy to include her. They were the opposite of everything she had experienced with the twins.

She was sorry when all three of Bob's children left at midnight. Charlotte was staying in the apartment downstairs, Francesca was going home to her boyfriend, and Dorian was meeting up with friends. Sydney told them she hoped to see them again before she left, and meant it, but Charlotte said she was going back to Shanghai the next day. Francesca and Dorian promised to come by the next night. They all hugged her warmly when they left. She was stunned.

She turned to Bob when they were alone in the apartment again with a look of amazement. "You have the nicest kids I've ever met."

"They're good kids, but I wish I could get them into decent clothes. Dorian's right, they look a mess." They were all slightly eccentric but in a very appealing way. And Bob had obviously let them be themselves.

"No, they don't," Sydney disagreed with him. "They just look like kids, and they don't have jobs you have to dress up for. I think they're wonderful." They were smart and affectionate and unpretentious. "I haven't had this much fun in ages. Sophie and Sabrina would love them. I wish we could get Dorian and Sophie together. She's kind of a bumbler about guys. You missed the last one, who was a total neurotic mess."

"I don't know why, but Dorian can never find decent girls. They're always crazy, or just out of rehab, or homeless, or have some huge problem he thinks he can fix."

"That's Sophie too. She always ends up playing psych nurse to some basket case."

"Dorian too, *and* he borrows my shoes and loses them *every* time," he said, laughing. "I think he hands them out to homeless people or gives them to his friends." They both laughed, and Sydney felt as though a thousand-pound weight had been lifted off her shoulders.

"I was terrified to meet them," she confessed.

"I know," he said gently. "That's why I invited them here tonight. I wanted to put you out of your misery quickly. They're not a very scary group. I knew they'd like you. I just didn't know how you'd feel about them. They're not as glamorous as your girls. Dorian is right about that too. You should read his novel. It's actually very good," he said with fatherly pride.

"I'd like to. And Sabrina always disapproves of the rest of us, but she can let her hair down too. I think Steve will relax her a little. And it's her job to look like that." She had acted like the fashion police since she was a little girl.

"They all told me how much they love you when they left. They think you're really 'cool.'" He was pleased, and proud of Sydney too, not just his kids.

"Well, I think they're 'cool' too. Very, very, very cool. And so sweet."

"Well, that's over. Now you can enjoy them the next time you see them," he said, sounding pleased and relaxed. The evening had been a success.

"I enjoyed them tonight." She smiled, and he walked over and kissed her.

"Let's go to bed," he whispered to her. "I gave up tonight for them, now I want you to myself." She laughed and followed him into his spectacular bedroom, and he closed the door and they fell into bed with each other, smiling and laughing and talking and teasing until passion overtook them, and they forgot about his children, and thought only of how much they loved each other. It had been a perfect night. And now she could relax and spend her time with him in Hong Kong. She had nothing to fear.

Fall from Grace

The monsters she had been so afraid of had turned out to be charming, funny, loving, bright young people. They had overcome a huge obstacle that night, and it only made her love their father more.

Chapter 20

Sydney told Ed about meeting Bob's children the next day while they set up the benefit together, checked the room, did a sound check, and went through the rehearsal with the models.

"You were right, they're adorable," she said, looking totally pleased with the evening. She was still coasting on it, and had seen Charlotte at breakfast before she went back to Shanghai. She had come to Hong Kong just to meet Sydney, and said she was glad she had. She gave her a big hug before Sydney left for work, and told her that she had to come to her next art show.

"I told you so," Ed said, pleased with himself. "They're a terrific family. They're all regular people. There isn't a snob in the bunch. Bob isn't a snob either. He's just a very successful guy, and he likes the good life more than they do. You should see the cars they drive. Dorian drove a ten-year-old mail truck all through school. They're all kind of hippies. Maybe it's a reaction to the money." But she liked that about them, and Ed did too. It made them seem younger than they were. There was an honesty about them that was very appealing. And Sydney complimented Bob on them again that night before the benefit. She had come back to the apartment to change, and was wearing a beautiful evening gown Ed had made for her for the event. It looked like vintage Chanel. It was finely pleated black silk with pale pink satin panels, and was spectacular on her slim figure.

Everything had gone smoothly at the hotel that afternoon, and was in good order when she went backstage before the show. Ed was wearing a tuxedo and looked very elegant, and Kevin was wearing one too. The guests had started arriving. Ed and Sydney checked all the models themselves. His mother came backstage a couple of times. And then everyone was seated at the tables, and the show started. They had rolled out a carpet for the models to walk on, which wended through the room, so everyone could see the clothes. It was perfect, even better than the New York show, because it was more relaxed. Ed and Sydney got a standing ovation when they took their bows, which were always quick.

And then dinner started and an orchestra played and people danced. They had paid a fortune for their seats, for a good cause, and they got their money's worth. Sydney enjoyed meeting Bob's friends, more than she'd expected to, and had a good time with them at dinner. He had invited four couples, bankers, lawyers, a doctor, and a journalist. They were accomplished people, and warm and welcoming to her. And when Bob danced with her, she was pleased to discover he was a wonderful dancer. They were among the last to leave the event at two A.M. The assistants had already packed up the clothes, with Kevin's supervision. And from then on, Sydney was on vacation and had nothing to do except play tourist with Bob around Hong Kong.

They sat on his terrace again until three in the morning and talked about what a success the benefit had been and then went to bed. In the morning, he was dressed when she got up, and anxious to show her around. They took the tram up Victoria Peak, above the Chins' home. He took her to the famous Ladies' Market, and shopping at Causeway Bay, where all the best stores were. They went to the best restaurants for lunch and dinner. Finally, after four days of visiting Hong Kong, he got up the courage to ask her what he had wanted to since Valentine's Day, and before. They were having dinner at Caprice, and were drinking champagne. He didn't want to wait till the last night to ask her.

"I want to ask you something, Sydney," he said cautiously, and she could see that he was nervous. She hoped that he didn't give her an ultimatum, or offer her something she couldn't accept. She had a feeling she knew what he wanted. "I know what happened and how badly your life has been shaken up for two years, but I have to ask you this, so I know where we stand." She almost winced when he said it, not wanting to hurt him or turn him down. "Is there any chance that you would ever consider retiring again, leaving New York and moving to Hong Kong with me, with or without marriage, your choice?" She looked at him sadly after he asked her. She didn't want her refusal to end what they had. It was too precious to her to lose. But she couldn't lose herself again either. She couldn't ever let that happen, even for him.

"No, there isn't," she said gently. She wanted to be honest with him. "I don't want to give up my career again. I love what Ed and I are doing, and I don't want to lose that. But I don't want to lose you either. I just can't do what I did before, give up working, become dependent on a man, and risk everything I am. If anything went wrong with us, I'd be screwed all over again." He nodded, and understood. It was the answer he had expected, and the question he felt compelled to ask, in case her response was different from what he thought.

"I would never let that happen to you," he said kindly. He didn't want to be critical of Andrew, but they were very different men, and he would never leave the future to chance. He was even slightly younger than Andrew had been. He told her that he knew that one day he would die, and he wanted to leave his affairs in order, and those he loved well cared for, and even protected from each other, if necessary. "I can promise you that."

"I'm sure you would. But if I give up my job for you, I'd be totally dependent on you. If I didn't work, I'd have no money. I did that once. I can't do it again. It would be a terrible mistake. And I don't want to be beholden to you. I want to be with you because I love you, not because you support me." She had loved Andrew too, but he had supported her completely and very generously. And when he died, it all ended. She didn't want to be in that situation again. "I'm not even fully back on my feet yet. I'm just getting there. I want to make my own money, not live on yours. I'd only marry again if I could be responsible for myself. It doesn't have to be equal, but I have to make enough to take care of myself." She had never realized how important that was until she lost everything.

"I understand," he said quietly. And then he thought of another question he had been wondering. "Could you work from here?"

"Maybe," she said honestly, but she didn't tell him that Ed had told her she could and even suggested it on the plane over. She didn't want to move to Hong Kong just for him. It was too much to do for a man. She wanted to make her own choices. She loved him, and knew she wanted to be with him. She just didn't know where, or how, or under what circumstances. She wanted to let it unfold between them, not force it or make huge sacrifices for him, like giving up New York and no longer living in the same city with her daughters, or retiring, as he had asked her. It could all blow up in her face if something went wrong. She knew instinctively that if one of them made all the sacrifices, it wouldn't work. And she was too afraid of the risks now. Life was too uncertain. But she didn't want to be unfair to him either. She wanted fate to make some of the decisions for them, not create them all herself, or for him to dictate the terms. But she recognized that he wasn't dictating. He was asking. "It's possible," she answered his question about her working in Hong Kong. "It will depend how the business develops. It's too soon to know."

That made sense to him, and she had left the door open. He liked that. It wasn't the answer he had wanted, but she hadn't turned him down flat either, which he had feared she might if he pushed her. He had tried to be careful not to, and to be respectful of her. They both needed a relationship based on mutual respect, which they'd had so far.

"I love you," she said, looking at him intently. "I'm certain of it. I just don't want to make any big mistakes this time. Or overlook something important. You wouldn't give up your business and move to New York. I don't want to give up mine after we just started it. I think I would always regret it if I did." And he knew she was right. She was a smart, sensible woman, who had learned a hard lesson and paid a high price for it. And he respected her career, and her talent, as much as his own.

"Would you spend time with me here? Maybe if we take turns traveling, it will work better in the long run." But he had business in New York frequently, and Hong Kong was far for her to come, and more difficult if she wasn't working there.

"I'll try," she said honestly. "I love being here with you. It's a wonderful place. It's just a long way from New York." He nodded and smiled at her, and kissed her fingertips.

"I love you, Sydney. We'll find a way to make this work for the long haul. I want it to," he said, and she nodded. She did too. She just didn't know how.

"Let's give fate a chance," she said softly. He kissed her on the lips then, and they went home a little while later and made love. A lot had been said that evening. They didn't need to say more for now.

Ed called her in the morning when they got up, and asked if she had time to see him that afternoon.

"Anything wrong?"

"No, the orders are going great in New York. I just want to ask you something."

"Do you want to come here?" she suggested.

"To be honest, I'd rather see you alone. How about Felix at the Peninsula at five o'clock?" It was a chic bar she'd been to with Bob.

"That's fine. I'll have Bob drop me off."

"I'll take you home afterward."

She told Bob, and she had no idea what Ed had on his mind or what he was going to say. She thought about it all day, and Bob kissed her when he dropped her off.

"I hope everything's okay." He could tell that she was worried.

"He said it was." She smiled at him and hoped so too. The purpose of the meeting was a total mystery to her.

Ed was waiting for her at a quiet table. They both ordered white wine and chatted for a few minutes and then Ed looked at her seriously. "I have a proposal for you, and a question. I had a long talk with my parents this week. They have an idea, and I think it's a good one. It wasn't what I had in mind. But the more I think about it, the more I like it. I wanted to open a store in New York once we're established, and I still want to. They want me to open a flagship here, and then open New York a year later. I thought it was crazy at first, but it's not. It would get us a lot of attention. As you know, many of the big-name fashion brands have opened flagships in Beijing. I don't want to. If we're going to do China, which I think we should eventually, I want to do it here, at Causeway Bay."

"Wow," she said, thinking about what he had just shared with her. She didn't think it was crazy at all, and he had terrific connections here. A store in Hong Kong could be a huge success, and position them a little differently from everyone else, which she liked. "When are you thinking? In about a year?"

"Now," he said, and stunned her again. "We're hot now. We're new. If we start now, we could be open here in six months. And do a flagship in New York a year later. My father owns a piece of real estate that would be perfect for a flagship here. It would be the hottest store in the city." It was an ambitious project, but she could see why he was excited about it. She was too. It could be a brilliant move for them, especially with his family behind them, who were so powerful locally.

"Do you really think we could have it open in six months?" It was a lot to ask. They were both based in New York.

"I do, with the right person in charge of the project and opening it, I think it's realistic. Hard work, but possible."

"We'd have to find someone," she said, considering what he'd said.

"There's only one person I know who could do that," he said earnestly. "You. You don't have to stay here forever if you don't like it. You could stay for six months, and then come back to New York, if you still want to. That's what I wanted to ask you today. Would you do it, Syd? You're the only person I would trust to open here." He was looking straight at her and she felt as though he had just blown her across the room and knocked the wind out of her. But she could see what it could do for their business. It might be the smartest move they'd ever make. He was right, and his family weren't fools either. A flagship in Hong Kong, followed by one in New York, could send them into the stratosphere, and if they had the real estate and he had their backing, how could they lose? But was she ready to move to Hong Kong for six months? That was the big question for her.

"How soon do you want to know?" she asked, looking at him intently. "It's not forever, but it's still a big move for me, even for six months."

"Apparently, my father's been sitting on this piece of property for a while. I didn't know about it till yesterday. He has a chance to sell it now, with a big offer. But he'll give it to us if we want it. I really do," he said honestly. "But I can't do it without you." She nodded. "He wants to know by tomorrow. And I'm serious, all you have to do is be here for six months to open it. And after that, go back to New York if you want to, or you don't. It's up to you. I think we could be a big presence here."

"I don't know if I'd want to stay here," she said thoughtfully.

"You don't have to. We could find someone. But right now, we don't have time to find someone to open. It has to be one of us. And I think I should be in New York." She agreed with him. He knew more about the technical side of the business than she did.

"I could do it for six months," she said, trying to think of everything at once. "How fast would you want me here?"

"We'd have construction to do on the site, not a lot, but some. And I want to find a great architect to design it. They work fast here. You could go back to New York with me. Could you come back here in two weeks?" Sydney laughed at him as she thought about it.

"You don't fool around, do you?"

"No, I don't." He was dead serious, and so was she. But she loved his idea, and she liked the offer and the idea of being there for six months with Bob, without throwing her whole life out the window to do it. And she had a valid reason of her own to be here now. Fate had stepped in, just as she'd hoped. It was what she had told Bob she wanted the night before. The hand of fate to help make the decisions. And fate had just taken a hand with the piece of property Ed's father was giving them. What more could one ask? She looked Ed in the eye and she knew it was right. This was her destiny. She had been meant to meet him at Lady Louise. It was the only good thing that had come out of it. And she had been meant to meet Paul Zeller on the plane, even if he was a crook and she got arrested and stuck in her apartment for three months. She had lost everything after Andrew, and now she had a chance to build something herself, with Ed. And maybe with Bob. She had met him through Ed too. It was all a chain linked together.

"I'm probably insane, but I'll do it," she answered him. "Six months. That's all I'm promising for now. We'll talk about it again in six months, and I'll come back to New York if I want. I'll need to be in New York for a couple of weeks to do Sabrina's wedding," she reminded him.

"Of course," he agreed easily. She stuck out a hand, and he shook it as his face broke into a broad grin. She had thought about her daughters too, but they were old enough to manage without her for six months. They were grown women with good jobs, and they could visit her in Hong Kong. And she'd fly back to New York to see them.

"Are we crazy?" she asked Ed with a stunned expression.

"Maybe, but I don't think so. My father's the smartest businessman I know, and he thinks it's a great idea."

"So do I," she said. She felt sure of it in her gut. She wasn't even scared. It felt right. He paid the check and they left the restaurant. He dropped her off at Bob's a few minutes later, and she went upstairs, amazed by what she'd just done, but excited and pleased too. She knew it was the right move.

Bob was working at his computer when she walked in, and he greeted her with a smile. "Welcome home." And he looked at her questioningly. "What did he want?" he asked, and she didn't know where to start for a minute. She walked toward him with an expression he'd never seen her with before. It was strength and determination, courage and excitement all at once. "What's up?"

"I'm moving to Hong Kong in two weeks, for six months. We're opening a flagship store here. His father is giving him the location, and I'm opening it for him," she said, as a slow smile spread across her face, and he looked at her and realized what it meant for them. "I only promised him six months here. We'll see after that." Fate had taken a hand, right from the first. For the business, for Ed, for her, for Bob, and for their relationship. And it all started with Andrew leaving her out of his will and leaving her destitute, meeting Paul Zeller on a plane that almost crashed in the Atlantic off Nova Scotia, and meeting Ed Chin, and Bob through him.

"Welcome home," he said softly again. "Thank you." He wasn't sure if he was thanking her or the Fates, who had just blessed them with an incredible opportunity. Anything was possible. Anything could happen now. The dice had been rolled. For all of them. The rest remained to be seen.

She smiled at him, as he put his arms around her. He knew just how amazing she was. She had fallen, and survived it, stronger than ever before. And just when she thought all was lost, she had won. And now so had he. The Fates had been extremely kind to them. And Sydney was brave enough to reach out and seize the opportunity. They both were. He knew, looking at her, that great things were going to happen. He was sure of it. They already were. This was just the beginning. Their time had come.

Danielle Steel

Turn over for more information about
Danielle's upcoming books . . .

IN HIS FATHER'S FOOTSTEPS

A tormented past. A hopeful future.

April, 1945. As the Americans storm the Buchenwald concentration camp, among the survivors are Jakob and Emmanuelle, barely more than teenagers. Each of them has lost everything and everyone in the unspeakable horrors of the war. But when they meet, they find hope and comfort in each other.

Jakob and Emmanuelle marry, and resolve to make a new life in New York. The Steins build a happy, prosperous life for themselves and their little family, but their pasts cast a long shadow over the present.

Years later, as the Sixties are in full swing, their son Max is an ambitious, savvy businessman, determined to throw off the sadness that has hung over his family since his birth. But as Max's life unfolds, he must learn that there is meaning in his heritage that will help shape his future . . .

Available for pre-order

PURE HEART. PURE STEEL.

FAIRYTALE

Charmed. Trapped. Magical.

Camille Lammenais has grown up in the beauty of the Napa Valley surrounded by acres of her family's vineyards. After graduating from Stanford, she returns to help manage her parents' chateau. But their fairytale ends suddenly with her mother's death. Her devastated father is easy prey for a mysterious, charming Frenchwoman visiting the valley. But Camille begins to see past the alluring looks, designer clothes, and elegant manners of the Countess . . .

Fairytale is an enchanting rendering of a much-loved classic, and a reminder that good prevails over evil in the end.

Available now in paperback

PURE HEART. PURE STEEL.

ACCIDENTAL HEROES

A journey they will never forget . . .

On a beautiful May morning at New York's JFK airport, a routine plane departs for San Francisco. Security agent Bernice Adams finds a postcard of the Golden Gate Bridge bearing an ambiguous message. Who left the postcard behind, which flight is that person on, and what exactly does the message mean?

As the plane bears down on its destination of San Francisco, the futures of these strangers will be changed forever by a handful of accidental heroes.

Coming soon in paperback

PURE HEART. PURE STEEL.

Danielle Steel

Have you liked Danielle Steel on Facebook?

Be the first to know about Danielle's latest books,
access exclusive competitions and stay in touch
with news about Danielle.

www.facebook.com/DanielleSteelOfficial